"Did you see, Mom? We almost cantered."

Sawyer sent Olivia a look as he led Hero out of the corral, Nick still grinning.

"Not quite," Sawyer assured her. "Hero's got good gaits, but I doubt I could keep up with him at that pace."

He wasn't even breathing hard, and Olivia looked away from his shirt, which was now plastered to his shoulders, chest and flat abdomen. He was saving face for Nick so he wouldn't feel as if he were on some pony ride at a summer fair. Of course he wanted to go fast. That was her son. Years ago, she had to admit, that would have been her, too, flying like the wind on Jasmine.

And that was, always, like Sawyer. His impulsiveness had cost Olivia her favorite horse. She found it hard to forget that when she was here at the Circle H... Yet watching him and Nick with the lovely gray gelding had made her heart ache in a good way. Here was Sawyer McCord, a cowboy again, though he'd turned his back on the ranch years ago.

Though he would probably leave again once more.

Dear Reader,

I'm so happy to bring you *Cowboy on Call*, this third book in my Kansas Cowboys series. Sawyer McCord is the bad boy of this group—I do love bad boys!—and he truly needs to find redemption.

In his defense, Sawyer hasn't had an easy time of it. After losing his parents when he was eight, he and his twin brother, Logan (from book one, *The Reluctant Rancher*), were raised by their grandfather, Sam. But after Sam and Sawyer had a falling-out, Sawyer left home. Long estranged from his brother, too, he has a lot to make up for. And not only with his family.

Sawyer is also carrying a heavy load of guilt over another tragedy that happened far away. But coming home again can't fix that, either. He's in bad shape as a doctor and as a man, and Sawyer certainly doesn't count on becoming a cowboy again—or meeting up with Olivia Wilson, the one true love of his life.

Divorced from Sawyer's brother, Olivia is determined to be the best single mom she can be for their son, and the last thing she needs is to fall for Sawyer. He won't stay long—just like before—and besides, they have a sad history.

I had a great time getting Sawyer and Olivia together, though it takes an unruly black colt to help get the job done. Ride 'em, cowboy!

I hope you enjoy *Cowboy on Call*. If you missed book one, *The Reluctant Rancher*, and/or *Last Chance Cowboy*, book two, they're also available. And please visit my website, leighriker.com, where you can also sign up for my newsletter.

As always, happy reading!

Leigh

HEARTWARMING

Cowboy on Call

——

USA TODAY Bestselling Author

Leigh Riker

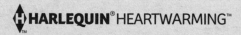

Recycling programs
for this product may
not exist in your area.

ISBN-13: 978-0-373-36860-0

Cowboy on Call

Copyright © 2017 by Leigh Riker

Printed in U.S.A.

Leigh Riker, like so many dedicated readers, grew up with her nose in a book. This award-winning, *USA TODAY* bestselling author still can't imagine a better way to spend her time than to curl up with a good romance novel—unless it's to write one! She's a member of the Authors Guild, Novelists, Inc., and Romance Writers of America. When not writing, she's either out in the garden, indoors watching movies funny and sad or traveling (for research purposes, of course). With added "help" from her mischievous cat, Daisy, she's now working on a new novel. She loves to hear from readers. You can find Leigh on her website, leighriker.com, on Facebook at leighrikerauthor and on Twitter, @lbrwriter.

Books by Leigh Riker

Harlequin Heartwarming

Kansas Cowboys

The Reluctant Rancher
Last Chance Cowboy

Lost and Found Family
Man of the Family
If I Loved You

Harlequin Intrigue

Agent-in-Charge
Double Take

Red Dress Ink

Strapless

Visit the Author Profile page
at Harlequin.com for more titles.

For Don

Still my favorite cowboy...happily-ever-after.

CHAPTER ONE

OLIVIA WATCHED HER ex-husband dance with his bride.

From the deep shadows along the driveway, in view of the ranch house where she'd once lived at the Circle H, she watched other people join the bride and groom and listened to the soft strains of the ballad the band was playing. And felt her eyes fill. She always cried at weddings, but this reception held special significance.

Overhead the stars twinkled like ornaments just for this summer night. Strung through the nearby cottonwood trees, fairy lights winked as if someone had matched the two displays, heaven and earth.

She wasn't really part of this. Olivia had been invited to the wedding earlier that day, but as Logan's former wife, it had seemed inappropriate to accept the invitation and she'd skipped the ceremony.

Carrying a large box wrapped in white with a silver bow, she stopped here and there to say hello to someone but didn't linger. She planned to leave her gift—a quilt in the classic wedding ring design from her antiques shop—collect her seven-year-old son, who'd been his dad's ring bearer, then go home.

What's done is done.

Three years after her divorce, Olivia bore no hard feelings. The bride looked lovely in her lace-trimmed gown and Olivia already liked her. After all, she was Nick's stepmother now, and Olivia's little boy adored Blossom. Besides, Olivia had finally made her peace with Logan, her ex.

If she felt slightly left out tonight, that was her problem.

She'd had her turn and blown it. Olivia had always half expected her marriage to disintegrate as her parents' had, and like some self-fulfilling prophecy, she now had the papers to prove it. Love clearly wasn't her strong suit—except her maternal love for Nick. In that, she could be as fierce as a mother tiger, and Olivia intended to be the best single mom on the planet. On her own again, she worked hard to provide the emotional security for him—the stability—that she'd never known.

She could handle feeling invisible; she'd had a lifetime of experience at it.

Taking her gift toward the house, she spotted her brother in the crowd but didn't get the chance to talk to him. Before she took another step, Olivia noticed yet another man crossing the lawn. And froze. At first, she thought he was Logan, that he'd changed from his khakis and navy blue blazer with the yellow pocket square to jeans with his white shirt. But it wasn't Logan.

After nine years, her ex-husband's twin brother was back.

Sawyer McCord.

Olivia turned then went the other way.

THE HEELS OF Sawyer's new cowboy boots sank into the grass, forcing him to slow his steps before he reached the large gathering of wedding guests.

He was late. Later than late, actually. He'd almost missed the whole thing. He'd been lucky to make it at all and he could tell the reception was already half-over.

With varying degrees of skill, half a dozen couples gyrated on the temporary wooden dance floor in the middle of the lawn to a fast tune. Classic rock, which the band had just launched into after the bride and groom's first dance. The cork from a fresh bottle of champagne popped loud enough to be heard over the music.

Sawyer glanced around but didn't see his brother. Maybe just as well.

He wasn't sure of the welcome he'd get. Weeks before, Logan had asked him to be his best man, but his brother's email and some missed follow-up calls hadn't caught Sawyer's attention until recently. In the small, far-off country where he spent most of his time these days, he'd had his hands full. He wondered if the epic landslide in Kedar and its aftermath would strike Logan as reasonable excuses not to show up until now.

He scanned the yard again, recognizing a high school friend here, a longtime neighbor there. No one had seen him yet.

Or...had she?

His heart sank into the ground like his boot heels. *Olivia*. But almost before their gazes met, she looked away.

Wouldn't you know she'd be the first person he saw?

Maybe he shouldn't have come at all.

Hoping to buy a little more time before he faced Logan, Sawyer halted steps away from the milling group of wedding guests—and saw his grandfather coming toward him with a slight limp.

"Well, I'll be. Sawyer McCord." Sam studied him, then looked down at his own navy blue jacket and the white rose boutonniere in his lapel. "Wouldn't be shocked if you didn't recognize me in this getup. But what happened to you?"

"Guess like Indiana Jones, 'it's not the years, it's the mileage.'"

In the past few weeks, while dealing with so much death and destruction, Sawyer had probably aged ten years. He hoped that didn't show, but it probably did.

Sam had changed, too. His still-thick hair had a few more gray strands among the dark brown, and there were lines in his face Sawyer hadn't seen before. But his blue eyes had stayed as sharp as ever and he was still whipcord lean. "When you were kids, no one could tell you apart from Logan."

"They will now," Sawyer said.

Sam's voice hardened. "About time you showed up."

"I would have come sooner, but..." He trailed off.

He didn't want to think about, or remember, his final screwup thousands of miles from here. The clinic he'd cofounded with his partner in Kedar was always in danger of attack from rival tribes, but bullets and bombs weren't the only means of devastation there. That huge landslide had brought half the mountain down, isolated the village and destroyed more lives than it should have. The disaster had tested his skills to repair, to heal, to save. And despite his lifelong urge to always step in, to help, Sawyer had failed. Was he as good a doctor as he'd believed he was, or—in violation of his Hippocratic oath—had he done more harm than good?

He tried to quiet his unruly thoughts. "How's your leg, Sam?" According to Logan, a few months ago Sam had been thrown by one of his bison cows that took offense to him getting too close to her calf. Now, Sam's cast was obviously off but his muscles must still be weak, even withered. At his age, full recovery would take time.

Sam was tough, though. "Good enough," he said.

Sawyer could almost hear someone say, *Go on, you two. At least slug each other on the arm as men do to show affection.*

But he was afraid to move. Sam didn't, either. They hadn't parted on good terms, to put it mildly. Over the years since Sawyer had left the Circle H instead of taking over the ranch, finished medical school, then based his practice overseas, they hadn't exchanged a single word. If Sam or Logan—or Olivia—had read about the landslide in the papers or online or seen the coverage on TV, they wouldn't have known he was there. And although he'd felt tempted to let them know he, at least, was unharmed, Sawyer hadn't tried to get in touch. He wouldn't worry them. There was nothing they could have done, except worry.

Sam continued to study him. "Never thought I'd see you again. Don't know if my heart's up to the shock."

Sawyer's throat tightened but he didn't say the words. *I love you, too, Pops.* Maybe he no longer had the right to call him that. He wasn't sure Sam or the others cared about him anymore. His fault.

Without another word, his grandfather stomped back across the lawn to join a group of other ranchers and their wives. A moment later, his laughter floated on the warm night air to Sawyer, excluding him. He hadn't been here twenty minutes and he was already in trouble with Sam. Nothing new.

He looked toward the spot where Olivia had been standing moments ago. In a wisp of filmy skirt and a silken swirl of blond hair, she was gone. He hadn't missed the look in her eyes, though. She was no happier to see him than Sam seemed to be.

He squared his shoulders, then plunged into the crowd, greeting former friends he hadn't seen in years. People, like Olivia and Sam, he'd never thought *he'd* see again.

THE LOUD MUSIC—the band played hard rock almost exclusively as the night wore on—made Olivia's head hurt. Sipping at her single glass of champagne, which she didn't really care for, she stayed on the fringe of the festivities, counting the minutes before she could leave. Avoiding Sawyer. Avoiding her father.

He and her stepmother had arrived from Dallas only that morning, her brother had told her. While she was glad her father had found a better life with Liza, she didn't want to talk to him. Or to her, either.

Olivia was still here only because Nick had balked at leaving.

"I'm having fun!" he'd shouted. Then he'd run off again with his new best friend, headed for the refreshment tables.

Olivia had left her gift in the ranch house, and she wished she could go home now. Other people were beginning to drift toward the makeshift parking lot on the far side of the yard, the hard packed dirt area beyond the grass that led to Logan's barn. She heard laughter, talk of some upcoming doings in town, a promise here and there to get together soon.

"Are you hiding?" Sawyer's familiar voice

snapped Olivia to attention. "I never thought of you as a wallflower. Yet here you are, keeping away from everyone. Or someone," he added, obviously meaning himself.

She looked away. "I'm about to leave. It's way past Nick's bedtime."

"Your son," he said.

She nodded. "Your nephew. The one you've never met."

That didn't surprise Olivia. Sawyer had cut and run long ago, and he hadn't come back—until now. Which reminded her of Nick's mostly absent grandfather. Her dad hadn't seen her son in a year. Nick was far closer to Sam Hunter, not that she would keep Nick from her father if he ever decided to play devoted grandpa at last.

She fought an urge to squirm. Seeing Sawyer appear so suddenly again had been a shock, but she hadn't confused him with Logan for more than a second. Olivia had always been able to tell the twins apart when most people couldn't. They had the same dark hair and deep blue eyes and almost identical builds, yet Olivia could see subtle differences. Their physical resemblance was strong but, for her, superficial.

Logan, who'd become a professional test pilot, was steady and calm; Sawyer was more intense and impulsive. She couldn't deny he was an attractive man, to put it mildly, but she couldn't bring herself to look at him again, and Olivia wasn't in the mood for a heart-to-heart chat—or anything else.

She searched for Nick, then spotted him marching around the yard carrying a big piece of cake in a napkin. The band launched into yet another earsplitting tune and Olivia took a step. "I'd better go."

Sawyer stopped her. "So this is how it will be, Olivia? Come on, I've already been stiffed by Sam. Haven't talked to Logan yet. Why not spare me a minute here? It's been a long time. Tell me how you've been since…the last time I saw you."

"Fine," she said. Her personal life was certainly none of his concern. Never mind that they'd once been friends. That had ended a long time ago in a field between the Circle H and Wilson Cattle, her family's ranch next door. "In fact, I've just heard about a possible opportunity to expand my antiques business. There's another store on the way to Wichita that I've been interested in for some time. The owner plans to retire." She bit her lip not to ask Sawyer about his life. They weren't friends anymore.

He looked past her toward Nick. "Which

would mean a move? Away from Barren?" He knew she wasn't fond of the Circle H, in part because of him.

"Possibly. I haven't thought that far yet," she admitted. "I'd probably want to be near both shops. There's a nice little town halfway between there and Barren, so I'd have an easy commute each way. I've heard good things about their elementary school. By September, when Nick starts second grade, maybe I'll be ready to move."

Olivia hadn't said the last word before Nick rushed up to them with his friend Ava, Olivia's niece. The two had gradually come closer but Olivia hadn't noticed. His deep blue eyes, so like his father's and Sawyer's, flashed. "No!" he yelled, making Olivia's ears quiver.

"Nick—"

"I won't leave the Circle H! I'll stay here with Daddy!" Then he pulled Ava across the yard, through half a dozen cars in the parking area and they raced toward the barn. "I'm going to see my kitten!"

The blood drained from Olivia's face. "I didn't realize he could hear us. I haven't talked with him yet or made a firm decision."

"He had a point, though. And what would Logan say?"

"He won't want us to leave town, but..."

She watched the children disappear into the barn and stifled the need to go after them. "I didn't mean to upset Nick. I'll give him a bit of time, then talk to him." She hesitated. "But I have to think about my business, too. Our means of support."

"Olivia."

Determined to avoid any more talk with Sawyer, she left him standing there and started toward a small group of other guests gathered near the porch. On the front steps, Blossom held her bridal bouquet aloft. An excited bunch of younger women were waving their arms, hoping to catch the spray of white roses, baby's breath and calla lilies and be the next to marry.

After she'd made the toss, Blossom came down the steps, her gait somewhat impeded by her gown and her obvious pregnancy. Her unhappy previous relationship was behind her now. This baby, although not hers with Logan, would be born into love, would be cherished… as Olivia cherished Nick.

Blossom said, "Thank you for the gorgeous quilt."

"My pleasure. Best wishes."

Olivia said goodbye to Blossom, then started toward the barn. She was halfway there when nine-year-old Ava burst outside and tore up the hill, her eyes wide as she barreled into Olivia.

She caught the little girl's shoulders. "What is it, Ava?"

Breathless, she could hardly speak. "Nick! He fell. I think he's dead!"

CHAPTER TWO

SAWYER HAD FINALLY found a chance to speak to Logan. They had just started to talk, when a little girl he didn't recognize shot out of the barn, waving her arms and shouting. Halfway up the hill, she ran straight into Olivia, and Sawyer watched Olivia's face turn white.

Logan was already running toward them. "Nicky!" he yelled. "Nicky!"

As if his boots were glued to the spot, Sawyer stayed where he was. For a guy who'd always responded to any crisis stat, who'd studied and interned, done his residency and practiced medicine under the worst trauma conditions, he couldn't seem to move.

Nicky. His nephew's name alone should have galvanized Sawyer but didn't. He heard the girl's words echo, sounding thick inside his head, as if both ears were plugged. *Dead.*

A dozen images of disaster flashed in his mind. *A man pulled from the rubble, one of his arms crushed. A pregnant woman, her cuts and scrapes ignored as she went into labor on the hard, rock-strewn ground, moaning in pain. A precious child…*

From behind him, Blossom loped across the lawn, holding up her bridal skirts, then passed him by. Several other late-leaving wedding guests rushed with her to the barn.

And still he didn't move.

After a long moment, he realized Olivia hadn't, either. With one hand over her mouth, her blue eyes wide circles of fear, she stood there, frozen like some ice statue. The little girl clung now to her skirt.

"Stay here," he said, finally forcing his legs into motion. On his way past, he lightly touched Olivia's shoulder. "Let me check out the situation."

She didn't answer. Pulse thumping, he left her and, like some caboose at the end of a train when he was used to being the steam engine, followed the last people into the barn.

He couldn't see through the circle of wedding guests in the aisle, their bodies blocking his view.

"Move back. I'm a doctor," he said but in a weak tone.

Logan was the last person to obey his order. He'd been down on one knee, bending helplessly over his little boy. Sawyer felt the same way. Those other images kept running through his brain.

He pushed the memories aside. "Let me see, Logan."

Logan didn't have a trace of color left in his face. He got up but his gaze didn't leave his son.

Sawyer's nephew—the small blond boy he'd never seen in person until tonight—lay half-conscious, sprawled on his back on the barn floor. His skin gray, his eyes closed, he looked almost peaceful.

Sawyer assessed his condition—airway, breathing, circulation. He preferred the few photos he'd seen of Nick, his birth announcement with a newborn picture attached to the email, the baby looking as if he were already able to smile, and later a first-birthday party shot of him in his high chair. Happy times in which he'd had pink cheeks and bright eyes.

He felt Nick's fine-boned wrist again for a pulse and breathed a sigh of relief. "Light," he said, adding silently, *and a bit thready*. He didn't want to worry people.

Blossom drew Logan close. He rested his forehead against hers. "Thank God."

His hand shaking, Sawyer raised each of Nick's eyelids to assess his pupils. He didn't like the look of them. "Come on, Nick. Talk to me. Squeeze my hand."

Show me something here. Though he knew Nick was still alive, the word *dead* kept spinning through his mind, reminding him of that other child who, because of Sawyer, wasn't breathing any more. He examined the boy's legs, his arms, searching for fractures.

"No obvious breaks," he said, turning to Logan. Sawyer wouldn't mention a possible skull fracture. Nick needed a more thorough assessment than he could provide here, and he was no neurologist.

The little girl who'd called for help had entered the barn with a woman who must be her mother. She was vaguely familiar, but his focus stayed on Nick.

Without glancing at her again, Sawyer asked the girl, "What happened here?"

Her voice quavered. "Nick was mad at his mom. We came to the barn. I thought we were going to see the kitten, but Nick climbed the ladder to the hayloft instead. He told me to go away." She began to cry. "I didn't see how it happened. But he fell."

Sawyer patted Nick's cheek to stimulate him. He heard a shuffle in the aisle. A couple of people shifted to let her through, and Olivia was finally there, moving like someone in a bad dream.

Sawyer said, "He must have hit his head pretty hard. He'll need a neuro consult, but first…" He looked around. "Where's Doc?" he asked, referring to the local physician who'd treated Sawyer as a kid. There weren't many choices in Barren, and Sawyer supposed he was Nick's doctor now. "I saw him earlier at the reception."

"He went home," Blossom murmured.

"*You're* here," he heard Olivia say in a firmer tone than he might have expected. Or no, it was exactly what he expected. It was almost an accusation, and another memory assailed him. Sawyer and Olivia, racing their horses across that nearby field until…he hadn't yelled a warning in time. Did she think of him now as a last resort?

His stomach heaved. *I can't do this, especially for my brother's kid. If I can't trust my judgment, what use would I be?* Once, he'd exuded confidence with what had amounted to a typical god complex. Kedar had changed that.

Sam hurried into the barn carrying a neck collar to stabilize Nick for transport. "Got this after I tangled with that cow. I called an ambulance."

"Won't get here soon enough. He needs to

go *now*." The collar was too big but Sawyer made a few adjustments. It would do.

He studied his brother and Blossom. He felt as helpless as they looked, even though he was the one who'd gone to med school. He'd practiced in a foreign country, often without proper medical supplies and equipment, especially in those days after the landslide when Sawyer's sense of powerlessness had finally overwhelmed him. He felt the same way now.

He glanced at the open barn doors, seeking escape.

THE COMPLEX OF buildings at Farrier General Hospital squatted just off the highway in the next town from Barren. Olivia hadn't been here in three years, since her marriage had ended after the spring flood when Nick almost died from pneumonia. Every smell reminded her of that night she'd nearly lost him.

Her nerves on edge, Olivia gazed down the hall again but didn't see a familiar form approaching. For the past few months Olivia had been seeing another antiques dealer from Kansas City, and she would have welcomed his presence now. But so far, Clint was nowhere to be seen. She'd left him a message about Nick, but she certainly didn't feel Clint's support.

Earlier, she had gone into Nick's ER cubicle

with Logan, concerned for their son's welfare, together in a new show of unity. Blossom had staycd in the waiting room where they joined her now while Nick was having tests. Logan was still pale and Olivia imagined she must appear chalk-white herself.

"I'm sorry your honeymoon is delayed," she said for want of something else to say.

Nick had been taken to the imaging center and Olivia tried not to imagine the worst again. At least he'd fully wakened in Logan's truck before the rush with Sawyer to Farrier. That was a good sign, wasn't it? She wished Sawyer would come back to the waiting room with a report for them.

"We can take a honeymoon anytime." Logan reached for her hand to still Olivia's constant fussing. "Try not to worry, Libby. I know how you are."

"As if you aren't just as worried."

"Does it show?" Like someone who had wandered in from some production of a play and was still in costume, Logan was wearing his wedding clothes. A few grains of rice dotted the shoulders and lapels of his navy blue blazer. He'd long ago given his yellow pocket square to Blossom who, in a chair opposite, was crying softly into her hands.

"It shows," Olivia said. She glanced toward

the elevators. Still no sign of Clint. Maybe she'd been right that even dabbling in the dating scene again was a bad idea. "Of course it shows. What's taking so long?"

"Don't ask me." He looked at her. "Reminds you of the flood, doesn't it? Being trapped at the ranch? I feel as helpless now as I did then."

Olivia shuddered. Nick's temperature had kept spiking higher, and she and Sam hadn't been able to get it down even with cool baths. "I thought you'd never get there."

He arched an eyebrow. When the waters started rising at the Circle H, Logan had been in Wichita for his job as a test pilot for a small manufacturer of private jets. Now he was a rancher again, though she wondered if that would last. "Lucky we did. After I reached your brother's place, we rode cross-country in the pitch-black, praying our horses wouldn't run into a barbed wire fence we couldn't see." That only reminded her of the horse she'd lost in that same field. "I'm still sorry, Olivia, that I wasn't there for you sooner."

Briefly, she leaned her head against his shoulder. "You came," she said. "That's all that mattered." And at one time, she'd thought he was everything she needed. "I shouldn't have spent so much time blaming you." Three years, she thought, until this past spring.

She straightened, her heart tripping. Sawyer was coming down the hall toward them at last. She couldn't tell from his face what, if anything, he'd learned.

Logan shot to his feet. "Well?"

Sawyer put out both hands, palms down. "Relax. He's okay. No real damage."

"Then why aren't you smiling?" Olivia asked.

Sawyer seemed not to hear her. "He doesn't quite know what happened at the barn but that's nothing to worry about. He'll remember. His pupils are equal and reactive now..."

Logan shook his head. "That reminds me of Sam. While he still had his cast on, he decided to take a horseback ride, prove he was fine— and fell in that same barn aisle. He still has some residual effects from his concussion."

"He had *two* falls? All I ever heard was he'd broken his leg."

"Maybe you should check in more often," Logan muttered.

Obviously, their reunion hadn't gone well, but she'd picked up on something that mattered even more to her. He'd said *no real damage*. "What's wrong, Sawyer?"

"Probably nothing, just me feeling twitchy." He shifted from one foot to the other. "The hospital wouldn't send him home if they thought he wasn't okay. They're going to release him tonight…into my care."

He didn't seem to want that responsibility, and Olivia wondered why. Although he'd finally come with them to the hospital, she'd resented his hesitation at first. True, he didn't know Nick very well—in fact, not at all—but did he not like children? Or was he holding a grudge? He and Logan hadn't been close for a number of years, but that couldn't be all. As a doctor, Sawyer was bound by an oath to treat those who needed him.

Had he been reluctant to help Nick because of her?

Because his "help" years ago had only led to tragedy for Olivia.

HOURS LATER, at the ranch, Olivia and Logan settled Nick into bed upstairs while Sawyer paced the family room. If he were the admitting physician at Farrier General, Nick would be in a room there overnight under observation. Or was Sawyer still in panic mode?

All he could think of was another pending disaster. The wrong diagnosis. Something Sawyer had missed at his clinic with someone else's child. Those nightmares haunted him every night and sometimes during the day until his hands shook and his heart beat like thunder.

If he had to diagnose himself, he'd say post-traumatic stress disorder. PTSD, like a soldier after battle, which in a way he supposed he was. Certainly the long hours, the deprivations, the constant stream of crises coming through the clinic door after the landslide should qualify as traumatic. For sure, his error in judgment did.

And then, as if he needed more, there was Olivia. Being back had already made clear her ongoing mistrust of him. Earlier, she couldn't get away from him fast enough.

He turned to make another circuit of the room. The house, the yard, were quiet. The reception was long over. The caterers had packed up and left, and not a single car remained in the makeshift parking area. The nearby kitchen looked immaculate. The neatness all around should have calmed him, its sense of order and all the trappings of civilization.

What could happen here? But of course, he knew, and not only because of Nick. Because of Olivia.

Footsteps sounded on the stairs and, before Sawyer could finish his thought, Logan walked into the room. He'd ditched his blazer and tie and rolled up his white shirtsleeves.

"He asleep?" Sawyer asked.

"Drifting in and out, I think."

Olivia had wanted to take Nick home to their house in Barren, to his own bed for the night, but Logan wouldn't hear of that. Olivia would stay here with Nick, and the newlyweds would spend their first night of marriage on the Circle H, close enough to make sure Nick was okay before they even thought about leaving on their honeymoon. And perhaps most important, this was where Sawyer would be staying. He was supposedly in charge for the night. Nick had been released only because a doctor would be present.

His palms began to sweat. And as he'd expected earlier, his brother wasn't happy with him. Nick's accident had only delayed their talk.

"I appreciate you finally coming back," Logan said. "Even if you didn't make it in time to be my best man. But I'm still mad."

"Because I showed up late? I'm sorry, but I'm here now." His brother appeared a lot calmer than Sawyer felt. His reluctance to explain himself warred with his longing to reconnect with his twin. He wanted to hear

Logan call him Tom again, as he used to do, a teasing play on his name.

"Hell, Sawyer, you didn't even bother to answer my calls."

Okay, he could give Logan this much. "I run a clinic in a remote area. You can't imagine how remote. I bet you've never heard of Kedar. In the heart of the Himalayas, the highest, most rugged mountains on earth. You think the Circle H can be hard to get to?"

"Hard enough," Logan murmured. "Three years ago, we nearly lost Nick right here when a spring flood blocked the roads to town and washed out the driveway. He and Olivia were stuck, trapped, in fact—I wasn't home—and Nick was very sick."

"I didn't know."

"If Grey and I hadn't forged our way from Wilson Cattle over the hill on horseback, he could have died of pneumonia. So yeah, I know *hard*."

"Maybe so, but those people I work with have very little. To them, the Circle H would seem like paradise—except they love those mountains. Even my sat phone doesn't always work there." He added, "If it did, I would have called you back." Yet his phone had been working fine before the landslide; his cell, too, most of the time. "I imagine Grey Wilson must have done a good job as best man in my place."

"He did. But how would I know about your sat phone—or anything else? Sawyer, the last time I talked to you, about Sam's accident, all I got was 'I'm here and there, doing this and that.' That was months ago. And then there was your silence about the wedding. We're *brothers*. Why didn't you tell me where you were? What you were doing?"

Sawyer took the verbal lashing. He had been secretive about his clinic, about his life there. For one thing, Sam wouldn't have approved. For another, Sawyer's decision to leave the Circle H—in part because of his feelings for Olivia—had been immature, and though he didn't regret opening the clinic, he was sorry for the way he'd left things at home. Not sharing much about Kedar had been a way to avoid dealing with how he'd treated his family. He wasn't proud of running out on them, but it was obviously his MO.

Logan wasn't finished. "After Mom and Dad died, you and I were never apart for more than a day or two until you left here for good. Left me with the Circle H," Logan said. "And that's all I get from you now? Some weak excuse? I mean, what's the point of living in a place like you describe?"

"I like to help people. I don't belong here anymore."

"What are you, really? Special Ops—and you don't want us to know? A spy?"

He didn't smile. "I'm just a doctor." *Or I was*. He wouldn't elaborate. If Logan couldn't accept his apology for nearly missing his wedding day, he could live with that. He had a bigger guilt to wrestle with—and that was on him alone. He wasn't about to share. "Listen. Just as you asked, I'll stay with Sam while you and Blossom take your honeymoon. I hope you have a great time." He held his breath. "We okay, then?"

Logan shrugged. "I'll see how you do while I'm gone. Think I'll try to get some sleep," he said, then turned and went up the stairs.

Sawyer let out a sigh. But he wasn't alone for long. Logan had no sooner disappeared than Olivia came down the steps. She looked wan, exhausted, and Sawyer didn't want to face her, not after their earlier conversation.

"You look beat. You can have my room, Olivia." The words sounded strange to him. Sawyer hadn't slept there in over nine years, but the wallpaper, the bedspread, the pictures on the desk were still the same. He'd left that room, this ranch, behind a few days after Olivia married his brother.

He tried a half smile. "I'll take my pillow, though, if you don't mind. Took me a long time to get that punched down just the way I like it. I've missed that." *Missed you*, he thought, but he could never say so and certainly she didn't feel the same way about him.

Olivia cleared her throat. "Fine. Or I could take this sofa."

"Wouldn't hear of it. You need a good night's rest."

"You don't?"

"I'll need to check on Nick periodically." He already dreaded that. The boy wasn't his responsibility and yet tonight he was. Being near Nick made him more than uncomfortable, afraid he'd do something wrong again, maybe with catastrophic results. Yet he owed Olivia—and had for years.

"Thank you, Sawyer." The sound of his name from her lips made every muscle in his body tense. "This certainly isn't a holiday for you. Leaving your busy practice, coming back for Logan…ending up with another case on your hands."

"For tonight." *For you*, he thought. He paused. "I'm not really practicing medicine now. While I'm here to help out at the Circle H, I'll need to make some decisions about my future."

"You wouldn't go back? To wherever you've been?"

Sawyer hesitated, then mumbled something vague about Kedar. Their friendship had ended, she'd married his twin brother instead...and Sawyer hadn't been the same since.

"Don't know," he said. "Don't need to know right now."

Olivia glanced down at the rug, then up again. Her eyes held his. "There must be some reason for your indecision." She waved a hand as if she were indicating his clinic, which seemed unlikely. She didn't know about what had happened there.

Sawyer had told Logan enough for one night. He wouldn't enlighten Olivia. No one else had to know about his mistake—not this far removed from the clinic, and certainly not at the Circle H, where he'd experienced the other two worst moments of his life. Losing both his parents at once and, later, driving Olivia away.

Anyway, he wouldn't be able to get the words out without crumbling into pieces. Olivia was the last person he'd confide in. He couldn't risk showing her his weakness, which would only reaffirm what she must still think of him.

"I need to check on Nick," he said and started for the stairs.

CHAPTER THREE

BY THE NEXT MORNING, Nick seemed much better. Olivia was not. Although she felt relieved about her son, a glimpse in the bathroom mirror had showed her a too-pale woman with dark shadows under her eyes. At the kitchen table, she sipped coffee and made plans to leave the Circle H as soon as Nick finished his cereal.

His face had color again and he continued to shovel in his breakfast as if he might never see another meal. Sometimes he astonished Olivia with the amount of food he could take in, which should have eased her mind. Her growing boy.

"Eat up, punkin. We need to go. I have an appointment out of town today."

Nick spoke around a mouthful of Cheerios. "Who's going to watch me?"

With school out for the summer, she'd have to rely on her usual babysitter, but in last night's chaos she had forgotten to double-check. "Susie," she said.

Olivia yawned. She hadn't slept well in Sawyer's bed, imagining his scent in the room, surrounded by the trappings of his younger life. And worried about Nick, she'd only dozed, waking with a start each time to wonder if he was okay.

Once in the night, she'd met Logan in the hall with the same intent to see their son, and another time she'd nearly run into Sawyer. Her mind foggy, Olivia had hurried back to her room.

"Why can't I stay here today?" Nick asked, nearly knocking over his orange juice. "I could ride Hero."

His new horse was a bone of contention for Olivia, who hadn't been consulted before Logan bought the gelding. She'd been working on becoming less protective of Nick but had a hard time keeping her mouth shut about this. Logan argued he'd rather see their boy on a steady mount than trying to handle one of the other, sometimes unpredictable, horses already in the Circle H stables. He was too big now for a pony.

She had to admit the gentle gray gelding with a showy black mane and tail took good care of Nick. She shouldn't worry, not about that at least.

"No Hero today for you." Logan had appeared in the kitchen doorway, and Olivia appreciated the backup despite wondering how long their united front would last. "Nicky, that's not a good idea. Grandpa Sam will set you up with the TV instead. You can watch a movie, play a video game..."

Nick gave him an assessing look. "Daddy, I want to ride."

Logan smiled at Blossom, who had joined him in the doorway. They both wore a visible glow this morning. He caught Olivia staring at them.

"A different wedding night than we'd planned," he admitted. "We both passed out as soon as our heads hit the pillows. We'll be talking about that for years." On his way by, Logan ruffled Nick's hair then headed for the coffee maker. "I know you're feeling better, but you took quite a spill last night. Hero can wait for a few days. Okay?"

Nick didn't answer. He crunched more cereal. Obviously unhappy, he refused to look at Logan, and Olivia saw the little frown between his brows that, in such a young face, always clutched at her heart. She set aside her coffee cup, then rose from the table.

"I appreciate the offer to keep Nick, but I'll see that he plays quietly today at home," she said, making a mental note to call Susie. Olivia turned to Blossom, who was pouring a glass of orange juice. "Are you guys leaving today?"

"The car's already packed." She hugged Olivia. "Thanks for coming yesterday. I know that wasn't easy for you, then Nick had his accident... That was quite a scare, but since he seems to be fine, yes—we'll start for the West Coast."

That had been Blossom's dream when she'd fled the nightmare of her previous relationship. On the run from her abusive fiancé and determined to protect her unborn baby, she'd thought if she reached California she'd be free. Olivia was glad she had a happier occasion to celebrate now and the coming baby to look forward to soon.

Blossom and Logan were driving west. Her pregnancy was far enough along that she didn't feel comfortable flying, and some airlines didn't permit that in the last trimester. They also wanted to see the sights on their way.

"I'm good," Nick said to his cereal bowl. "My head hardly hurts at all."

Another pair of footsteps clattered down the steps and Sawyer came into the room. He looked at Olivia as he spoke, his tone thin. The conversation must have drifted up the stairs to him. "He really should stay here." As if he didn't want him to but felt he had to suggest that. "With Sam," he added.

Was he omitting himself? Sawyer had always had a passionate streak, taking chances, riding the rankest horse. Olivia felt certain he'd carried that into his career as a physician, one who must deal often with trauma worse than Nick's fall yesterday. His history of making quick decisions, taking risks, would be an asset.

Yet she saw a new difference in him. Olivia couldn't put her finger on what that was, but she saw it in his eyes. He seemed to be hiding something deep inside.

She stared into her half-empty cup. The riskiest thing she planned to do was to possibly move away from Barren.

"Did I hear my name?" When Sam wandered into the kitchen in search of coffee, too, she almost groaned. He and Nick liked to hang out together and she expected Sam to weigh in about Nick, but he surprised her. "Sorry, won't be here today. With Logan gone, I have work to do." He didn't mention Sawyer.

She felt almost sorry for him. He still had his troubles with Sam and Logan.

Olivia gathered her bag and the sweater she'd brought yesterday in case the air grew cool during the reception. "My sitter can watch Nick. I'll fill Susie in on his fall so she'll make sure he takes it easy. Let's go, punkin."

She wondered if she imagined the relief on Sawyer's face.

AFTER OLIVIA LEFT with Nick, Sawyer wandered down to the barn. Aside from last night, he hadn't been there in nine years. The familiar smells of hay and leather and manure assailed his senses, taking him back to another time when life had seemed simpler—when as a boy, then during college, Sawyer had lived for this barn, these horses. Back when he'd expected to take over the Circle H one day.

Then, after Sawyer's first year of med school, Olivia had married his brother, and Sawyer had stopped coming home. Sometimes he thought part of his reason for opening the clinic in Kedar three years ago had been to get so far away from Barren that he'd never feel tempted to contact Olivia again.

This morning he couldn't get past his new feelings of guilt, and to make matters worse, he was still worried about Nick.

My head hardly hurts at all. Sometimes, as Sawyer knew only too well, kids tried to cover up or downplay their symptoms, or they couldn't articulate what was wrong until it was too late. Yet, even the Hippocratic oath couldn't convince Sawyer it was his place to make Nick stay at the ranch or to watch over him. Olivia had decided to leave, and she was Nick's mother.

In the quiet sunlit aisle of the barn, he talked for a few minutes with a couple of ranch hands. The pair was saddling a bay mare and an Appaloosa gelding. Willy and Tobias were getting ready to ride fence, he supposed. Once he went back up the hill, he'd be alone in the house. He had nothing to do. "I could ride with you," he offered, although he hadn't been on a horse much in recent years.

Willy, a tall man with dirty blond hair and a sly manner Sawyer didn't like, eyed him up and down, obviously noting his new jeans and boots. "Rough work," he said. "Wouldn't want to mess you up."

Tobias, who was older and had a wiry build, snorted. "Fancy duds."

Sawyer flinched. They didn't want him to go with them. Okay, he got that. Once he'd been a pretty fair hand. Now, with rusty skills, he'd only get in their way. He'd likely cut himself on some barbed wire and remember he was overdue for a tetanus shot.

Tobias and Willy mounted up. With a tip of their hats, they ducked low to ride out of the barn, looking more comfortable in their well-worn saddles than they did on two legs. As their horses trotted toward the pasture gate, he heard the two men laughing.

Leaning to open the gate, Willy called back. "Come over to the Wilsons' later if you want to help. We're rounding up some missing cattle." A wedding guest last night had mentioned a trio of rustlers who'd tried to clean Grey Wilson out, but they'd been caught and the local ranchers had offered to help bring the cows home. "Logan's prob'ly got some old clothes you can borrow. Pickup keys are in the black truck."

Sawyer watched them go. He was only here to help Sam and get his own head together. After Logan returned from his honeymoon, Sawyer would leave. Yet Grey was an old friend. How could he not drive over to Wilson Cattle, at least offer to pitch in?

But Grey was also Olivia's brother. What if she was there later, too? He didn't relish another awkward conversation with her.

He half wished Nick had stayed, a ready excuse for Sawyer to remain at the Circle H all day, not that the kid had exactly taken to him. He'd examined Sawyer with curiosity, confused him at first with Logan, then seemed to dismiss him.

Besides, Nick reminded him of that other

child he hadn't been able to save. The memory of that boy, who like many others had been pulled from the landslide rubble, made him feel guilty all over again. His dreadful mistake had cost a young life, and he couldn't seem to forgive himself for that, either.

How possibly to atone?

There was no way to bring back that dark-haired, dark-eyed child or to relieve the sorrow Sawyer had seen in his parents' eyes. He could only guess how that must hurt.

At the age of eight, Sawyer had lost his mother and father in a road accident. They'd been on their way home the day before his and Logan's birthday. It was Sam who'd raised them, adopted him and Logan, who'd been here all these years like a father to them.

The memory of his parents had saddened him. It seemed that everyone he loved, he lost.

Sawyer drifted down the barn aisle, stopping here and there to say hello to each horse that sidled up to the stall bars and poked out a soft nose. He didn't realize Sam was in the next stall until Sawyer walked up to peer at the black colt inside.

The horse's ears flattened against his skull. His eyes rolled, showing the whites. Not a good demonstration of his nature.

Sam lifted his head. "Better keep back." At

the horse's side, he'd been bent over, picking the colt's hooves. "He doesn't like strangers."

Sawyer obeyed. He didn't fear the horse, but he wouldn't agitate him and get Sam into trouble. Moving around in an occupied stall could be dangerous.

He assessed the animal with a cool eye. He had good conformation—beautiful, in fact. His glossy black hide shone in the soft light coming through the stall window that opened onto the barnyard. The colt danced around, reminding Sawyer of another horse years ago, shifting his hindquarters one way, then the other as if he were doing a samba. "He looks like a real handful."

"Oh, he is," Sam said but with apparent pride. "Picked him up at a sale. Guy there told me this one's daddy was a prizewinner—champion barrel racer—but his baby showed no signs of following in his hoofprints. I got him for a song." Still hunched over, Sam glanced up again. "Cyclone has no manners. And he bites."

"You love him," Sawyer murmured. He could see that in Sam's eyes.

"I will." He straightened, then lightly swatted Cyclone on his near flank to shift him over. "Once he learns how to behave."

"Has he had any groundwork?" The horse,

which appeared to be a yearling, wouldn't be
ready to ride until he was three, but he needed
to learn some of those manners long before
that. Sawyer's hand all but twitched to feel a
lunge line in his grasp, with one flick of his
wrist to get the colt moving with a fluid, forward gait in the corral.

"Logan offered to work with him," Sam
said, "and so has Grey Wilson, but neither one
has gotten around to that, much less breaking
him first."

Sawyer didn't like the term *break*. It im-
plied ruining an animal's spirit. He preferred
a gentler touch.

Years ago, he'd not only been a better ranch
hand in the making than his twin brother, he'd
also trained a few horses. One of them, at an
advanced age and probably now in retirement,
still lived in the end stall by the barn doors.
On his way through, Sawyer had slipped him
an apple. Another, Sundance, was Sam's horse
and now Logan's part of the time. Another…
had belonged to Olivia, but that horse wasn't
here or at Wilson Cattle.

"I could give the colt a try," he said, testing
the waters. He wasn't the only one to remember that other horse. He doubted Sam would
trust him with the colt.

Sam blinked. "Been a while since you handled a green one like Cyclone."

"I'm willing to try, though. While I'm here," he added.

"He'll need lots of attention. You plan to stay that long?"

"I don't know. Depends on what you mean by long." Yet Sawyer felt his spirits begin to lift. Frankly, this morning he'd been feeling sorry for himself. Regretting his reluctance to take responsibility for Nick's care. Knowing he wasn't part of the Circle H anymore, part of anything, really. His partner, Charlie, in the clinic had seemed half-relieved to see him go. Sawyer's presence was a constant reminder of what had happened there, and he guessed Olivia felt similarly about him. He'd be doing her a favor to keep away from her.

Sam was right. He wouldn't stay long, didn't know where to go when he left, much less how to find redemption for his sins. Still…

He reached through the stall bars, taking the chance to stroke the colt's nose. For his first attempt at friendship, he got a sharp nip that broke the skin on his index finger. Sawyer snatched his hand back.

"Told you." Sam shoved the horse aside to slide open the door. "Saw him take off the tip of someone's ear a couple months ago." He stepped out into the aisle, then threw the bolt, shutting Cyclone inside.

Sawyer looked at the colt for a moment. It seemed suddenly important to establish his temporary niche at the Circle H, give himself something to do while he was here. Maybe with Cyclone he'd do better than he had with a scalpel in his hand in Kedar. By the time he left, the black colt might have the foundation to become a decent horse. If Sawyer didn't fail again.

"I'll try anyway," he told Sam.

OLIVIA WAS STILL fuming as she parked her car in front of the antiques shop where she had a meeting with the owner, who wanted to sell. Without warning and after Olivia had called to remind her, Susie had cancelled, which was becoming a habit for Nick's babysitter. More than once this summer, Olivia had been forced to work from home, which had meant closing her store and losing business for the day, to stay with Nick. Her primary concern, of course, was her son, but she'd had to bring him with her today, and Susie's frequent no-shows were a problem.

Now, because Olivia hadn't let Nick stay at the ranch, he was sulking. Still mad, too, she supposed, about their possible move.

Even so, he was unusually quiet. She shut off the car's engine, glanced at Nick in the rear seat, then opened her door. Maybe it was better that he'd come with her so she could watch him. From what she'd seen last night and earlier today, she wouldn't want Sawyer to look after him. What kind of doctor was he?

"Nick, Mr. Anderson is waiting for us."

Theodore Anderson met them at the door. His stooped posture, the frail look of him, alarmed Olivia. The last time she'd seen him, he'd appeared much stronger. His watery eyes and the fringe of white hair around his scalp added to the impression. Olivia hoped her dismay didn't show on her face.

"Ted, how nice to see you." She reached out for a hug. "This is my son, Nick."

He shook Nick's hand. "How do you do, young man?"

Nick mumbled a response. Ted had the old-fashioned manners of a nineteenth-century gentleman, which suited his profession, but Olivia caught a faint flicker of unease in his gaze, to which she could relate. Like hers, his shop was filled to the rafters with furniture and delicate collectibles. Every tabletop held glass paperweights, exquisite crystal, ceramic figurines. Olivia spied a graceful Lladró statue of an elegant lady in gray with sweeping, sculpted skirts, one of the first designs the esteemed Spanish manufacturer had issued. Her mouth watered.

"What gorgeous things you have."

Ted's expression fell. "Apparently, I need to get rid of them. My son and his wife want me to move to Florida."

What did *he* want? Olivia felt sorry for him. He was obviously under some pressure, but Ted's wife had died several years ago, and she could see he'd declined since then. He probably felt he was losing his independence now.

"Do they live there?"

"No. My son has a small ranch not far from here. He's convinced my arthritis will improve once I get away from our Kansas winters. They've found me a lovely condominium down South." He didn't sound enthusiastic.

Giving up his shop would be hard for Ted. He knew each item and where to find it in this magnificent clutter of a place. She didn't doubt he loved every single piece.

"I take it you're not wild about a move, but warmer weather might be nice," she said. "I don't care for snow myself."

He smiled a little. "Then maybe *you* should buy that condo. I'll stay to run my shop—and yours."

"That wouldn't work for me," she said, "but

I'm interested in buying you out here if you do want to sell."

His thin shoulders slumped even more. "Let me show you around."

Nick trailed behind, his fingers busy on the tablet she'd bought for his birthday, his gaze intent on the screen. He'd recently discovered Minecraft. Although the game was educational and creative, if she didn't set limits for him, Nick would play all day and night.

Ted gave her a tour of the shop, pointing out an especially valuable English silver tea set here, an exquisite Victorian fainting couch upholstered in lush plum velvet there, while Olivia held her breath. She'd always loved his store. Ted had exquisite taste. He had carefully acquired an amazing and expensive collection, a good percentage of which Nick, lost in his game, could easily blunder into.

As they returned to the front of the store, Nick raised a hand to rub his forehead with a frown. He bumped against a round mahogany drum table from the eighteenth century, rattling its display of fine Lalique perfume bottles. Olivia barely righted one in time to prevent it from breaking.

Her heart slid back down into her chest. "Sorry," she said just as Nick crashed into a small nearby liquor cabinet, a priceless-looking

Tiffany vase on its top shelf. To her horror, the vase wobbled, then fell, shattering into pieces on the floor. Shards of glass, splintered with light into a full spectrum of colors, scattered everywhere.

Olivia cried out, then dropped to her knees to begin picking up the mess. "I'm so sorry, Ted. Of course I'll pay for the damage." *Or try to.* She felt too shaken at the moment to ask what this particular vase had been worth.

"No need to apologize. We'll work it out." But he looked upset himself. He was simply too polite to lose his temper, and he hastened to reassure Nick, who seemed dazed as he mumbled an apology.

Ted led them past the front counter, where an ancient computer sat gathering dust. Beside it was a vintage cash register that he'd once claimed still actually worked. He said, "Just tell me you have an offer I can live with. About the shop."

Keeping one eye on Nick, Olivia named a figure.

Ted wrinkled his nose. "I had something a bit higher in mind."

Olivia tensed. "You know I'll take special care of all your treasures." Remembering the broken vase, she winced. "I won't let a single one go for less than a good price. I'll love them as you do."

"Well…" He didn't go on.

"Think about this," Olivia said, not wanting to press him any further. "Call me if you want to counter my offer. And let me know about the vase."

Ted ignored that part. "Those kids want me to move soon. Not much time to inventory everything and then…leave," he added. "I'll be giving up my livelihood. My passion, as it were."

Olivia laid a hand on his arm. "We'll talk." Her gaze strayed to Nick, who was now sitting cross-legged on the wooden floor, still furiously thumbing the tablet as if nothing had happened. "I'm sure we can come to some agreement." She hesitated, then tried to sweeten the pot. "Once we do, I promise to keep you in the loop, ask your advice on things. Goodness, I can't possibly know as much as you do. That way you can keep your hand in and the shop can still feel like yours. Which it always will be." Another pause. "I want you to be happy, Ted."

His expression told her he didn't think that was likely, but Olivia left him to ponder her offer, hoping he'd come around. She badly wanted his business. When a deal was done, she could think about a move away from Barren, away from her memories, some of which Sawyer had stirred up with his unexpected return. She told herself he'd probably be gone before she packed a single box.

In the car, Olivia sagged in her seat. "Oh, Nick." How would she pay for the vase? She had a rough idea of its value, a figure that made her want to groan. She hadn't wanted to make a scene in Ted's shop, but Nick hadn't been paying attention. And now his carelessness might have cost her a deal with Ted. Nick needed to learn there were consequences to his actions. "Sweetie, the vase you broke was very expensive." Not that Nick had a true understanding of the money involved. "I hate to do this, but I think it will be a valuable lesson. You'll have to help earn the money to pay back Mr. Anderson."

"How?" he moaned. "Mom, I don't feel good. I still got a headache."

Her breath caught. "I didn't mean today. We can work something out later."

Nick's frown deepened as they headed out to Wilson Cattle, where Olivia planned to pitch in wherever she could with the return of Grey's cattle. At Ted's shop, she'd thought Nick was simply bored and cranky. Then she'd assumed he felt terrible about the broken vase, though he'd said nothing after his brief apology. Now she wondered. Was he just tired? Doubling down on the sulking because he'd have to do added chores to pay off part of the debt? Or was it something else?

She drove faster, trying to run through the numbers to adjust her offer to Ted but worrying more about Nick as she neared Barren.

"It really hurts," he said with a groan.

Her pulse suddenly pounding, Olivia checked her rearview mirror. Nick's face was ashen, worse than it had been last night. She wanted to pull over, but traffic on the interstate made that a dicey proposition. She'd risk getting hit while parked on the shoulder.

She gripped the steering wheel. "Hang on, baby. We'll be there soon."

She tried to tell herself he just needed something for the pain, that this was normal after what he'd been through last night. It wasn't an emergency, was it?

She glanced again in the mirror.

Nick had slumped to one side. Dozing, as he'd often done in the back seat since he was a baby? Or had he passed out again?

Panic hit her as if a rock had been thrown through the windshield. "Nick!"

His eyes opened, then closed again. "I'm sleepy."

A quick look at her GPS told Olivia they were nowhere near the hospital.

She grabbed her cell phone from the seat beside her and called Doc but only got a recorded message. *Gone fishing. If you have an emergency, contact Dr. So-and-So...* Olivia barely listened and missed the name. But no one answered at the clinic on Main Street, either.

She didn't have a choice. The ranch wasn't far now.

She hit Speed Dial for the Circle H and asked for Sawyer.

CHAPTER FOUR

SAWYER DIDN'T TAKE the black ranch pickup. An hour or so after Willy and Tobias had ridden out, he saddled up Sundance, then started over the hill to Wilson Cattle. Although he hadn't ridden in years—unless he counted the few house calls he'd made in Kedar, climbing the side of a mountain on a tough Asian pony—he relished the feel of Sundance's much bigger, warm horseflesh between his legs.

The steady, rhythmic clop of iron-shod hooves on the hard dirt path of summer, the feel of leather reins guiding the horse around stony obstacles or out from under the occasional tree branch, made him happy for the first time since the landslide.

All by himself, Sawyer grinned. Once, he'd loved this place and never wanted to leave. *Funny, the different trails life takes you on*, he thought as he crested the low hill. For the first time since he'd walked into his brother's wedding reception last night, he wasn't thinking about Kedar or even Olivia.

That is, until he realized he was riding the same path he had with her years ago. Below, the neighboring ranch was a bustle of activity. Trucks parked everywhere. People milling about. Laughter and talk rising into the heated air. He spotted Everett Wilson with his new wife, Liza. They must have decided to stay longer instead of flying right back to Dallas after yesterday's wedding.

A rig towing a stock trailer had just rolled in, stirring up dust and filled with bellowing cattle. Sawyer wondered if they were irritated at being herded into a metal pen on wheels with the others or if they were calling out in recognition that they were home again.

Wearing a black Stetson clamped over his light brown hair, Grey met him at the bottom of the hill. "You here to join the fun? We could use more help." As he said the words, two other monster pickups with slat-sided trailers barreled along the driveway to the barn.

"Whatever you need me to do," Sawyer said. He saw Willy and Tobias heading for the first truck and nodded in their direction. Willy tipped his straw cowboy hat as if to acknowledge the worn jeans and Western-style shirt Sawyer had filched from Logan's closet. "Looks like you nearly lost a big bunch of cattle, Grey. How many?"

"A good percentage of my herd," Grey agreed. "I'm more than glad to have them back." He couldn't seem to stop grinning, his blue-green eyes alight but not only for the cattle, Sawyer noted. The dark-haired woman he had seen with Grey the night before was coming across the ranch yard with the little girl who'd alerted everyone to Nick's fall. As she came closer, Sawyer finally recognized the child's mother—Grey's long-ago girlfriend.

Grey scooped her close to his side, then ruffled the girl's hair. "You remember Shadow?" he asked. "And this is Ava. Our daughter."

Sawyer glanced at the diamond ring on Shadow Moran's hand. He didn't see a wedding band, so... "Congratulations. I knew you before I left the Circle H. You were behind me, though, in school. What, three, four years?"

"Five." Her dark eyes warmed. "At first, when I crossed the yard, I thought you were Logan—then I remembered he and Blossom are on their honeymoon."

Ava gazed up at him. She looked like her mother except for her eyes, the color of Grey's. "You and Logan are just the same."

"Yes, we are," he said, then pointed at the small scar by his right eye. "You can always tell me from him because of this."

"How did you get it?"

"Doing something I shouldn't have been doing." He touched her shoulder, then turned back to Grey. He wondered why Grey was just now getting around to marrying Shadow, though it was none of his business. "Point me in the right direction. I did work the Circle H before Sam decided to run bison instead of cows, and I don't think I've forgotten how to handle them." He hoped not. "Nice-looking Black Angus you have, by the way."

"Thanks, Sawyer."

He had started toward one of the trucks to help unload when he stopped again. "Who stole these cattle, anyway?"

Shadow shifted in Grey's embrace. Her mouth turned down. "My own brother—and two other men."

"One of them a ranch hand of mine." Grey kissed the top of her head. "The sheriff's not happy with them, and they may still be in trouble with the law, but I refused to press charges. Shadow's baby brother got off on the wrong foot in life. We'll try to change that if we can."

Sawyer was still digesting that when a car coming up the drive cut around several pickups and stock trailers, then braked to a stop right near him, spraying dirt everywhere. The cloud of dust choked Sawyer and he was coughing when Olivia got out. Eyes wide, she left her door flung open and charged up to him.

"Nick!" she managed to say, then pointed at the car.

In the dim light inside, Sawyer could see the boy leaned over in his seat, eyes closed, his body limp. Sawyer's pulse jumped.

"I called the Circle H," she said from behind him. "No answer at Doc's or the walk-in clinic, either. Then I remembered everyone was here today and we were only minutes from Wilson Cattle, too. I hoped Doc had stopped by on his way to go fishing—"

"Why didn't you head for Farrier General?" The ER there had Nick's chart from the night before.

"It's no closer today than it was last night." She mentioned her visit to the antiques shop. "Frankly, I didn't expect to find you here."

"Yes, you did," Sawyer murmured. He doubted she'd come in search of Doc, but he couldn't blame her for saying that.

Olivia told him about Nick's headache, which had obviously gotten worse since that morning when Sawyer had worried about it. He could see for himself how drowsy Nick was, if not in danger of slipping into a coma. He didn't want to scare her, but this wasn't good.

Last night, he'd hesitated to even approach

Nick. He couldn't stall now. "Olivia, stay with Shadow." He glanced at his friend. "Grey, keep everyone away."

The last thing he needed was a crowd. Sawyer hunkered down in the open doorway and reached into the car, checked Nick's pulse, made sure his airway was clear, his heartbeat strong. This was the sort of basic triage care he'd practiced with the victims of the landslide, and as he performed the quick movements again, he didn't need to think. To doubt himself. He only had to act—and do the right thing.

Finally, he turned to Olivia. "Get in," he said.

She'd been standing with Grey, her brother's arm around her, but hurried back to the car. "Is he—"

"Olivia, let's go. I'll drive."

OLIVIA FELT COLD all over. If she didn't keep a tight grip on herself, she would begin to shake and wouldn't be able to stop. She clenched her jaw to not let her teeth chatter. She'd been sitting in the Farrier General waiting room again for what seemed like hours.

Shadow sat beside her. Grey had offered to come with them—insisted upon it—but Shadow had told him to stay behind for now.

He had his returned cattle to oversee, and their daughter, Ava. They would keep him posted, and he could come to the hospital later. Olivia had hoped that wouldn't be necessary, that Nick would be released as quickly as he was last night, but the staff members' words so far didn't reassure her.

She tried to think of something—anything— else to stay sane. Like her plans to trade in her car soon. She needed something bigger, maybe an SUV, to deliver purchases to her customers. But she couldn't concentrate on that. Feeling anxious, she kept looking around but didn't see Sawyer anywhere.

Shadow patted her arm, her voice low and soft. Her liquid dark eyes held Olivia's gaze. "I'm sure one of the doctors will be out soon. They need to focus on Nick right now. Get him stabilized."

Olivia nodded but only felt worse. "I'm a bad mother," she said. "I should never have left the Circle H this morning." She could feel hysteria rising inside her. The longer she sat here, even with Shadow for company, the more worried she got.

"You're a wonderful mother," Shadow insisted, tucking a strand of her long, dark hair behind one ear. "Far better than I was to Ava at times. He's going to be all right, Olivia."

She peered down the hall, as if also searching for Sawyer. "Nick's a tough little boy. He's a fighter."

"He's also seven years old and small for his age—" She broke off. Shadow was right. Olivia wasn't making sense. More than anyone else, she knew how strong-willed Nick could be. "I'm sorry, I'm such a mess." Shadow was aware of how overly protective she'd been of him since the flood at the ranch. "I was making good progress," Olivia said. "Now this. I can't stand waiting." She gestured at the Staff Only sign. "I want to charge through those doors—"

"Of course you do." Shadow drew her close and gently pressed her head against her shoulder. "Try to relax. Deep breaths. I'll tell you as soon as I see someone coming."

Olivia wasn't sure whether she meant a nurse, a doctor or Sawyer, or which one she should hope for.

"Nicky's back in the hospital?" Logan asked, sounding tense. Sawyer could hear the hum of the highway in the background, the blast of a horn from what sounded like a semi blowing past Logan's car. "Why?"

He'd told Olivia he would call his brother, the last thing he'd said to her before he escaped the waiting room.

"He's being admitted." Sawyer tried to downplay the seriousness of the situation. He'd made a quick report to Olivia after first speaking with the doctors, but he didn't know exactly how bad Nick's condition was yet.

Sawyer had been pacing the hospital cafeteria for the past hour. He'd memorized every food item available, but the sight of bins of meatloaf with onions swimming in gravy, pale yellow corn and anemic-looking peas, limp french fries, and slices of lemon meringue pie turned his stomach. With every step, he'd been debating with himself. Rush back to the waiting room? Be there for Olivia, assuming she would want him by her side? Or—and he was leaning most strongly toward this option— hurry out to the parking lot and borrow her car? Get away from here? He could pick her up later or Shadow could drive her home. On the other hand...

He was licensed to practice in the state of Kansas. He'd gotten his degree, done his internship and residency here after he left the Circle H for good. And then, overseas, he'd failed in the most basic way when someone needed him most.

Nick is a different person, he told himself. Nick was his nephew, as Olivia had pointed out. But to Sawyer, that was splitting hairs.

He didn't have an affiliation with this hospital. *You could study his chart, though. You could discuss his treatment plan. You could screw up again.*

"What did the doctors say?" Logan was asking. "What do you think?"

Sawyer couldn't answer. He didn't want to admit he'd all but recused himself from the case, as he had every right to do. Nick was a close family member, and because of emotional involvement, Sawyer could opt out—as if he'd been asked to take part. But Logan was his only brother. Didn't he owe him more than that? Wasn't a nine-year absence from all their lives enough? If he couldn't atone for Kedar, he should at least try to make up for that. And the other doctors were willing to talk to him as a professional. He could share his views. Although they had disagreed, he suspected Nick's headache might be due to a hematoma. Had they since scanned his head?

"I'm turning around," Logan said.

In the background, Sawyer heard Blossom agree. "We have to make sure Nick's okay. Poor little guy…"

Of course they did. Sawyer didn't try to dissuade them. Maybe by the time they got here, Nick would be out of danger and released again, and they'd all share in various expressions of relief sprinkled with laughter, as if they'd been foolish to even think he could be in real trouble. In any event, Sawyer knew Logan needed to see his boy for himself. "Drive safe," he said.

After the call ended, he resumed his circuit of the cafeteria. The lemon pie's meringue was starting to curl with beads of moisture glistening from the overhead lamp. The meatloaf's gravy had congealed in its steel bin and... *You're a coward.*

Sawyer made an about-face. What kind of brother, uncle, friend—ex-friend, to Olivia— was he? He'd been trying to protect himself to the point of being unable to protect a vulnerable child. Nothing new there, but not very admirable, either.

He marched toward the exit, out into the hall and down another back into the emergency department to collar Nick's doctor. Even the well-known smells of antiseptic, of medications and of illness and fear, including his own, didn't stop him.

Olivia was nearby, waiting. Reason enough.

She didn't need him to treat her child, but she did need his knowledge.

Sawyer went to see about that scan.

CHAPTER FIVE

"TELL ME," OLIVIA SAID, rising from her seat as soon as Sawyer reentered the waiting area. While he'd been gone to call Logan and she'd been trying to hang on to her sanity, the small TV on the wall had kept playing the same video loop over and over again, informing any viewers about the most recent treatments for diabetes and elder incontinence. Olivia had been about to lose the rest of her mind. The only ailment she wanted to hear about was Nick's. Leaving Shadow, she marched out into the hall with Sawyer following.

He ran a hand over the nape of his neck. "Try to be patient. The doctors are doing all that's necessary, Olivia." Sawyer focused on a point beyond her shoulder. "This is all I know right now—we've finally agreed that Nick has a hematoma."

She felt her body drain of strength. "Sam also had a blood clot, or whatever," she pointed out. "Didn't he?"

"No. Well, as far as I know, he had a concussion. This is subdural."

"What does that mean?"

Sawyer rubbed the back of his neck again. "I didn't like the look of his pupils last night and this morning—"

"Then why didn't you say something? Do something?"

"I'm not practicing right now. I'm not his primary physician. All I could do was make sure his head stayed elevated during the night in a midline position and that he remained responsive. Otherwise, I don't make the decisions—for which you're probably glad." Sawyer's explanation made her head spin, but he went on. "Nick's initial score on the Coma Scale we use was around fourteen when Nick was sent home last night, meaning he didn't need to be admitted. But today, as you know, his condition became worse." He softened his tone. "He's had a CT scan now, which they didn't do last night. With kids, we worry about the radiation exposure, so we avoid CTs if their initial scores indicate only mild head trauma. As in a certain percentage of cases, he has a faint linear skull fracture and now, some brain swelling."

Olivia shook her head to clear it. "Does that mean surgery?"

Sawyer cupped her elbow, as if he guessed

she might faint. "I hope not. His other signs are pretty good. Unless the swelling gets worse, and fast, it's likely a wait-and-see scenario. In lots of cases, the swelling goes down on its own. But I'll talk to his doctors again later."

She was shaking now, and she poked his chest with her index finger. "Your silence— your *selfish* silence—could have resulted in tragedy for Nick. It still might, from what I hear. You might not be his doctor, but you still could have said something last night, if you thought— And you haven't even bothered to visit his room. All you can say now is that waiting's just part of medicine?"

"Olivia, he's getting good care. What else would you have me do?"

She glared. "Nothing, I suppose. Or no, maybe I should be grateful you didn't intervene like years ago when—"

His mouth tightened. "Seriously? You want to bring that up now? Compare then, and a horse, to your own child? It's not the same, Olivia."

"I know it's not. But you were guilty then. As far as I'm concerned, you're guilty now— and this time it's *my son* who has suffered."

Sawyer's blue eyes darkened. He seemed to collect his thoughts before he said, "Fine. You want to rehash the past? Okay, let's. If you remember, *years ago*, yes, I challenged you to that race across a dry field littered with stones. There'd been no rain for weeks, but I had a sudden urge to fly like the wind. To hear you laugh," he said. "I knew we shouldn't, but it wasn't like we hadn't done it before. All of us."

Her mouth turned down. Olivia didn't welcome the memory, but she'd started this. And that day they had been alone, not with their brothers. By then, she and Sawyer had been seeing each other for about six months, their childhood friendship left behind for a new relationship that was turning into love...until her feelings for him had led to tragedy.

Her eyes filled with fresh tears, and he tried to reach for her hand but Olivia stepped back. She knew they were both picturing the same moment: galloping neck and neck until, suddenly, Jasmine had lurched, stumbled, then fallen, taking Olivia down with her. Reining his horse to an abrupt stop, Sawyer had jumped off, dropped to his knees to make sure she was all right. Bruised but unbroken, Olivia had already started to cry. It took Sawyer another second to realize how badly hurt her horse really was.

Her beautiful black mare lay on her side, breathing hard, her normally calm brown eyes wide with pain and fear before they rolled back in her head. Her left foreleg had been shattered by the fall.

"I'm sorry, Olivia. I should have known better. If I hadn't argued with Sam again that morning, maybe I wouldn't have suggested the race at all. But I did. And that's no excuse. I'm not sure if I've told you before, but we were fighting about med school. About my being away from the Circle H so much. Sam wanted me there more often instead. I had so much anger then. Probably still d—"

"She *died*." Olivia's tone held the unshed tears that had filled her eyes, partly for the horse, partly now for Nick. Maybe—no, definitely—it was best that Sawyer hadn't tried to treat Nick. "You didn't even give her a chance. You *shot* her, right in front of me."

"I put her down," he said, and she bristled at the euphemism. "We were a mile from the ranch yard, the barn, probably an hour or more from the vet getting there. What else could I do?" He'd repeated the question he'd asked about Nick. "Like Logan, Grey and me, you'd been riding since you were two years old. You knew why I had that rifle with me, why any other rancher would have one, too. Warding off coyotes isn't the only reason. There wasn't *time*, Olivia."

"You don't know that."

"Would you rather have watched her suffer?" Sawyer shook his head. "Jasmine broke her leg in about a hundred places. There was no putting her back together. Trying to reconstruct that foreleg would only have caused her more pain and wouldn't have worked in the end. She'd have gone crazy shut up in a stall for weeks, maybe hurt herself again with the same result."

She pressed her lips together, then said the words anyway. "Is that how you manage your *human* patients?"

Sawyer turned pale. "I'm not managing anyone. I told you that."

He started to walk away, but Olivia went after him, grasping his arm and feeling the hard muscle under her fingers. His whole body was taut. Her voice trembled. "You just can't say it, can you? That you were wrong—she might have survived—that you made a bad decision. That was my horse—the best horse I ever rode—a horse that could have been a national champion barrel racer." She hadn't ridden since, perhaps another reason she'd been against Nick getting Hero. "A horse I loved with all my heart. How am I supposed to forgive you for that?"

"You're not." He removed his arm from her grasp, then touched the corner of his right eye.

Hysterical at seeing her horse destroyed, Olivia had struck out, cutting Sawyer with a ring she wore. "But if it makes you feel any better, I haven't forgiven myself, either. I wish I'd had another option. I wish there was some way I could…make amends. Atone."

He was halfway down the hall, and Olivia was still shaking, before the thought crossed her mind. He hadn't just meant Jasmine. He hadn't even meant Nick.

LIZA WILSON STEPPED out into the hallway of the pediatric neurosurgical wing. She'd gone in to visit Nick again until she could no longer blink back tears, so she'd finally left his room to get control of her emotions. Since his admission several days ago, she'd been running back and forth from Wilson Cattle to see him, but worry was never far from her mind. Liza didn't have children of her own, and she'd taken a shine to Nick the instant they'd met.

The feeling seemed to be mutual, bless his heart. Which only made her worry more for his well-being. So far, surgery hadn't been on the schedule and for that she felt grateful, but Nick wasn't out of danger yet.

Understandably, Olivia was still a wreck, but she wasn't inclined to lean on Liza, who had left her in the waiting area with Blossom,

Logan and Everett. Liza knew Olivia liked her, yet they weren't friends, much less step-mother and stepdaughter—family—except in legal terms. Neither Olivia nor Grey had fully accepted her, and Liza couldn't blame them. As adults, perhaps they felt they didn't need another mother, especially one who was only four years older than Olivia.

At thirty-six, Liza was twenty years younger than Everett Wilson. And his grown children already had a mother. A mostly absent one, Liza thought, but still... She might never be accepted, and the reality saddened her. The Interloper. Liza didn't fit in here. But oh, she wanted to.

Halfway down the hall, she spied Sawyer and her opportunity to learn more about Nick's condition. He was standing at a window that looked out onto the parking lot, his broad shoulders hunched, hands in his pockets.

Liza laid a hand on his forcarm. "There you are." Her pulse beat heavily. Why had he left the waiting room? Overcome, like her, by his feelings for Nick? Sawyer knew him less well than Liza did, not that that precluded concern. But, she realized, she hadn't seen him in Nick's room once. Had he just heard bad news? Or, no. Maybe he felt unwanted as she did. The Prodigal Brother.

"Hey, Liza." Sawyer turned, forcing a smile. "I couldn't take all the gloom and doom in there," he said with a wave toward the waiting room. "Thought I'd catch some air, but no one opens windows here. The AC doesn't cut it for me. Summer in the mountains of Kedar can be brutal, but here in Kansas..." Outside, heat and humidity shimmered off the pavement. Liza was used to that in Texas.

She couldn't keep from asking. "What have you heard?"

"Nothing more. 'Watchful waiting,' his doctors say."

"Do you agree?"

Sawyer glanced out at the blacktop. "They don't need me to. I'm lucky to get a look at Nick's chart now and then and try to read the scribbles. Olivia seems convinced I can read 'doctorese,' but that's only my own. You'd think Farrier would have gone to electronic records by now, but handwriting's closer to what I'm used to at my clinic. Or was," he added.

"What do those scribbles tell you?"

"The brain swelling isn't any worse—but it's not that much better, either."

"I see." She'd been wrong. Apparently something hadn't gone well between him and Olivia. If only her stepdaughter would let Liza hold and comfort her. Yet even in Nick's room, standing together by his bed yesterday, Olivia had kept her distance and Liza had taken to seeing Nick alone or with Everett.

"I'm sure Olivia is grateful to you for staying close," Sawyer said. "Grey told me he's glad you and Everett decided to extend your visit."

"Did he?" Her spirits brightened. Maybe Sawyer had noticed Olivia giving her the cold shoulder and was trying to comfort her. Liza had already seen that he was a sensitive person, one with a deep-seated pain he tried not to reveal to anyone else. "Grey's a good man. Everett is proud of him." *So am I*, she thought, though he probably didn't want her approval.

Sawyer smiled without it reaching his eyes. "I hear Grey went through some hard times with the ranch, but he sure looks happy now. His cattle are back, and he's engaged to Shadow. Guess there'll be another wedding in your family soon."

Liza couldn't smile. *My family*. She wasn't about to tell him that was a first for her, as if she truly belonged. She didn't care to ponder her own painful past. "Everett and I eloped to Palm Springs. We had just the two of us and a pair of witnesses we tapped from among the other resort guests."

"You didn't want a big wedding here?"

Liza decided they were both sticking to safe topics. "No," she said, not willing to mention that at the time Olivia had seemed to oppose the marriage, possibly wondering why her father needed to tie the knot a second time with someone so much younger than he was. Grey had said little and Liza had chalked that up to his usual reticence to talk about his feelings. Oh, they were both polite to her and included her in family events now, so maybe this would be a gradual thing, but Liza could always feel their reluctance to consider her a real part of the group.

Or was that her insecurity showing? "I was more than happy with a quiet ceremony and—" she added with a smile "—a good glass of wine to celebrate."

"Grey tells me you also took a cruise for your honeymoon."

Liza laughed at the memory. "Yes, would you believe? To the Galapagos on one of those expedition ships. As you can imagine and after living in a remote area yourself, it was quite a challenge—Everett's idea. I always tell him he was hard to keep up with. I did enjoy seeing the unusual flora and fauna there. Thank goodness for my new hiking boots. And, of course, I loved just being with my new husband." With Sawyer, she didn't need to hide her love for Everett.

Sawyer glanced toward the waiting room. His eyes had turned from that compelling deep blue to indigo.

She touched his arm again. "Sawyer, what is it other than Nick? I know being home again after so long has its issues, but I'm sure Logan is pleased—"

"He tries hard not to show it." He paused. "I almost wish he and Blossom had continued with their honeymoon."

"But there's something even more, isn't there?"

He shrugged. "Nothing right now." He turned away, as if casting about for a reason to leave. "Think I'll try to get another look at Nick's chart. The neurologist was here just before I stepped into the hall."

Liza didn't get the chance to say more. Sawyer kissed her cheek, and with what appeared to be a self-assured stride, he went back toward the nurses' desk. Despite his show of confidence, he looked to her like another lost soul.

Like Liza.

SAWYER STAYED AT the hospital for as long as he could manage without coming out of his skin. He felt constantly torn between being there for Logan and Olivia, as if she wanted him, and the desire to flee before the very smells made him fall apart. Liza was in the waiting room again, too, and he didn't want to continue their hallway conversation within earshot of Olivia. Frankly, his problems—here or in Kedar— were no one else's cross to bear.

Sawyer had a hard enough time keeping his mind off Nick. Before he'd left today, he'd bought a teddy bear wearing a Superman costume and a big, encouraging grin in the gift shop, then left it with Olivia, whose murmured, if cool, "Thanks," was the only word she spoke.

Nevertheless, it had conveyed the message: Sawyer should have delivered the stuffed bear himself instead of handing it off without ever stepping foot in Nick's room. He shouldn't have discussed the horse tragedy with her, either; revisiting that had only raised his self-doubt.

Feeling like a heel, he strode down the hall, then through the main lobby and outside to the truck—into a blast of summer heat. Knowing earlier that he wouldn't be able to stick around too long, he'd borrowed a ranch pickup for the ride to Farrier General today.

Olivia would probably spend another night by Nick's side, in a chair that supposedly turned into a bed. An uncomfortable one, he thought, her sleep interrupted if not by her worried thoughts, then by the constant stream of staff checking Nick's vital signs, giving him medication or inspecting his IV lines.

Sawyer suppressed another twinge of guilt for escaping again, then got in, started the engine and sat there, letting the AC start to cool the interior, letting his pulse settle. He hadn't put the truck in gear before his cell phone rang.

Sawyer tried to sound calm, in control, but his most recent talk with Nick's doctors hadn't eased his mind. Nick's brain swelling was now worse. So was Sawyer's approaching panic attack. Olivia was right to resent him for keeping his distance from her son, for not stepping up, just as she'd been right to blame him for Jasmine's death, but Sawyer was having enough trouble holding himself together. She probably didn't want him taking part in Nick's care now.

"Hey, Charlie."

At the other end of the line, Charles Banfield IV, a true Boston Brahman who'd attended Exeter and Harvard before meeting Sawyer at KU School of Medicine, launched into all the reasons why Sawyer should be in Kedar. Yesterday. He finished, "I'm doing what I can, but the twenty-hour days are taking their toll. I've lost ten pounds and I look like hell—so bad I've been avoiding the mirror when I shave."

"Sorry, Charlie. I don't know what to tell you."

"Tell me you're coming back."

"I had the impression you didn't want me there."

Charlie ignored that. "The other day we had—I should say, *I* had—a dozen kids come in. There are no more hospital beds since the landslide leveled the infirmary. I haven't had saline solution in over a week, so I can't even hang IVs. Two women gave birth in the clinic last night. One of the babies, a preemie, sadly didn't make it. And I'm still stitching up cuts, treating abrasions as well as I can without enough gauze, bandages, disinfectant..."

As Charlie trailed off, Sawyer remembered all too clearly the day he'd left Kedar as if he were being chased off the mountain by his demons. He'd left Charlie to handle everything in his absence, the one he wasn't sure wouldn't be permanent.

"I couldn't stay there. Not after what happened to... Khalil," he said. But now, after dealing with the clinic's overload of desperate patients for a while, Charlie needed Sawyer, though he probably didn't want to.

Was Olivia right? Had he made the wrong decision years ago with Jasmine, too? At least he hadn't tried to manage Olivia's son's case.

Sawyer rubbed his neck. His pulse beat in his ears so loud he could hardly hear himself. His palms grew damp.

Charlie only said, "When are you coming back?"

Maybe I'm not. At the same time, Sawyer knew he wouldn't be able to live with himself unless he returned, made up for his mistake somehow. Still, he feared he couldn't make the trip to the Himalayas again. Not yet. "How's the road in?"

"Still blocked much of the way. Helicopters have been flying in whatever supplies are available. Sawyer, I know we had a pretty bad fight before you left. I apologize for anything I said that may have come across as, well, blameful. We're still partners, aren't we? The clinic needs you." He hesitated, as if he hated having to say "So do I."

Sawyer cleared his throat. Through the windshield, he watched a man walk out of the hospital, an arm around a crying woman's shoulders. Then he saw Everett and Liza coming across the parking lot holding hands, and he fought an urge to slink down in his seat so as not to be seen. But if they were leaving, that was a good thing, right? Nick must still be holding his own. He didn't want to talk to them, though.

"Listen, Charlie. I have to go." Briefly, he filled him in about Nick. "I hope you can understand why I have to stay here a while longer."

"Of course." But Charlie sounded disappointed. No, resigned.

"He's close to…Khalil's age." And Sawyer hadn't said five words to Nick. Why use him as an excuse?

But Charlie understood family. He was an only child whose parents, a Harvard archaeologist and a well-known pediatrician who headed her department at Boston Children's Hospital, had left him to be raised mostly by nannies before shipping him off to boarding school when he was Nick's age. He'd often spent his college breaks and summer vacations with other people's families.

When they'd founded the clinic a few years ago, full of great plans to give back and make a difference in the world, Charlie had truly come alive. He'd found his passion. Before that, during his training, he'd met Piper, and they'd married and had two children. Sawyer had never seen a man take more readily to having a family of his own, as if to make up for his lonely childhood.

"I hate to let you down, Charlie. But I need more time."

For a few minutes longer, they discussed Nick's case as if they were together at the clinic, treating him rather than scores of needy people with more drastic conditions and worse prognoses. Struggling to cure diseases that couldn't be cured in the end, performing surgeries that often failed to make the difference they'd hoped to make.

"How much time?" Charlie asked, his tone strained.

"I don't know. I'll keep in touch." After he hung up, Sawyer wiped his damp hands on his jeans, then stared off into the distance.

An ambulance raced toward the ER entrance. A young couple, the wife holding what appeared to be a newborn baby, got into a waiting car, headed home to begin their family life together.

He seemed to be letting everyone down. Including—no, especially—Olivia. He could almost feel tonight's nightmare coming on.

Where did he belong? Here, or there with Charlie?

Or in neither place?

Sitara, Kedar...last spring

THE EARTHQUAKE HAD come first. Without warning, the land began to shake, tremors shifting the simple huts of the village, sending people running into the street. The few two-story buildings swayed and windows shattered.

From his office at the clinic, which was shaking right along with the rest of Sitara, Sawyer watched it happen. There was little he could do. Such quakes happened now and then, more often than he cared to think about. People huddled together, babies cried, dogs and chickens ran for shelter.

After a minute or two, the quake subsided. Sawyer peered out the window but saw little damage. During the monsoon season after summer, he'd worry more about landslides, but in spring...

The thought hadn't left his mind before he heard the rumble of sudden movement, and to his utter horror the whole side of the mountain that reared up at the end of the main street began to shift.

People looked up, screamed, then ran again, fleeing toward the clinic where he stood, waving their arms, looking back with their mouths open, gaping in terror.

Sawyer froze. In a wide swath of grayish-tan dirt and a gathering cloud of dust, rocks and boulders swept toward them, toward him, ripping trees out by the roots, consuming houses and sheds and farm animals like some giant hand clearing the green mountainside, the growing crops and anything else in its path. Like some monster, roaring like thunder. He would never get that sound out of his head.

Before he could move—but where to go?—some of the townspeople had swarmed into the waiting room of the clinic, weeping and moaning. Others hadn't been as lucky; the landslide had buried them at the end of the street, sliding past the clinic but destroying the outbuilding that served as his and Charlie's hospital. He knew the people inside would be crushed as the infirmary collapsed under the weight of rock and soil.

A woman rushed through the clinic door, one arm hanging, obviously broken. A compound fracture. He had to move, to help.

But shock had stunned him, and where was Khalil? After seeing him at the clinic earlier for a minor complaint, Sawyer had sent the boy back to school. Sawyer tried to move but couldn't. He felt stuck, as if in cement or quicksand, and people were still yelling. *Help us!*

IN THE MIDDLE of the night, Sawyer jerked awake. He'd been dreaming, just as he'd expected he would, but the horrific images followed him into consciousness. He fell back against his pillow, sweating, remembering how he'd failed in Kedar.

CHAPTER SIX

"UNCLE SAWYER BOUGHT me this?"

Two days later, after yet another brief scare that had taken ten more years off Olivia's life, Nick was released from the hospital. To her vast relief, the edema in his brain had begun to resolve and his numbers had improved enough that he could be sent home—or rather to the Circle H.

Olivia drew a chair up beside his bed in the spare room. She and Nick would stay here until Logan and Sawyer felt satisfied that it was indeed safe for him to go home. His primary care doctor, Cyrus Baxter, was scheduled to make a house call tomorrow.

She tried to smile as Nick turned the Superman bear from Sawyer this way and that, examining its satin cape, then tracing a finger over its broad grin.

"Yes," she said, trying to suppress a fresh wave of anger. She hadn't seen Sawyer since they'd reached the house—hadn't talked to him since that day at the hospital. Apparently he was still making himself scarce, sending gifts through someone else as if to show he cared.

"Why doesn't he come to see me?"

"I don't know, Nick. Maybe he's busy helping Grandpa Sam."

Sawyer wasn't the only one among the missing. So was Clint. She'd enjoyed his company, but he hadn't even called after Olivia first sent him the news of her son's injury. Which said something about him, too.

"But Daddy's here," Nick said. "Uncle Sawyer doesn't need to help."

Olivia had no answer for that. She was surprised, to be honest, that Sawyer hadn't already packed and left for—what had he called the place? *Kebir?* A few times, as she'd asked him to, Sawyer had talked to Nick's doctors. He'd "translated" for Olivia. Then, after their talk about Jasmine, he'd relayed answers and she'd sent questions through Logan or Blossom. Even her father and Liza had delivered information to her. She hadn't seen Sawyer again at Farrier General—not once.

Now she would have to. Nick was at the Circle H. So was Sawyer.

Olivia could feel thankful that her son was getting well. After hours of playing Minecraft with him, she was getting to be pretty good, but she felt exhausted. Her eyes had crossed from staring at the tablet screen all afternoon. "I'm glad you like your bear," she said.

Nick considered for a moment. "But I don't know if I like Uncle Sawyer."

Neither do I, Olivia thought, which unfortunately didn't seem to change the unwise attraction she still felt. She rose from her chair. "Why don't you and your new friend take a nap? Grandpa Sam promised to come watch a movie with you after he feeds the horses. Your dad and Blossom are going to read a new book with you after dinner. Then maybe you can all watch a baseball game on TV tonight."

Nick yawned. "Where are you going?"

"Downstairs," she said, "to help Blossom with dinner."

He gave her a sleepy grin. "You just don't want to play Minecraft. Do you?"

"Tomorrow," she said, then kissed the top of his head. "Rest, punkin."

Her heart full, Olivia paused in the bedroom doorway to take a last peek at Nick, who had already snuggled into his pillows, the bear in his arms. For now, their potential move seemed far from his mind, and she'd loved their closeness today. As she shut the door behind her, she could hear him tell the stuffed animal, "I'll take you to meet Hero as soon as I get out of bed."

She turned away, blinking back happy tears. And ran into Sawyer.

They each stepped back as if they'd been scalded. "Sorry," he said.

"Oh. I didn't see you."

He glanced toward the room. "Nick okay?"

Olivia looked at the floor. "He's good. His headache's still there but not as bad as it was. He still doesn't remember his accident."

"He will, or maybe he won't," Sawyer said. "Sometimes our brains protect us from painful experiences."

The words reminded her of Jasmine, yet Olivia could still recall her horse shrieking in agony as if it were yesterday. She was still holding that against Sawyer, which if he hadn't known before, he did now.

"Kids are resilient," he continued. "Other than a bit of confusion now and then, which should resolve over time, he'll be fine, Olivia." His gaze met hers. "And I should apologize. At the hospital, I—"

"You were there but you never visited Nick. Why not?"

"Do you really want to know?" He didn't wait for her answer. "I wouldn't bring this up—risk making you question my judgment even more—but I want you to understand." He avoided her gaze. "This may not surprise you, but a month or so ago I lost a patient. In Kedar. A boy roughly Nick's age." Olivia guessed he knew exactly when that had happened. "He *died*, Olivia. Two strikes against me. I never want that to happen again."

She frowned. "That's why you've stayed away from Nick?"

"First, do no harm," he murmured. "But I did. With your horse, as you believe, and in Kedar, I did. I'll be trying to make up for that the rest of my life. Somehow. But I have to figure out the how. I'm sorry you feel I've neglected Nick but I'm not in the best shape right now—which must be pretty obvious." Still talking, he started down the stairs, then stopped. "Olivia, my mistake was so basic that my license should be taken away. It's not as if that boy came in with grievous injuries that no one could have fixed." He glanced at her over his shoulder. "He should have survived." His back to her, his voice gathered steam. "Like Nick, he should be with his family, putting their lives together after the landslide. Playing with his friends. Hugging his mom and dad. Instead, he's in a makeshift *grave* on the side of a mountain that could come down again at any moment." He took a breath. "I won't chance making another bad judgment call."

"Sawyer."

"Nick is better off without my 'help.' And so are you."

"EASY, BOY," Sawyer murmured, reaching a hand toward the black colt.

Cyclone seemed aptly named. He danced out of Sawyer's way, then pawed the straw bedding of his stall with a well-shod hoof that could deliver a lethal blow. Sawyer had left Olivia on the stairs at the house, and with his surprise confession still spinning through his brain, strode down to the barn.

Years ago, after his parents were killed, this had been a place of refuge for him. Then, after he'd put down Olivia's horse in the far meadow, she'd abruptly ended their fledgling romance and he'd begun to disengage from the ranch. Olivia had turned to Logan, and after their wedding, Sawyer had left. He doubted he'd find peace here now. He hadn't meant to spill his guts tonight, especially to her.

Cyclone snorted, his nostrils flaring and teeth bared.

"This horse needs to be gelded," Sawyer said to Logan, who had just come out of the nearby tack room carrying a bridle. "At least he didn't bite me this time."

"You got off with a warning." Logan cracked a smile. "I think he likes you."

Sawyer eyed the horse. Cyclone eyed him right back, as if he understood what Sawyer had said and didn't like that any better than he'd liked him poking his hand through the stall bars again.

"Whether he likes me or not, he's showing serious signs of becoming a stallion. You really want to deal with that?" On the Circle H, the horses were all geldings or mares. "From what I've seen, his temperament isn't the best to begin with and he's not going to be easy to train."

"Sam says you volunteered for that."

"I welcome the challenge. But the last thing you'd want on the Circle H, especially with Nick around more often, is a rogue horse. Nick could get badly hurt, and his fall from the hayloft would seem like a minor scratch in comparison. I don't mean to scare you—"

"No, you're right." Logan nodded. "Guess I'd better give the vet a call."

"I could do that." Sawyer wanted to make the appointment. Dealing with the horse would keep his mind off Olivia and Khalil. "You and Blossom planning to resume your honeymoon now?"

Logan fiddled with the bridle in his hands.

"As soon as Doc Baxter says Nick is okay to go home. To Barren, I mean."

Doc, he'd said. Logan hadn't asked for Sawyer's medical opinion lately, and while he didn't want to practice himself or be responsible for Nick's health, that hurt. Logan's resentment ran deep, and Sawyer was still on probation. He'd be as useful as he could without prescribing pills or sewing up wounds. He would have to deal with the emotional ones, though, tricky as they might be to heal.

Logan gestured toward the row of stalls. "You want to go for a ride?"

The invitation surprised Sawyer. "Sure."

Logan headed for a stall. "Before Blossom and I take off again, I'm going over to Grey's place. Have to return a post-hole digger I borrowed. Thought you might like to catch up with him and I need to give Sundance some exercise. Take Ginger. She'll go easy on you."

Sawyer snorted. "You think I need 'easy'? I could always take you, big brother." They'd been born just shy of five minutes apart. "How about we sweeten this deal? Twenty bucks says I win." He could already feel the horse, hooves pounding the ground, the exhilaration of galloping flat out with the wind in his hair. Then he remembered that field…and Olivia.

Logan's face clouded. "No race," he said.

"I'm a family man, not a daredevil kid." He was referring to Sawyer as a teen. "I need to be in one piece when our baby comes."

"Spoilsport." But Sawyer got that message, just as he had Olivia's. He'd messed up again.

They said nothing more to each other until they had saddled the horses, mounted up and were halfway to Grey's ranch. Then it was Logan who spoke first.

"Well. I'm married now—a happy man. Grey's engaged to Shadow and he hasn't stopped grinning since they made their announcement. What about you, Sawyer? I guess you've never tied the knot." He paused, letting the words hang there for a moment. "Not that you'd probably tell me."

"No," Sawyer said, in regard to being married. He reined Ginger around a big rock in their path. On the way by, one hoof grazed it and the bay horse's iron shoe clanged as if landing in a horseshoe pit. He wanted to enjoy the ride, which felt even better to him than he'd expected. Ginger had a smooth, fluid gait that, at a lope, gently rocked him, lulled him into the state of peace he'd been seeking earlier. But Logan wouldn't let the topic rest.

"You seeing someone? Anyone serious?"

"No," Sawyer said again, running the fingers of his right hand through Ginger's mane.

Olivia's image flashed in his mind. *As if*, he thought. "I'm too busy in Kedar to build a relationship." *Or I was*. "The only woman I see other than local residents and patients is my partner Charlie's wife. I love her to pieces, but not in that way."

"Huh," Logan said. "At the risk of us sounding all touchy-feely, I'd hate to see you end up alone. You going to spend much more time in, where is it, Kedar? From the little you've told me, the place sounds dangerous."

The memory of the landslide, his dream, briefly overwhelmed him. "Can't deny it's a dangerous spot," Sawyer said. "I'll never forget the sound of the landslide there, rushing and roaring like it was warning everyone. But not in time. The whole mountain came down, Logan. It barely missed the clinic—and me."

He omitted the part about Khalil. He'd done enough talking with Olivia. Still, Logan's knuckles whitened around Sundance's reins. "The way I live is pretty much camping, except a tent might be fancier. I wash my clothes in a freezing mountain stream. My kitchen is a hot plate and a battered cooler when I can get ice." But his personal comfort wasn't the point. He didn't want to sound as if his work at the clinic was some kind of sacrifice. He'd chosen that lifestyle. At times, he loved it.

"I have a palace compared to most of my patients. At least I have a roof over my head, not too many leaks."

"You serious?"

"Yeah." *Deadly.* He wondered now how many of those patients had lost everything in the landslide. How many hadn't survived. He'd have to ask Charlie about everyone next time. During their last call, he'd been so caught up in his weak explanation for his continued absence that he'd forgotten. Or maybe he'd simply wanted to avoid asking, to avoid feeling guiltier than he already did.

Logan frowned. "You don't have to live like that, Sawyer."

"I don't mind roughing it. You should come visit," he said, trying to lighten things up.

Logan shook his head. With a slight movement of his legs, he nudged Sundance over the top of the hill. "I'll pass. Blossom and I would like to help, though, with people there in such need."

"Thanks. I'll let Charlie know."

"On the other hand, you can help here, Sawyer. That is why you've come back, isn't it? I know Sam worries and we never know what's going on with you. You never came home during med school or your residency, and we didn't even know where you were for the past three years. A good thing, in a way. If Sam had known about the clinic, that landslide, he'd have worried even more. So would I."

"That's why I didn't tell you."

"Maybe it's time you came home for good. Settled down. Found someone to be with."

Had this been the whole point of their ride? "I figure that will happen when—or if—it happens. Wherever it does."

Logan grinned, looking a bit smug. "Most likely when you least expect it."

"Like you and Blossom? I'm happy for you, but I'm…okay on my own."

"I don't think you're okay," Logan muttered just as they rode into Grey's yard.

"WHAT'S THE VERDICT, DOC? You think Nick and I can go home today?"

Olivia stood with Cyrus Baxter the next day in the Circle H foyer. He had sharp blue eyes that didn't miss a thing and still-dark hair sprinkled with gray. Just like Grey, Logan and… Sawyer, Olivia had been his patient growing up. She'd known him all her life. Now he was Nick's doctor—there were no pediatricians in Barren—and she badly wanted his blessing.

"In my opinion, Nick's good to go." He glanced up the stairs. "I was glad to see him so bright and alert this morning. A far cry from the forlorn little boy I saw in the hospital. That hairline fracture should heal up nicely at his age. Of course, you'll want to watch those headaches, but the analgesics seem to be working well. He seems comfortable."

Doc hefted his black medical bag, the same one Olivia had always feared as a girl. She still didn't like needles or being poked everywhere and only last spring she'd had a brief health scare. She had to hide that uneasiness in front of Nick, though Doc's touch with him was always gentle and his words reassuring.

"Don't you smother him now, Olivia," he said. "Your boy has quite the spirit. I wouldn't let him near Hero for a while, though. That's all he talks about, isn't it?"

"Pretty much," Olivia agreed with a smile. "His horse and Minecraft."

Doc laughed. "I didn't let him drag me into that. I have other patients to see and those video games are beyond me."

Olivia saw him to the door. "I can't believe you still make house calls."

"I'm a country doctor, Olivia. Sometimes I'd rather go to a person than make them come into town when they're feeling poorly. Gets me out of the office, too," he said with a twinkle in his eye. "Now and then Ida's voice can shred my nerves—and how that woman loves to gossip."

She lightly poked his arm. "You adore her, Doc."

"Yes, I do. But after forty-plus years as man and wife, I need fresh air and a change of scene sometimes. Speaking of which—"

The back door opened before he could finish. Sawyer walked in from the kitchen to the front hall. When he saw Doc, he grinned. "Hey, great to see you again." He folded Doc into a warm embrace, the two thumping each other's backs in some ritual male greeting.

Olivia wondered if Sawyer had seen Doc at the hospital, or if he'd avoided him as he had Nick. At least now she knew why.

"Heard you were back in town," Doc said, easing away. His gaze roamed over Sawyer's face and body with a critical eye. "Bit thin there, youngster. Need to put on some weight."

"I've had so much on my mind lately. I forget to eat."

But Olivia, who sometimes forgot, too, wondered if he was telling the truth. Or if, in Kedar, there wasn't enough food. She thought he looked just fine, but she could imagine Sawyer giving his portion away to someone in greater need. Like the child he'd told her about. As much as she resented the way he'd avoided Nick, she'd been able to see the pain he still felt.

"We had a landslide in Kedar at the clinic where I work," he told Doc. "With so many people who needed help, there wasn't often time to fix a meal."

"Heard about that slide," Doc said. "Near Tibet?"

"And Nepal. It's a tiny country, without much infrastructure—even less since the disaster. They'll have a hard fight to come back. Other than a bit of agriculture—they're great farmers—there was a small tourism industry, but the landslide wiped that out, too. And foreign investors are wary right now." Sawyer added, "Then there are the various tribal groups, always on the verge of war with each other."

Doc shook his head. "I admire you, Sawyer. Not sure I could practice in such a remote area. But then, I'm much further along in my career than you are."

Olivia stood back, enjoying their talk. She always enjoyed Doc.

"I don't know how much longer I can practice," he said. "The hours alone are killing me. We've got a small walk-in clinic now, which is progress, and they handle emergencies and overflow, but I'm the only doctor with a regular practice and an ongoing client list."

"We all rely on you," Olivia put in. "You aren't really thinking of retiring?"

"Thinking about it, talking, is all. I'd need to find someone to buy my practice so Ida and I can travel some. One of our boys is in Chicago, the other lives in Seattle," he told Sawyer. "We don't see them nearly enough and we'd like to while we still can. The grandkids, too, of course. Oh, and then there's Ida's notion. She thinks we need to see Eastern Europe. That's on her bucket list, she says. Her people came from Poland, you know."

"I didn't know that," Olivia said. She noticed Sawyer had stopped talking. He had a faraway look in his eyes, as if the conversation about Kedar had brought back the memory of that lost boy. His fault, he'd claimed. Which must hurt even more.

Doc switched his medical bag from one hand to the other. "Well, better be on my way. Promised I'd stop by the Sutherland ranch to see Ned. He's been feeling down since his stroke. Needs regular cheering up. Between me and Shadow Moran at the Mother Comfort agency, we manage." He smiled. "Don't know if he'll feel that cheery when he sees me with this bag. Most people don't." He shook Sawyer's hand. "Take care of yourself. Don't forget to eat. I'll finish my calls by lunchtime. Then Ida and I are off for a few days to see Vegas."

"You won't be here?" Olivia tensed. Who would care for Nick?

"Didn't Logan tell you? I talked to him on the phone before I left the office. Told him I'd make sure Nick is all right before we leave. Gave him the go-ahead for that honeymoon. No, we're taking a brief holiday. Haven't had a vacation in years."

Olivia blinked. "But then who—what if Nick needs—"

"That young man who runs the clinic is on call—if he's not out in his boat fishing or on a hike." Doc glanced at Sawyer. "And you have a doctor right here. You make house calls, Sawyer?"

Olivia saw him flinch. "In Kedar, yes."

Doc fished in his pocket for something, then pressed a set of keys into Sawyer's hand before he could object. "Supplies and charts are in my office. If need be, you can make one in Barren."

CHAPTER SEVEN

THE BELL RANG AGAIN, but Olivia didn't get there in time. Nick dashed past her shouting, "I'll get it!" He flung open the front door.

"You're supposed to be in bed, young man," she said, then stopped.

On the steps to her house in downtown Barren stood her stepmother, blinking in the afternoon sunlight with Olivia's father behind her. In the few years she and Nick had lived here, Everett had never come to visit—certainly not before he married Liza.

"Gramps," Nick said, barreling into his arms.

Absorbing the boyish impact, Everett let out a whoosh of breath. "Hold on, there, Nicky. Let us come in first. Then you can see what we've brought." He was carrying a big bag from a toy store in town and held it out from his side so he wouldn't crush whatever was in it. "We can come in, can't we?" he asked Olivia.

"Liza, Everett," she said weakly. She hadn't

called him *Dad* in years. What on earth were they doing here now? Well, obviously bringing her son a present. Since Olivia had been thirteen and moved away from Wilson Cattle when he and her mother had divorced, Everett had come bearing gifts. Like the Trojan horse. Only this time the gift was for Nick.

Everett had called him *Nicky*, which only Logan had ever done, and Olivia stepped back from the doorway. Maybe Everett wanted to be a better grandfather, if not to make some deeper emotional connection. It was a thoughtful gesture. Nick had had a rough time lately. "By all means, come in."

Liza kissed her cheek. Her square-cut diamond engagement ring sparkled on her slender hand, anchored by a slim platinum wedding band. As usual, she wore an attractive dress, this one a summery teal blue with sandals.

Smoothing her dark hair, she said, "We're on our way back to Dallas, but we didn't want to leave town without checking on Nick." She drew him close, making Nick grimace. Since his seventh birthday last spring, he'd decided hugs and feminine attention were taboo. "How are you doing?" Liza asked. "Feeling better?"

"I'm better enough to ride," he said. "But Mom and Dad won't let me."

Taking a chance, Liza kissed the top of his head. "Listen to your parents."

"Thank you," Olivia murmured. She ushered them into the living room just off the narrow front hallway.

Her house wasn't big or fancy, like the condominium Everett and Liza owned in Texas, but she and Nick had made a home here, and Olivia wouldn't trade it for anything—except a larger place. They had outgrown the space, but if they did move, it would be hard to leave, unlike the Circle H, where that spring flood, like a last straw, had put an end to her marriage.

And not like Wilson Cattle, either. After that painful move into town from the ranch with her mother, she'd spent some miserable summers and occasional holidays there, mostly avoiding Everett. Her mother blamed him for their broken marriage and so, then, did Olivia. With Grey, her father had the common bond of the ranch and he'd been eager to teach her brother the ropes. She'd become a rebellious teenager, acting out whenever she saw Everett until, finally, she rarely did see him. She'd imagined he must have felt relieved.

Her best, and earlier, memories were of spending time with her brother, Logan and Sawyer. Building snow forts by the barn after a blizzard, dragging home the Christmas trees they'd cut down for each of their houses and putting on the lights, hanging the ornaments, singing Christmas carols. Splashing their horses through the creek on a lazy summer afternoon.

Then later, Sawyer kissing her in the hayloft for the first time, altering their friendship forever. Thinking she was in love. Racing with the wind in her hair...before Jasmine had tripped in the hole.

That memory had changed everything again. Olivia didn't trust easily, and she couldn't trust Sawyer. Now he was home, at least for the time being, bringing all those memories alive. Churning up her emotions. Had she always felt this drawn to him even when, clearly, he wasn't good for her?

In the living room, Everett presented the shopping bag to Nick as if it were filled with precious gems. And apparently to Nick, it was. When he saw the huge Lego Minecraft set, he whooped in delight. "Wow! Mom! Look what I got from Gramps!"

"And Liza," Everett put in, giving Nick a nod in her direction. Her father's eyes lit up when his gaze met hers.

"Oh. Yeah, thank you...too." Nick had told

Olivia the night before, their first night home again, that he didn't know what to call Liza.

"Did you get it from the toy store here? Daddy bought me a black truck like his there and I love it. How did you know what I wanted?" Nick stared, as if transfixed, at the detailed image on the box.

Olivia could tell he was barely restraining himself from tearing it open, scattering the million or so pieces everywhere and starting to put them together. Or trying to. Olivia thought the model looked far too hard for a seven-year-old boy even though Nick had excellent fine motor skills and liked building things.

Liza sent him a fond smile. "Your dad may have made a suggestion. I'm glad you like it, Nick." The look she gave Olivia was more pointed. "Maybe you and I could make coffee, take time for a little girl talk while Nick and Everett start on the Legos."

The not-so-subtle hint galvanized Olivia. "Of course. I should have offered sooner." She was not only a bad daughter; she was being rude. "I think we have some cookies left. Nick loves the chocolate chip ones from Annabelle's Diner." She led the way into the kitchen, leaving Everett and Nick to admire his Minecraft set.

Olivia didn't want to be a wet blanket, and her father was always more than generous, but she imagined she'd be finding stray pieces in the carpet or under chairs for the next year, long after Nick's interest had moved on to something else.

She focused on setting up the coffee maker, her back to Liza as if she was putting up a fence. "Did the newlyweds leave?"

"Early this morning. We stopped over as they were loading the car—reloading, I should say. Blossom said that seems to be a habit of hers, setting out, then coming right back, but that's some kind of in-joke with them. They're still worried about Nick. Logan promised to call every day—unless someone calls him first."

"I hope they have a good time." Olivia hadn't forgotten Doc's house call yesterday, or how he'd prodded Sawyer to fill in with his patients while he and Ida were gone. In Nick's case, she wasn't sure she'd let him.

"I wanted Nick and Everett to spend time together," Liza said, gesturing toward the living room. "They're so cute." She glanced at the coffee maker. And came to the point. Liza had an uncanny ability to see Olivia's innermost thoughts. "Are you holding it against me that your father married me?"

"Of course not."

Liza lowered her gaze. "That isn't the impression I've been getting."

Voices drifted into the kitchen, Everett's low and amused, Nick's higher pitched and excited. The coffee maker burbled away on the counter while Olivia counted minutes until she could pour two cups and find something neutral to talk about. Thankfully, Liza didn't press the issue. Not that one, anyway.

"Everett wants to know Nick better, and I think Nick wants that, too. I must be a bit harder for him to figure out," Liza admitted. "Maybe I need to suggest a name for him to call me. I'm not sure I like the idea of being Grandma."

Well, that was an honest statement, but Olivia decided not to say anything. Had Liza meant her, as well? That Olivia didn't know what to make of her, either?

Liza mused aloud. "Maybe Gi-Gi, Nana… no, or the French *grand-mère*." Liza threw up both hands. "Anyway… Olivia, you didn't say one word to your father when we came in."

"I said his name."

"Yes, and every time you do, I can see the sadness in his eyes." She hesitated. "I can see the anger in yours."

"I'm not the one who broke up our family,"

she said. "You weren't here then—you don't know how that hurt. It still does. Because of what my parents decided, I had to leave the only home I'd ever known."

Liza's voice cooled. "Your mother was half of that decision, at least. I don't pretend to know exactly what happened between them, but you don't really know, either. You were still a child, Olivia. And from what Everett has told me, your mom insisted that you live with her. She made it nearly impossible for you to spend time at Wilson Cattle."

Olivia fought a wave of regret. Until recently, she'd treated Logan much the same way when it came to seeing Nick.

"Do you think your father didn't want you there?" Liza asked. "I know he did—and every time you turn your back on him, *he* hurts a little more."

Olivia winced. "You make me sound cold. I'm not, Liza." Her stepmother's words had shocked, even moved her. "But I suppose you're right. There's still that little girl inside me who hasn't forgotten. Most of my memories of Everett are like that big bag he brought today for Nick. Beautiful presents, clothes he thought I'd like but that were too small for me by the time I got them." She could see Liza's point. Maybe that wasn't his fault, but… "And then there were the promises," she said, "to see me again soon. To have me at Wilson Cattle for the whole summer next year or every Christmas."

"At least he tried."

She hadn't thought of that before. With her mother's constant criticisms, Olivia's heart had gradually hardened until she didn't need any more obstacles put in her path to visit Wilson Cattle, or him.

"Your mother," Liza began, then stopped. "No, this isn't my place. It's for you to make peace with Everett, to finally understand— as an adult—what happened to your family then. To be able to move on, to make something new." She paused. "Maybe I shouldn't say this, but…you've done so with Logan. You and he are in a better place now, for Nick's sake—and your own." She touched the back of Olivia's hand. "Please, try to do the same with your father."

SAWYER HAD SPENT the morning doing chores in the barn. When he'd come in, Cyclone had ambled over to, well, if not to greet him, at least to see who was there. Sawyer had left him an apple and a few carrots. A blatant attempt to win him over, perhaps, but also a sort of apology. He'd spoken to the vet earlier and scheduled an appointment. Cyclone's days as a stallion in the making were numbered.

Then at the house, he'd realized how quiet and empty it seemed. Enraptured by each other, Logan and Blossom were headed again for the West Coast. Everett and Liza Wilson had stopped by at breakfast time to wish them well. Nick and Olivia were gone, too. Sam had ridden out with Willy and Tobias to look for a stray bison cow and her calf, which had wandered off. They hadn't invited him.

Almost glad to get away for an hour or two, Sawyer decided to drive into town. Logan had said he needed to buy more feed but Sawyer didn't stop at the ag store first. As he passed the storefront medical clinic on Main Street, he noted it was open for business, and Doc's words stopped playing in his head.

He wouldn't be needed after all. He probably wouldn't see Olivia again before he left the ranch to return to his clinic overseas…or, if he couldn't, to go somewhere else.

In front of Annabelle's Diner, he swung into an open parking spot. Sam had promised to cook dinner tonight, but at lunchtime, Sawyer's stomach was growling. At the Circle H, he'd decided against making himself a sandwich. He wanted more than that, and he'd missed eating good food that hadn't been fixed over a hot plate.

The popular local restaurant bustled with activity. Every table was filled. A slender brown-haired woman holding a glass coffee carafe spotted him standing in the entrance. She broke into a broad smile, then rushed over to him. "Sawyer! Is it really you?"

More or less, he wanted to say. For a second, he didn't recognize her. Then, "Annabelle Foster." Why be surprised to find her here? "I haven't seen you since graduation."

They'd gone to school together in Barren. She'd been a class behind his, but they'd become friends and sometimes hung out in a group with Logan, Grey and Olivia.

With the coffeepot in hand, she gave him a one-armed hug. "I heard you were in town. For Logan's wedding, I suppose."

"I didn't see you there."

She raised an eyebrow. "I couldn't get anyone to fill in here that day. I'm so sorry I missed it. Everyone says it was a beautiful wedding and the reception was lovely. We all like Blossom—and of course we love Logan. I hope they got my gift."

He shrugged. "I'm sure you'll be getting a thank-you note after they get home from their honeymoon."

"In time for the baby's birth," she said, then leaned closer. "You'd think we'd never had a baby born here. Everyone on Main Street is excited. Sherry, who runs Baby Things across the street, has put together an entire layette, and Ida Baxter is knitting the most gorgeous afghan. It looks like a rainbow. We're throwing Blossom a baby shower when she gets back."

"That's very nice of you. I'm sure she'll appreciate that."

"Blossom is one of us now."

Sawyer looked into her green eyes. "And what about you? I mean, obviously you're still at the diner." Which her parents had named after her when she was a baby. "I remember you working here during high school. How are your parents?" Annabelle's mother and father ran a tight ship. She'd missed her junior and senior proms to work, just as she'd missed Logan and Blossom's wedding. Maybe nothing had changed.

Annabelle's mouth tightened. "They're both gone," she said.

"I'm sorry. I didn't know." In fact, he'd hoped Annabelle had left town by now to find a better life than she'd had living under her controlling parents' thumbs.

"I inherited this place—that's about all they

left behind. As long as I can make a go of it—
if the café at the other end of Main doesn't
drive me out of business with their new up-
scale dinner menu—then I guess I'm here to
stay." She gave him a bright smile that seemed
forced.

Sawyer had never understood why she didn't
just pack her bags and leave right after graduation. He had eventually, and so had Shadow
Moran—even Logan for a while. Certainly,
Annabelle's folks hadn't treated her very well.

She glanced around the diner. "Enough
about that," she said, flushing. "I see a space
at a table in the back."

With a determined step, Annabelle led him
to the rear of the restaurant, but the table she'd
mentioned was already occupied. A tall dark-
haired man wearing jeans and a denim shirt
sat there perusing the menu. "Sheriff, we're
so crowded today. Do you have room for one
more? This is Logan Hunter's brother."

"I don't mean to intrude," Sawyer began,
feeling uncomfortable. He wasn't good at
small talk these days. Maybe he'd get his food
to go, eat in the truck or save it until he got
home rather than sit with a stranger. Feel on
display.

The sheriff wasn't wearing a badge or a

uniform, which struck him as odd. Maybe he liked to ambush people.

He looked Sawyer over. Sawyer could see him catalog every feature, make a mental note of his hair and eye color and his height as if Sawyer was in a lineup or being booked for a crime. Not that he wasn't guilty of something.

Then the sheriff turned back to Annabelle and smiled. "Sure, why not?." He handed Sawyer the menu. "Take a seat. I recommend the beef patty melt today."

"It's our special." Annabelle refilled the sheriff's mug, then hurried away, the coffee carafe still in hand and her cheeks as rosy as a Western sunset.

"She forgot to actually introduce you," the sheriff said with a smile. "Annabelle's a sweetie but sometimes her heart isn't here." He stuck out a hand. "Finn Donovan."

"Sawyer McCord."

He frowned a little. "You looked familiar and now I know why—but Logan's *brother*? Obviously, I see the resemblance, but I don't recognize the last name. I'm fairly new in town. Enlighten me."

"I've been gone for a long time, but I'm back to help out while I can."

"Ah," Finn said. "The honeymooners. And Sam. Logan pressed me into service as a groomsman. Didn't notice you at the wedding. I missed the reception. Had a call I needed to respond to."

Sawyer didn't explain his lateness. "You're not from around here, are you?"

"Chicago PD," Finn said, then fell silent as if he didn't want to explain himself, either. There was something more going on behind those keen eyes.

Sawyer waited a beat before saying, "My parents—and Logan's—died in a car wreck when we were kids." As always, the memory turned him inside out. "Sam and Muriel, my grandmother, who was a widow when they met, adopted us. They raised Logan and me."

"But then—" Finn prompted, as if he were interviewing a suspect.

"Sam and I had a falling-out." He was not about to bring Olivia into the conversation. Sawyer's long-ago yearning for her was just that, long ago, and although she looked even better to him now, and he admired her for being a good mother to Nick, a strong woman who could take care of herself, even put him in his place, that was none of the sheriff's concern. Or Sawyer's, for that matter. "Eventually I changed my name from Hunter back to McCord. My dad's name and his father's. The original name of the ranch."

Finn mulled that over. "What's the deal now? With you and Sam?"

"A work in progress," Sawyer said, pretending to read the menu.

"Aren't we all. Sorry, I didn't mean to pry."

Sawyer didn't quite believe him but Finn signaled their waitress over to take their order while Sawyer was still digesting that. The sheriff's gaze kept drifting, assessing the other customers in the diner as if for threats, and Sawyer guessed he was seated at the last table with his back to the wall for a reason. Of course he'd meant to grill Sawyer. That was his job, off duty or not, he supposed.

"You having the melt?" Finn asked.

The daily special held appeal but Sawyer opted out. "No, I'll try Annabelle's veal stew. If it's her mom's recipe, it should still be more than good." The woman had had a mean streak, but she sure could cook.

He wasn't as certain how he felt about the sheriff. Finn Donovan had an unassuming manner, but Sawyer would have to watch himself. No more impromptu lunches with the local law. Not that he'd done anything wrong.

Not here, at least.

CHAPTER EIGHT

OLIVIA TRIED NOT to eavesdrop. In the living room, Nick was talking to Logan on the phone. Each night for the past three nights, her ex had called to check on him. The first day, Nick had reported after the call that his dad and Blossom had stayed near Denver, the second in Wyoming—or was it the other way around?

She was glad they were enjoying their wedding trip, just as she was happy to be home, not at the Circle H. Olivia had gradually settled back in to her daily routine except for one thing.

Nick, who was still under what her brother Grey called "house arrest," wasn't any happier with her now that he was feeling better than he'd been right before he fell from the hayloft. Several times Olivia had tried to talk to him about their possible move from Barren, but Nick had retreated to his room or gone back to work at the dining room table—which he and

Olivia never used for eating—on the Lego set her father and Liza had given him.

As she finished their supper dishes at the sink, she heard his voice, sounding so excited at first about the progress he was making, and Olivia had to smile. The elaborate Minecraft display was coming to life with every piece Nick fit into the whole.

Olivia liked to think his dedication to the project helped him to heal, and that his view of their move might soon improve, too. He'd just groused to Logan about the light chore list Olivia had made for him to help pay for the Tiffany vase. But then, a few seconds ago, his tone had changed.

Nick scampered into the kitchen, holding out the phone.

"Daddy wants to talk to you."

Her heart sinking, Olivia dried her hands on a dish towel. Logan hadn't asked to speak to her since he and Blossom had set out on their honeymoon for the second time. Olivia wondered if Blossom was okay. "Everything all right, Logan?"

"You tell me." His tone didn't reassure her.

She shooed Nick back into the dining room, noting that he ducked out from under her hand when she tried to ruffle his hair. Then she changed her mind, not wanting him to overhear her conversation. "Nick, would you pick up those Lincoln Logs in your bedroom? And put them away? We made quite a mess this afternoon. I'll count that as one of your chores." She waited until he was gone. "Where are you?" she asked Logan.

"Lake Tahoe." He paused. "Blossom wanted to see the area, which is beautiful, and I'd never been here, either. We're zigzagging a bit, meandering our way to the coast," he said. "Probably to San Francisco first. What's this I hear about you moving?"

Olivia sighed. "Nick told you." Which explained the change she'd heard in his tone. She'd been afraid of this, but maybe she deserved to be put on the spot. Last spring she'd told Logan that Nick gave her a full report after each visit with his father. Now the tables were turned. "I haven't made a firm decision yet, but you know my house is too small for us. You know I've been planning to expand my antiques business."

"In Barren, yes."

She told him about Ted Anderson, who hadn't yet countered her offer. To be fair, she hadn't called him, either; she was still trying to find money in the budget to pay for the vase Nick had broken. Concerned for Nick, she hadn't broached the subject of a move before with Logan. Maybe she should have, but she'd also been enjoying their new truce and she'd suspected he wouldn't take this well. "If I can't come up with more money," she finished, "I may have to wait for a different opportunity."

Logan's voice hardened. "And that leaves me waiting for the other shoe to drop." He sounded so cool just when she'd hoped all the unpleasantness between them was over. "When Nicky told me, he didn't seem happy. Is this what caused his accident in the first place?"

Her spirits plummeted even further. The night he'd fallen, she'd told Logan that he'd run away from her. "I think so, probably, yes." Olivia had felt guilty ever since. In her zeal to be the best single mom she could be for Nick, to provide not only financial security but emotional stability as well, she'd only made things worse with Logan. And her son had been seriously injured in the process.

"Libby. Do I have to remind you? Our divorce agreement has a clause that prevents you or me—"

"From taking Nick out of the county to live. Yes. I know." That had been a sticking point about their settlement, but Olivia had finally given in, not planning to relocate any time soon. But that had been three years ago.

"Yet you've gone ahead with this anyway."

Olivia thought of her offer and Ted's refusal, then of Nick and the broken vase. "Logan, nothing has 'gone ahead.' Or changed. And I'm grateful for Nick's child support. I know I can count on you to make those payments every month, and I know how much you care about him—"

"I don't think you do."

"—but if I can earn more, do more, to secure our future, I will. I've opened a college savings account for him—"

"Nicky won't have to worry about that," Logan said. She could almost see the taut line of his mouth, the hard look in his eyes that had become too familiar during their battles after she left him. "I've told you before. The Circle H will see to his education." He heaved an obviously frustrated sigh. "Why do you worry about things you don't need to?"

She sighed. "I know you mean well, and I do trust you, Logan. I'll try to worry less about finances, but what about my ambitions? And look at Grey. He almost lost all his cattle, which would have ruined him. There are no guarantees in life. I need to make sure things are good for Nick."

Logan knew her well enough to know how her family's breakup had affected her and Grey—how she'd come to mistrust her father's promises and too often felt as if she were alone in the world with only herself to rely on. Or her mother, and they still rarely agreed on any best course of action. Last summer, Olivia had gone with her to Thailand, and delightful as the country was, they'd almost killed each other.

Feeling cornered, she said, "I *worry* about my son." Then Olivia suppressed a groan. She shouldn't have said that. "Our son, I mean."

It was as if all the progress she and Logan had made this spring and summer vanished with those few words. Was she turning into her mother? Always ready to do battle with her ex?

In the background, Olivia could hear Blossom's soft voice encouraging Logan to take a deep breath. From the bedroom down the hall, Olivia heard Nick drop another bunch of Lincoln Logs into his toy box with a clatter.

The last thing she'd wanted was to antagonize Logan. He had every right to want their child near, especially when he'd given up so much of his flying career to be with him now, with Blossom, with Sam at the Circle H. Secure in Blossom's love, Logan wasn't the same man Olivia had left three years ago. But had she changed?

"Logan. We wouldn't be moving that far. I don't want to argue," she said, her voice shaking. "Please. Try to understand my side of things."

"I've bent over backward to do just that. I thought we'd managed to make peace with each other. I'm on my *honeymoon*," he said. "You think I want to fight about this?" He took that breath Blossom had suggested. "I don't. I also won't stand by and watch Nicky move to…wherever it is you *plan* to go."

"The next county," she admitted. "If the deal with Ted goes through, I'd be back and forth, in Barren quite often. You could still easily see Nick. And if it doesn't, then I'll be right here for at least a little while longer."

"Great." His voice dripped with sarcasm. "That's reassuring. Nicky has friends here, Libby. He and Ava are inseparable—or they were before he got hurt. When I talked to Grey yesterday, Shadow told me Ava misses Nicky. You should get them together. He's finally settled after our divorce and you'd uproot him again?" He paused for a brief moment. "That's not going to happen. Hear me?"

"How could I not?" She said, "I wish Nick hadn't told you like that."

"So do I. He was practically in tears. *You* should have given me a heads-up."

She glanced toward the hall. She heard no further sound from Nick's room. Either he'd finished putting his toys away and was distracted by the new pile of books they'd checked out earlier from the library, or he was trying to listen in. She could imagine his ears pricked up at their conversation. "I'm sorry, Logan. I'll talk to him."

"To tell him what? That you're going to take him from his father again?"

Olivia had no answer for that. Maybe she hadn't thought this through clearly.

"Logan," she heard Blossom say, but he disconnected the call.

Olivia stood there, the cordless phone in her hand. She would have to smooth things over again, somehow. Yet she had to think of her future—and Nick's.

Soon, Logan and Blossom would have their new baby to care for. She wouldn't let Nick become an afterthought, as Olivia had years ago. She knew Logan wouldn't want that to happen, but it could happen all the same.

She had to find another solution.

WITH A SIGH, Sawyer answered the phone in the ranch house kitchen. He was alone in the house and hoped Doc Baxter would get back to town soon. Who had given what seemed like most of the population of Barren, many of whom he didn't know, the phone number for the Circle H?

Well, of course they'd know the number, he thought. Sam and Logan were popular in town, a big part of the close-knit community. And since Doc had left for Vegas and Sawyer's impromptu lunch with Finn Donovan, the phone hadn't stopped ringing, or so it seemed to him.

Usually, he let Sam answer or those people left a message: someone's toddler had a cold; a woman thought she might be pregnant; another's rash hadn't gone away despite the steroid cream Doc had prescribed before he left town.

None of the calls, thank heaven, had been emergencies, and Sawyer had returned them, but now—

"There's blood all over the place," the caller said after he'd identified himself. "Can you come out to my ranch? Stupid accident, a lapse on my part—"

Sawyer tensed. "I'd suggest you head for the ER at Farrier General."

"We went there the other day when my wife ruptured her Achilles tendon," Fred Miller said. "She can't drive. Plus, we had to wait five hours before anyone saw her."

Sawyer searched for another option that didn't include him. He had no idea where the Bar B&J Ranch was located, except that it was near Farrier. He had horses yet to feed tonight and he was bone weary. All afternoon, he'd chased bison cows around the Circle H, corralled late calves for branding and had even spent half an hour working Cyclone on a lunge line for the first time. That hadn't gone well and every muscle in his body hurt.

He rubbed the nape of his neck. "Can you call a neighbor?"

"Already did. None of them answered."

Here he was, thousands of miles from Kedar, determined not to make yet another mistake, as he had more recently with Olivia's son, incurring her wrath, but... "How bad is the arm?"

"I've gone through two towels already."

"Mr. Miller, you or your wife need to call an ambulance."

"Didn't you get the message? I can't afford another visit. Doc never charges me what the ER did."

Sawyer rethought the issue. Cash flow, health insurance, the cost of medicine could be a big problem for ranchers, especially smaller outfits. It sounded like Fred Miller was one of them. Sawyer softened his tone. "Then you need to get to the clinic here in Barren. That'll be cheaper than the ER. I know it's farther from you than the hospital, but it's your best altern—"

"I told you. I can't drive, either." The man's voice faded. "I feel kinda faint."

That alarmed Sawyer. Similar to kids, who sometimes masked their symptoms, ranchers were well-known for downplaying any injury. Years ago Sawyer had seen his father do a day's work with one arm in a makeshift sling, paying no mind to the powerful animal that had nearly broken his arm. Years later, at his clinic in Kedar, Sawyer had seen more of the same, local people who kept going when they should have been in a hospital.

This guy sounded no different. Sawyer hoped he didn't have an artery spurting. At least he'd called for help…

He asked a few questions, then said, "Listen to me. Sit down. Put your head between your knees and keep pressure on the wound. Your wife there with you?"

"Yeah, but frankly, I think she's closer to passing out than I am. What's wrong with you? Are you a doctor or ain't you?"

"Look, I—"

No excuses. None left. It was one thing to turn Nick's care over to Doc and the other physicians at the hospital then make his retreat as quickly as he could. Nick had been in better hands, but this man could be bleeding out while he spoke to Sawyer, and he seemed too stubborn to do what he was told.

Hanging up after he got directions to the Bar B&J, Sawyer snatched a few basic medical supplies from the bathroom, left Sam a hasty note saying he'd be back in a while and to eat without him—then borrowed the newest ranch pickup, which had a built-in GPS device.

On his way to town, he phoned Willy to ask him to feed horses in his place. Apparently, Sawyer was going to make a house call.

Twenty minutes later, he pulled up at the ranch. The gate stood open.

Fred Miller met him at the door to the house, his arm wrapped in a towel. Blood had seeped through the white terry cloth and his face looked deathly gray. "Thanks for comin'," he said, pushing the door open and leaning against the frame to prop himself up. "I kind of wondered if you would. After that mess with Grey Wilson's cattle, and all."

Sawyer gave him a blank look. "I wasn't here," he said. Grey had told him about the theft but few details. Had Miller been in-volved?

"My nephew Calvin and his friend Derek... rustled part of that herd. Hid them here at my place. I know you and the Wilsons are long-time friends."

Sawyer didn't need to hear what part Miller had played in the theft. All he needed was to inspect the man's wound. If he was lucky, he'd only need some gauze and a good-sized bandage.

Fred Miller wasn't that lucky.

"This needs stitches," Sawyer told him, bent over Miller's wounded arm at the kitchen table. His wife was nowhere in sight.

"You can sew, can't you? You're a doctor."

"I can, but—" *I won't*, he wanted to say. This wasn't a simple slice but jagged and rimmed with dirt. The repair would take skill, and he couldn't fix the arm, not here. "How did this happen, Fred?"

"Bull pushed me into the fence. Pinned me. The arm caught in the barbed wire. When he dragged me off—this arm just kept tearing."

In spite of himself, Sawyer's stomach rolled. He'd seen the worst wounds after the land-slide in Kedar, tried to fix most of them, and he didn't mind the sight of blood, even saw it as a challenge to stop the flow. But his short time at the Circle H had helped to blunt his former enthusiasm, and for sure he didn't trust himself. "When was your last tetanus shot?" Without one, Miller could die.

He looked perplexed. "Don't rightly know. Some years ago, I suspect."

Which could mean never, Sawyer thought. Who knew if this man ever went to a doctor? He might be more likely to call the vet for a sick cow or calf and ignore his own health like Sam did.

"I can't do this," Sawyer said. "We need to get that cut properly cleaned and stitched under sterile conditions." It wasn't his medical judgment he doubted now—it was clear what Miller needed—but his technical skills. What if the rancher got an infection, or suffered complications from blood loss or shock while Sawyer sewed him up? He'd worked in conditions worse than this in Kedar, but the ordeal with Khalil, and then Nick, had apparently eroded too much of Sawyer's confidence for him to go on.

He helped Fred Miller up from his chair. "I'm taking you to the clinic. The wait will be shorter there. Don't worry about the cost. I'll cover it."

CHAPTER NINE

"WELL? WHAT DO you think?" Olivia squirmed while Barney Caldwell studied her numbers. As the chief loan officer of the Barren Cattlemen's Bank, he had agreed to meet with her the morning after she'd talked to Logan, and Olivia didn't want to wait.

If Barney okayed the amount she was applying for, she could take her revised offer to Ted Anderson, then hope he accepted her slightly higher number before someone else showed up to buy his shop. She could cover the damage Nick had caused—also using his chore money to prove the point about taking responsibility—and worry about Logan's reaction to her move later.

Barney gazed at her across his broad desk, a lock of his nut-brown hair falling over one too-small eye. There wasn't a scrap of paper or a family photo on the polished walnut desktop, and Olivia thought the folder she'd brought with her looked lonely.

"I admire your grit, Libby."

Olivia tried not to frown. Logan and Grey might call her by the shortened form of her name, but she didn't know Barney *that* well, and the familiarity bothered her. She sensed he'd never speak like that to Grey, with whom he'd been strictly businesslike when he'd denied her brother a loan.

Barney glanced down at the documents she'd brought with her, focusing on her most recent profit-and-loss statement, thumbing through the pages again. "I was sorry when you and Logan split up. But you've made a new life for yourself—something I've never had the courage to do," he added with a tinge of color in his face that spread across his cheeks and stained them a dull red.

He cleared his throat. "However. Although you posted a tidy profit here last quarter, I doubt the bank can authorize further funds for your expansion. The dollar value you put on the business doesn't square with what you're asking. Your margins are lower than they should be."

Olivia folded her hands. "I know. I'm trying to remedy that, but the antiques business goes up and down. Trying to determine what the market will bear in terms of price for the items I buy and sell is always, um, something of a guessing game."

"You sell beautiful things." He cleared his throat a second time. "My mother bought a Tiffany lamp at your little store only last month."

That's Olivia Wilson Antiques, not some "little store," she thought. Was he trying to demean her?

"Yes, I remember." Barney's mother was a pillar of the community, and she liked everyone to recognize that. She'd been quite a challenge, but they'd finally settled on a sum for the lamp that pleased Mrs. Caldwell, if not Olivia. If she didn't miss her guess, Barney's mother controlled his life. He'd never married. "She chose a stunning example of that studio's work."

"She's very happy with it." He half smiled. "I'm sure she'd lend you this amount in a heartbeat. However," he said again, "she's not the vice president of loans here." Barney shook his head. "I'm sorry, but unless you can bring me better numbers, Libby, I have to decline your request."

Olivia's jaw tightened. "That seems to be an ongoing issue with my family."

"You mean Grey?" Barney looked toward the front windows of the bank as if he expected her brother to be standing there. "I'm glad he's been able to turn Wilson Cattle around —at least as far as getting his stock returned, I hear—but I had no choice. His figures didn't add up for me, either."

Olivia frowned. Grey had told her he and their father intended to reapply for a loan here, and Everett expected to get it. Just like their father to renege on another promise. He and Liza were back in Dallas, which had made Olivia breathe easier, but she hated to think he'd let down Grey this time.

Barney pushed back his swivel chair. He stood, indicating their appointment was over. "I do regret having to signal this decision. If you'd still like to fill out the application form—"

"No, I understand. Thanks for your time, Barney."

He walked her to the door. Several tellers looked up, and with surprise Olivia saw that one of them was Susie, her former babysitter. She couldn't blame her, really, for seeking greener pastures. The bank even smelled of money. Susie had graduated from high school in June. She had to think of her future—as did Olivia. She gave Susie a quick wave and mouthed *hello*.

Barney held on to the door handle. He glanced around, then leaned closer to Olivia, his voice lowered. "Annabelle's special at the diner tonight is her always-excellent chicken fried steak. Would you join me? Mother has her bridge club."

Olivia was stunned. Was he putting the moves on her? If she went to dinner with him, would Barney change his mind and rubber-stamp her application for the loan? She doubted that and the thought shamed Olivia. Maybe she was only flattering herself. And he was lonely.

Barney seemed to notice her hesitation. "Or, if that doesn't appeal to you, we could try the new menu at the café."

"I'm sorry, Barney. My seven-year-old is waiting for my 'special' chili and corn bread tonight."

The reminder that she wasn't exactly free and had to think of her son first did its job. Barney opened the door and gestured for her to step out onto the sidewalk.

"Maybe next time, then," he said.

SAWYER KICKED A metal water bucket in the barn aisle. The cut on Fred Miller's arm had required more stitches yesterday than Sawyer had expected, and he hadn't been impressed with the clinic doctor's work. Still, Max Garrett had been there and willing to take over, even if the guy seemed in over his head and claimed to be flummoxed by the long hours he had to put in during Doc's absence.

Fred would have an impressive scar, but at least he was on antibiotics to prevent infection, he'd gotten that needed tetanus shot, and who was Sawyer to criticize? He'd felt like an idiot walking into the clinic on Main Street, despite knowing he couldn't handle the case—unless he used Doc's keys to open his office on Cottonwood Street.

Sawyer had resisted the urge. In addition to his fears about making another mistake, he worried one stop at Doc's would lead to his keeping office hours until Baxter got back.

Earlier today, Sawyer had called Miller to make sure he was okay. He'd called the others, too, checking on the toddler's cold (better), that rash (improving) and the might-be-pregnant woman (she still hadn't taken a test). Miller had been the most appreciative, but frustration simmered inside Sawyer.

He'd done what he could; what he'd been comfortable doing. And Miller had gotten the treatment he needed. So why did he feel as if he'd failed again?

He took another swipe at the metal bucket. It rang like a gong and half the horses along the aisle danced in their stalls, ears laid flat against their heads. Cyclone let out a definite stallion whinny and Sawyer winced. He knew better than to rile them up just because he was frustrated. Or something.

"Temper, temper," a voice said from the open doors that led out to the ranch yard, but Sawyer couldn't see who stood in the bright light beyond the dim interior. It wasn't until the man came closer that he recognized him.

"Grey." Sawyer felt his neck heat up. "Pardon the tantrum. Sam's off with his men and I— What brings you over here?"

Grey resettled his black Stetson. "Hey. Didn't get a chance to talk with you the day you came to help with my cattle," he said.

Sawyer had just gotten there when Olivia showed up with Nick and they'd headed for the hospital.

"I wasn't much help." Here at the Circle H, his skills at handling the herd had proven to be pretty rusty, as he'd expected, and like Fred Miller, Sawyer had nearly gotten pinned against a fence by a bison bull. "Didn't really get a chance myself to say more than 'good for you' when Logan and I came by, either. About you and Shadow."

Grey grinned. "You took the words out of my mouth. I can't wait."

"Set a date yet?"

"That's the other reason I'm here. I don't

have a brother. Logan and I are friends, of course, but he has Blossom to take care of, and a new baby on the way, so—would you be my best man?"

"That depends on when the wedding is."

"We haven't decided," Grey said. "Soon, I hope."

"How long have you two...been together?" Sawyer asked. He remembered them dating when they were in high school, but... He thought of the little girl, Ava, and felt there must be a story there. He should probably learn it if he was going to be Grey's best man.

"I fell in love with her when I was seventeen." Grey frowned. "Her dad wouldn't let us date until the next year when Shadow turned fifteen. We had two years together, then right after we broke up, her brother was killed, and I went back to college for sophomore year."

"That was a rough time, Grey."

He nodded. "She left home soon after that and I never knew we had a daughter until recently."

"I'm glad it's all worked out for you."

Grey studied the floor for a moment, but when he looked up, his eyes shone with love. "If it were my choice, we'd be married already. On the other hand, Shadow's still turning over options for the wedding. I figure if I do my part now, I won't have to worry about the rest of the plans." He finally smiled. "After taking part in Logan's wedding, whatever she decides will be fine with me."

Sawyer felt a twinge of guilt. "I missed most of that day. I owe you for stepping in. You sure you'd want to rely on me?"

"If you say you'll be there, I know you will." Grey paused. "There's no hurry, is there? You going back to the clinic? I thought your partner was handling things."

"He is…" Sawyer eyed the bucket again. He'd been feeling this way ever since he first saw Fred Miller. No, since he'd answered that initial phone call and another stranger's plea for help. "Charlie's got more than he can manage right now, but I'm not…" *Ready*, he couldn't bring himself to say. *I don't know if I ever will be*.

And if he wasn't, what then? He'd let enough people down just in the past few days. And Doc's keys were in his jeans pocket again like a rebuke that gouged him every now and then.

Any other doctor worth his salt would have opened the office, treated Doc's patients, including Miller, filled in as Doc had obviously hoped he would. As Max Garrett had done at the walk-in clinic instead. Sawyer had paid the bill but he didn't feel any better.

Grey studied him. "Man of mystery," he said. "If you're that uncertain, maybe you don't belong there anymore. I know Sam would love to have you home again, to stay."

He worries about you, Logan had also said, but Sawyer wasn't sure.

Without a backward look, his grandfather had ridden out early that morning with Willy, Tobias and several other hands to do whatever they needed to do today. No one had informed him. Sawyer had used the past few hours to muck stalls, fill water buckets—and try to talk to Cyclone. He'd given Sawyer the silent treatment, as if the colt knew about his appointment with the vet.

"Look, Grey. I know how you feel about Wilson Cattle. But me? Maybe I was gone too long and the Circle H went on without me." Which he probably deserved.

The same thing would happen with his clinic if he didn't return soon. Or if he waited until Charlie didn't need—or want—him anymore.

Grey shifted his weight. "I'll nudge Shadow tonight. Urge her to pick the date so you can be here. Maybe we'll just run off somewhere and drag you with us. You and Olivia," he said.

Just hearing her name sent a wave of longing through him. He hadn't seen her recently, but he'd sure been thinking of her. And not only because he'd made her mad.

AFTER SHE LEFT the bank, Olivia crossed the street to the diner, which sat on the opposite corner from her antiques shop. She wasn't hungry—her talk with Barney Caldwell had ruined any appetite she might have had—but she often stopped in during the day for a bracing cup of coffee. A quick one, she thought, before she headed home early.

Worrying about her morning appointment, she hadn't slept well last night. She still felt muzzy, and all through her meeting she'd worried about Nick.

Olivia had left him home with his new sitter, their first time together. Her imagination ran wild. Phone calls with a boyfriend while Nick played, unsupervised, in the backyard, where he was determined to climb the old oak tree. Or he might fall from his swing. He wasn't even supposed to be outdoors yet. His balance could be unsteady and his headaches weren't entirely gone. What if he fell again?

Or what if he and the sitter didn't get along? Nick might do something mischievous or foolish or…decide to run away, to hitch a ride to the Circle H to see Hero.

As soon as she entered the diner, she pulled

out her cell phone. "Deirdre? It's Olivia. How are things going?"

"Fine," the girl said.

"May I speak to Nick?" Olivia envisioned him passed out in his room, the hematoma growing worse again while Deirdre watched television, oblivious to the fact that Nick needed emergency help. She had sounded distracted, or bored. Or was Olivia being unfair?

A brief conversation followed in the background, but Nick didn't come to the phone. "He's very into his Lego thing," Deirdre reported. "I'm making lunch. You did say he could have tomato soup and grilled cheese?"

"They're his favorites." Olivia raised one finger at Annabelle, who was bustling around to serve other customers. Pointing at the spot she wanted, Olivia slid into a nearby booth. Logan was right. She worried way too much. Her heart rate began to slow. Her bones relaxed. "Thanks, Deirdre. I'll be home soon." Still, she wasn't nearly as overprotective of Nick as she had been last spring. Was she?

Annabelle came over with a menu, which she didn't need.

"Hi, Olivia What can I get you?"

"Just coffee today. I won't take up this booth longer than that. I can see how busy you are." Olivia nodded toward the town's mayor, who was eating a hamburger, his chief aide sitting across from him. She smiled at a neighbor who lived down the street from her and often stopped to suggest that Olivia should plant some flowers in her empty front yard. There was still time this summer, she'd say. Every time she came by. A man Olivia thought was Grey at first turned out to be a stranger who simply wore a similar black hat.

Annabelle blew a stray hair off her cheek. Her face looked pink, her nose shiny, probably from the kitchen heat. They were basically diner friends these days and otherwise rarely saw each other. Maybe Olivia needed to make more of an effort with their friendship. She sometimes thought she'd only ever seen Annabelle wearing her pale blue uniform and carrying a coffeepot.

"I'm not sure being this busy is a good thing," Annabelle admitted, glancing around the nearly full restaurant.

"Really? The more people who come into my shop, the better I like it."

"I'll send you some customers."

Her remark made Olivia sit up and take notice. Annabelle was unfailingly cheerful, but today she seemed stressed, verging on unhappy. "Long hours?"

"Every day this week. I know. I should be

dancing on my way to the bank. My folks would be out of their minds with glee. But sometimes I feel overwhelmed."

Olivia touched her forearm. "What if you hired more help?"

"Even with business this good, I can barely afford to pay the servers I have. I shouldn't complain," she added. "This week is just… hard. One of them has been out sick with a summer cold, and another is pregnant so she's decided to cut back on her hours, at least during her first trimester." With an obvious effort, Annabelle squared her shoulders. "Listen to me, whining. I need to carry on, as they say. I'll get you some fresh coffee. And maybe a piece of pie? I made blueberry this morning."

"Goodness," Olivia said, grinning. Her stomach growled. "And you bake, too."

Annabelle gave her a twisted smile. "If I want to stay in business, I do. Otherwise, Jack Hancock down at the café will have my profits instead. His dinner service has brought a lot of people into town."

If I want to stay in business…

She could say the same thing about Olivia Wilson Antiques, but she noted something else in Annabelle. Did she actually want to run this diner? For years, she'd worked for her parents, but they were dead now. If Annabelle didn't want to stay here, she didn't have to. Why not go elsewhere?

Or was Olivia just caught up in her own dreams of buying out Ted Anderson and moving out of Barren?

CHAPTER TEN

"HOUSE CALL."

Shifting from one foot to the other, Sawyer stood on Olivia's front porch, a bunch of flowers in his hand and what he imagined must be an ashamed-of-himself look on his face. As soon as she'd opened the door, he'd decided this was a bad idea. An even worse joke. The only other "house call" he'd made was to Fred Miller.

Standing in the doorway, Olivia seemed speechless. Maybe she was remembering their last encounter at the Circle H when he'd told her about losing Khalil. He half turned to walk down the steps, wondering if he was here under false pretenses. Had he come to see Nick at last—or to lay eyes on Olivia again? She looked motherly, sweet, her blond hair pulled into a low ponytail, no makeup except for the faint tinge of pink on her lips—gloss or natural?—her blue eyes wary.

"Who are the flowers for?"

"You. Nick," he said, waving the bouquet

he'd put together with Blossom's flowers in the backyard. A few asters, a couple of petunias that had already begun to wilt in the heat, several pink and blue dahlias with showy blooms and some daisies. "Whoever wants them—if either of you do."

He sure couldn't tell if he was welcome here. He glanced behind himself. The grass needed mowing out front, all the shades had been drawn when he pulled up in the short driveway and only a few lights were on inside. He'd wondered if Olivia was home or if she and Nick had already gone to bed. Caring for her son alone must wipe her out. And in spite of that, Olivia was wearing her mama-tiger expression, which didn't ease his mind.

She hesitated. "All right. Those need a vase. Come in."

Sawyer blinked. Was she serious? She certainly looked serious. But then, so was he. He'd been trying for days to think of some way to make amends with Olivia, to take back what he'd said at the ranch.

Nick is better off without me.

Not that he'd changed his mind, but as long as he was staying at the Circle H and she was here in Barren, they'd likely run into each other. Burying the hatchet made sense. But no, he was lying to himself. He'd wanted to see her, to hear her voice, to find out how Nick was mending.

Sawyer followed Olivia into the house, trailing her through the entryway and into the living room. The furnishings were minimal, the walls painted a light tan. In fact, everything he saw was neutral—as if this were indeed a temporary space.

At the dining room table across the way, Nick sat hunched over some Lego pieces. He didn't look up even when Olivia gave him a pointed glance. She turned back to Sawyer and he handed her the flowers.

She said, "Have a seat. Would you like something to drink?"

Sawyer sat, then clamped his hands between his knees. He needed to steady his nerves before he imploded like some dying star in the galaxy. "A beer if you have one."

"I don't," she said. Olivia glanced again at Nick.

"Then nothing, thanks. I, uh, just came by to see how Nick's feeling." As if the Circle H was around the corner from her house when Sawyer hadn't been to town in days. He was still trying to make himself useful at the ranch.

She arched an eyebrow. "Really?"

"Yeah." He lowered his voice. "I may not

want to treat him—didn't want to before—but how are the headaches?"

Finally, Nick piped up. "Gone," he said, moving a plastic piece from one side of the table to the other. Sawyer had no idea what he was building, but he'd clamped his mouth tight in concentration.

"Completely?"

Nick nodded, then stopped for a minute as if his head were spinning. "I'm fine to ride Hero now."

"Nicholas Hunter," Olivia said in the chiding tone that Sawyer imagined every mother used. He vaguely remembered his own mom speaking like that when he was late for dinner or had taken another swipe at Logan just because he could.

"I am, Mom." Nick smiled. "If I finish my Minecraft Lego, that will prove it."

"He has a point," Sawyer said.

"Too bad his mother doesn't agree." Holding the flowers, Olivia sat on the sofa opposite the chair he'd chosen and ran a hand over her forehead as if she were the one with the headache.

The room was small yet cozy in its oddly bland way. Or not so odd, if she really was planning to move and hadn't wanted to put down roots. A small plaque on the wall read

Family. "Nick, you haven't thanked Uncle Sawyer," Olivia said.

"Thank you for the bear," he muttered, still not looking up.

"You're welcome. I thought you could use his superpowers to get well."

Nick grinned. "See, Mom?"

She sent Sawyer a look. "I was hoping you'd be a good influence." But her tone said otherwise.

"I doubt you hoped that." He rose from his seat. "Nick, would you show me the bear? After all, this is a home visit. I'd like to make sure he's being cared for." The boy's head snapped up before he froze and simply sat there. Sawyer imagined he was having a bout of vertigo from moving too fast.

To his surprise, Olivia hastened to help. "Nick has a whole collection of stuffed animals that will absolutely knock you out. There must be a hundred."

"Most of them are in the closet," Nick said, then shot a sour look at Sawyer. "I'm getting too old for stuffies."

"Well, before you send them off to the toy orphanage, maybe I can give them all a quick exam. See how they're doing."

Olivia mouthed a quick thank-you, as if she could trust him when the last time he'd seen her, Sawyer had told her about Kedar. About Khalil. "While you and Nick do that, I'll find a vase…make some lemonade. Put out a few cookies."

The simple offer stunned Sawyer. He knew she hadn't forgiven him for Jasmine's death, for virtually ignoring Nick at the hospital. Now she was entrusting him with her son, not that Sawyer meant to conduct a full examination of the boy. Probably she knew that, too.

With a heavy sigh, Nick pushed a pile of Lego pieces aside. He led the way down the hall to his bedroom and Sawyer didn't know where to step.

Like the rest of the house, the room was tiny, but unlike the other rooms it was full of clutter. The bedspread flung on the floor. Several Lego models strewn about. A pile of clothes. At least the room had more color. The rich blue walls made a perfect backdrop for the Star Wars decals and matching Millennium Falcon–patterned comforter.

Nick opened his closet, rooted around inside, then popped out holding at least ten stuffed animals. A battered Curious George, several bears other than the one Sawyer had given him, a white lamb with its stuffing coming out and a yellow character Sawyer didn't recognize. He took a seat on the bed. "Who's this?"

"Wubbzy. I had him for a long time."

"Pretty good friend, is he?"

"They're all good friends," Nick said, as if that should be obvious. He frowned. "Are you going to give them shots?"

Sawyer smiled. "No, I'll just take a look."

Really, he meant to study Nick from a short distance as he had in the barn and the house at the Circle H. While Sawyer poked and prodded the various stuffed figures, he also checked Nick's pupils, making sure they remained equal and reactive. Doc was still away and Sawyer owed Nick as well as Olivia. He teased him, as he had often teased children who came into the clinic in Kedar looking fearful—including Khalil, who'd had every right to be scared, as it turned out.

Finally, he said, "Tell me about the headaches."

"I did."

"No, you told your mother and me what you wanted us to hear. How are you really, Nick? This is just between us…men. Does your head still hurt sometimes?"

Nick's mouth turned down into a pout. "Not much," he said. "But when it does, it… hurts a lot." He glanced at Sawyer, showing that same fear as the kids at the clinic. "I'm okay now. I want to ride Hero."

"I know you do, but the adults here need to make certain you're ready for that. You wouldn't want to ride and get hurt again, would you? Or hurt Hero?" The image of Olivia's horse flashed through his mind. "I know you wouldn't mean to, but when you're on him you need to be feeling your best. In control."

Nick's deep blue eyes looked huge. "I'm not going to die, am I?"

With a start, Sawyer sat back on the bed. A sudden vision of Khalil had run through his mind. "No, of course not. Have you been worried about that?" Nick gave a small nod. "You don't need to, Nick." If only he'd been able to reassure Khalil like this. "You're going to be all right. Just take time to rest, to let yourself heal. I realize that can seem frustrating at times—it's hard not to be able to do what you want to do—but try to be patient."

Nick considered that. "How long?"

Sawyer fought a smile. "I can't tell you. But if you push too hard and ride Hero before your body is all better, you could get into more trouble. Then you'd have to wait even longer to ride again."

Nick reached for the new bear on his pillows. "I need more superpowers," he said, burying his face in the animal's fur.

"Well, that's what this guy is for. Never doubt Superman."

Gathering up the rest of the stuffed animals, Nick scrambled off the bed to put them back in the closet. His voice was muffled. "Is there really a toy orphanage?"

"What do you think?" It was the same question that during his training, Sawyer had asked kids who wondered if Santa Claus was real.

"No." Nick emerged from the closet. "But if there was, I wouldn't let them go there. I'll keep them in my room—even when I don't play with them anymore."

"Sounds like a plan," Sawyer said, trying again to suppress his smile.

Nick looked him up and down with a critical eye. Nothing wrong with his vision. He gave Sawyer a thorough once-over before he said, "You're a good doctor." Then he took the bear and left the room.

Sawyer sat there, thinking, *Out of the mouths of babes*. Wondering. Wishing that were true.

He might be a wizard with the toy bears and Curious George.

Beyond that…not so much.

"So, um…" Olivia took another sip of lemonade, the ultimate soother on such a hot summer night, yet she still felt edgy. She set the glass on the end table, wondering what to say to Sawyer.

Much of her conversation these days was with her seven-year-old. She'd put Nick to bed a few minutes ago but didn't linger to read another story with him as she usually did. Sawyer had been waiting in the other room.

He sat across from her, making the space feel even smaller, looking as uncomfortable as Olivia felt. She didn't date much—not that this was a date!—and she hadn't seen Clint in weeks, but here she was with another very handsome man in her house, which Olivia rarely allowed. She always met Clint for dinner or a movie in town, or occasionally in Kansas City. But since Nick's fall, Clint still hadn't so much as phoned to ask about her son. She guessed their relationship was over. She should miss that more, but she didn't and she had Nick to consider.

Maybe now Sawyer wished he'd left before Nick went to bed. Whatever they'd spoken about in his room was between them, but by leaving sooner he could have avoided this awkward time with Olivia. She would have been spared, too.

But Sawyer had taken the time to come by. He'd been surprisingly gentle, even humorous, with Nick, so he probably didn't dislike children in general, as she'd first thought. And his coolness before had more to do with what had happened in Kedar.

"Thank you for being so good with Nick tonight."

He frowned. "Meaning I wasn't good with him before."

Olivia couldn't argue with that. Still. Instead of resenting Sawyer or wondering what else he held so deep inside, maybe she should focus on how much he appealed to her: his dark hair and deep blue eyes and the way he fit his body and how he almost seemed to read her mind at times. As if that could be any safer.

"I talked to Logan last night," Sawyer said at last. "And from what he said and you told me the night Nick fell, you're thinking of moving away from Barren."

Olivia silently groaned. "That idea didn't thrill Nick—or Logan." Then, before she could stop herself, she explained about Ted Anderson's shop and her meeting with Barney Caldwell. "I don't know what else to do," she finished. "I'll explore other avenues for financing, but Barney had a point. I did value my business too highly. I'll have to get more creative, adjust my numbers...because I don't want to give up."

"The next county, Logan says. Would you sell your store here, then?"

"No, but going back and forth between Main Street and Ted's shop could get old pretty fast. If I let Nick stay in school here, let's say he gets sick, which happens every term, or there's a snow day—I'd have to drive all the way back here to get him. I could cut my commute in half by living between the two shops."

Sawyer gazed at her over his lemonade. "But if Nick doesn't want to relocate, why do it? He's been through a lot lately..." His eyes darkened. "Oh, wait. Does the move have something to do with your feelings about the Circle H? Getting stuck there in that flood with a sick child must have been difficult—"

"I don't blame Logan for that—now—but I don't like to stir up those memories," she admitted. Or another of Jasmine, years ago, that still made her sad...and made her blame Sawyer.

He must have known what she meant. "I guess Nick having his horse there makes that tougher. For you."

Olivia couldn't disagree. Though she welcomed Sawyer's input about her business in theory, he'd made her feel selfish about Nick. She leaned forward. "I would do anything to make Nick happy. I know how he feels about Hero, about Ava, about all his other friends here but—"

To her surprise, Sawyer half smiled. "You forgot to mention his stuffed toys."

Olivia couldn't manage to smile back.

She stiffened. "So you're taking Nick's side—and Logan's—when the move is my decision to make. Just as you made your choice years ago."

Now this conversation wasn't only awkward, it was coming close to a more personal issue for her with Sawyer. She didn't need to think about his attractiveness.

Sawyer glanced toward the hallway. "You mean because *I* didn't stay here? I couldn't. I had to finish med school—"

"Then move more than halfway around the world?"

"The clinic is my *job*, Olivia. It's my business just as Wilson Antiques is yours. It's what I do. The difference is that I don't have a kid to think about."

But he did have a family. People who cared about him. Missed him. Pointing that out would only reveal how she'd felt about him leaving, though.

Instead, she said, "That *was* your job, until your patient didn't survive." He paled and she regretted having been so abrupt just to protect herself. "Sorry, that was…unfair, Sawyer."

He was on his feet before she said his name. He carried his glass to the kitchen, where she heard him rinse it at the sink, then put it in the dishwasher. He came back to the living room and stopped in the doorway. His eyes looked indigo blue.

"Olivia. I'd hoped you understood why I kept my distance with Nick."

"But I still don't know what really happened over there. Sawyer, please. Tell me more. I do want to understand." She let out a breath of frustration. "What exactly was so bad that you don't think you deserve to be a doctor now? I mean, I understand that people die, even kids sometimes." Olivia fought back a shudder. "That can be inevitable." As it might have been when Nick fell.

Sawyer only shook his head. "It wasn't inevitable, and that's on me. Good night, Olivia. Tell Nick I'll keep an eye on Hero for him."

"Sawyer," she said. "I didn't mean to bring it up like that—"

"Good luck with your business."

He was out the door before she could say

anything more. Sawyer carried a huge burden, and she'd made it worse.

"Thanks for the house call," she murmured to the empty room.

CHAPTER ELEVEN

LIZA PACED THE vast living room of the high-rise condominium she shared with Everett in the heart of Dallas. Her steps had worn a path through the thick white carpet. The fading late-afternoon sun filtered through the gauzy curtains across the windows but she scarcely noticed the soft slant of red-gold light, and although she was already dressed for the evening's charity event, her thoughts were far away.

Wilson Cattle wasn't her home, yet she wanted it to be so she could feel like a part of Everett's family when she knew she wasn't. Leaving Barren, leaving little Nick behind had left a huge hole in her heart. She wouldn't count on Olivia or Grey coming around—though she had certainly tried to win them over—but Nick…she couldn't get the image of him, delighted with the Lego set she and Everett had given him, out of her mind.

He was such a darling, and after a lonely childhood spent in her family's mansion with only servants for company much of the time, she had so much love to give away. If only…

"Liza." Dressed in his tuxedo and fussing with his bow tie, which he never got right, Everett stepped into the room and her pulse quickened. "We'll need to buy new rugs if you keep going."

She knotted her hands at her waist. "Is it so obvious? I'm afraid I'm not in the mood tonight for a party. Dinner, which is always the same filet of beef or chicken, so many people crowding in—" She now preferred the space and big sky in Kansas, a change in her outlook that had surprised her.

Everett covered her hands with his. Warm and solid, he had a tendency to calm her with his very presence. "We can stay home if you want."

"No, we have to go." During the winter season that would begin all too soon, there would be dozens of such events to dress for, socialites to smile at and various causes to write checks for, all of which were worthy, of course. For too long, these events had been the largest part of her life. As a teenager, she'd made her debut, a rite of passage into society that had cost her parents thousands for her dress alone. "Sometimes I wonder if we made a mistake.

Selling my house in The Woodlands, moving here."

Liza came from big money. She'd inherited her parents' place, redone it several times without ever thinking of it as her own, then met Everett—and for the first time, fell instantly in love.

Their age difference didn't trouble her at all. No, not that. For a man in his midfifties with two grown children, he looked remarkably youthful and fit. His brown hair had a few streaks of distinguished gray and his earnest blue-green eyes could have belonged to his thirty-year-old son. And actually, they did.

Everett's years of running Wilson Cattle before he turned the ranch over to Grey had guaranteed the still-hard muscle in his arms, the flatness of his stomach. He remained a vigorous man, and tonight he was wearing cowboy boots with his tux.

My, look at you, she thought with another rush of warmth inside. *You can take the cowboy out of the ranch, but you can't take the ranch out of the cowboy*. Of course, he wouldn't be the only man in boots tonight— the hall would be full of oilmen. It astonished her how Everett had fit right into the world she'd known before him.

He drew her to the windows. They took in

the sweeping sight of skyscrapers, the faraway rush of heavy bumper-to-bumper traffic on the many freeways that snaked through the area and the first wink of city lights coming on. "Look at that view. This whole town is ours, Liza. I thought you were happy here."

They'd bought the condo a year ago to celebrate their first wedding anniversary. He and Liza had picked out every paint color, each piece of furniture and all the accessories and still…for her, like her family's mansion, it wasn't truly a home. Always, something seemed to be missing. At least here she had Everett.

"I didn't say I'm not happy."

He put an arm around her. "You don't look happy even in that spectacular dress. What's the color called?"

"Seafoam green—or blue, whichever you prefer. You like it?"

"I do," he said. "I love anything you wear." His voice turned thick. "You always look amazing, and I think what a lucky man I am. After all those years with the wrong woman, I finally found the right one. Needle in a haystack," he murmured, bending his head to kiss the curve of her neck.

Liza moved closer to him. "Now see what you've done. You've managed to sweet-talk me out of a bad mood." She reached up to redo his bow tie, which had been hanging lopsided on his snow-white pleated shirt.

"And you've managed to turn me from a lowly rancher into a high-society guy. Good thing I like it."

"Not lowly," she said, patting the tie. She was in awe of his quick adjustment to Dallas; Liza hadn't had the same opportunity in Barren. "Wilson Cattle is a wonderful place. I enjoyed our stay there for Logan and Blossom's wedding—despite the stress of Nick's accident." She paused before admitting, "I hated to leave."

He moved back to study her face. Liza didn't meet his eyes, but she could sense his thorough scrutiny. "What's this? My bride—the woman I love with all my heart, the toast of Dallas's elite who has turned this cowboy into a city slicker—is yearning for the ranch?"

"I wouldn't say yearning…" Aching, perhaps. "I miss Nick, especially. After all, he's my best chance to be a…grandmother."

Everett laughed. "Most women your age wouldn't be as eager for someone to call them Granny."

She frowned. "Nick doesn't call me anything at all, but he makes me smile just to see him."

He took another step back, letting his arms drop. "So. You're homesick."

Yes, she thought. *I am.* Not only for Wilson Cattle, or even Nick. She'd meant Olivia and Grey, too.

And, of course, there was something else she yearned for, but she couldn't tell Everett. She tried not to even think about it.

Instead, she tucked her arm through his. "I'll be fine. How could I not feel simply grand tonight with such a handsome man to escort me? I'm ready now," she said, determined not to dwell on something she could never have. "Fly me to the moon—or at least through all the maddening traffic to the Hyatt Regency."

Although they'd been married just a few years, Everett read her like a favorite book. "Guess tomorrow we'll have to plan another visit to Barren."

"Does Uncle Sawyer live at the Circle H?" Nick asked Olivia.

In her room, making one of his morning visits, he sat on her bed, feet swinging. He'd been bombarding her with questions ever since Sawyer's surprise visit.

Two weeks later, he hadn't paid another "house call" to Nick, yet his presence seemed to linger, teasing Olivia's senses every day with the faint scent of his aftershave, the sound of his murmured voice floating to her from Nick's room as it had the night he came. Nick seemed to have acquired what Olivia feared could become—for her—an unwise interest in the uncle he barely knew. In her mind, they were both better off without that.

"For now, he does."

Nick paused to rub his temple and Olivia's maternal alarm system went off again. She could see his progress every day, and he could play in the backyard now, if not on his swing set, while she watched from the kitchen window. His balance had improved, but she didn't trust him to stay safe. Were his headaches worse than he let on? For a second, she felt tempted to phone Sawyer, then suppressed the urge.

She didn't want him here again, didn't really want him around her child, but Nick's initial distrust of his uncle had changed since their talk in his room that night. In Logan's absence, maybe Nick was looking for a surrogate father. Certainly Sawyer looked much the same, but the last thing *she* wanted was to get close to him. She had nothing to gain from that, and Nick risked getting hurt if—or when—Sawyer left.

Nick frowned. "Why doesn't he stay all the time?"

"You'd have to ask him. Your uncle lives in a faraway place," she said. "He'll probably go back soon." A prospect that both eased Olivia's mind and tempted her to already miss him.

Nick's gaze stayed steady on hers. "How do you know?"

"Because that's where his job is." And the source of the pain she saw in Sawyer's eyes whenever he let down his guard. Most recently, she'd been the cause of that pain in her own living room after she'd put Nick to bed. Olivia still felt bad about that.

Nick stayed silent for a moment while Olivia checked her cell phone again. Earlier, Ted Anderson had finally called with his counteroffer to her second bid on his shop. Even the sound of his voice had perked up her spirits. She wanted this deal, badly, but then the newest numbers he'd quoted had stunned her.

Ted had rushed to complete his inventory, and his stock was worth more than he'd thought. She could barely afford what she'd already offered him, and after her disappointing meeting with Barney Caldwell, she didn't have the option to up her game. Olivia wouldn't go on a date with Barney to help her cause, but she felt half inclined to speak to Barney's mother as he'd jokingly suggested. Her deep pockets might be just what Olivia needed——assuming Mrs. Caldwell actually wanted to do business with her. And vice versa.

"Does Uncle Sawyer ride horses?"

A loaded question. She should have known. "Nick," she said, guessing what would come next. A day didn't pass without him finding some way to bring up Hero. Because of Jasmine, she could understand how much he missed his gray gelding, but that didn't mean she was going to let him ride yet.

There were no new messages on her phone, which she laid aside on the desk. Olivia conducted business from here in the evenings, her "home office." The small surface of the rosewood antique desk was, as usual, littered with paperwork. She really needed to catch up. And she was stalling with Nick. "What have we talked about? If you're not ready for your swing in the yard, then you're not ready to ride Hero."

His mouth turned down. "Mom." He drew out her name. It had become increasingly rare for him to call her *Mommy*. "School's going to start soon."

"You have time." Weeks, because August had barely started, but Nick was right. The days of summer were racing past.

"When I have school, there won't be time. I'll have *homework*," he said in a dramatic tone. "I'll never ride Hero *again*."

Olivia tried to smooth a hand over his hair, still rumpled from sleep, but he ducked away. Nick hadn't wakened until after ten o'clock this morning, which she struggled not to take as a bad sign.

"I know that's how you feel right now, but didn't someone tell you to be patient?" As soon as she said the words, she wanted to take them back. Nick pounced on that.

"Uncle Sawyer did. Maybe we could ask him if it's okay?"

Maybe we shouldn't. But Doc was still out of town. He and Ida had extended their vacation, going from Las Vegas to the Texas Panhandle. They were reportedly having a great time, staying on Padre Island. And Sawyer was, supposedly, still filling in for Doc. She couldn't deny that a check-up might help ease her fears about Nick's progress. But no, she didn't want Sawyer making another house call, invading her personal space and leaving part of himself behind.

Most women, she supposed, would have no problem with that. They might welcome having a handsome man around, but Sawyer's attractiveness wasn't all there was to him. If she'd needed that, she could have stayed married to Logan.

Sawyer had left here the last time rather than unburden himself any further about Kedar, and she didn't want to see that sorrowful look in his eyes again. She didn't want to care, or feel guilty, yet she did. For Olivia, that was a dangerous admission. She didn't want another relationship—and Sawyer clearly didn't, either.

"I think we'll wait a bit longer, Nick. Your appointment with the neurologist is coming up soon. We can let her make the decision."

"She's at the *hospital*." Nick had developed a definite aversion to that.

But Sawyer was at the Circle H. Seeing Nick's ploy, Olivia shook her head. He had taken the passive approach first, asking about Sawyer in a roundabout way as if his interest in his uncle didn't really involve Nick. Of course, that had led to Hero.

She didn't avoid the Circle H now as she had for the past three years, and Sawyer had picked up on her feelings, but she didn't go out of her way to visit the ranch, either—just as she seldom went to Wilson Cattle.

Still. That was all her problem, not Nick's. *I would do anything to make Nick happy.* How could she deny him the chance to at least see the little horse he loved?

"All right," she said at last. "Let's go visit Hero."

"Yay!" Nick bounced up and down on her bed. "Thanks, Mom."

She sighed, then couldn't resist the warning. "This doesn't mean you're going to ride today."

Her caution fell on deaf ears. Before she finished speaking, Nick was off the bed and shooting across the hall to his room with all the speed of a barrel racer. She could hear him rummaging in his closet, probably for his boots, banging drawers as he searched for a Western-style shirt and clean jeans. He never went near the Circle H these days without dressing the part.

Smiling, Olivia tidied the stack of papers on her desk. She guessed they could wait. She could indulge Nick in this simple pleasure. If Sawyer was there, she'd ask him to check Nick over again. But *she* wouldn't dress the same way. She was no longer the cowgirl she'd once been.

Olivia was now a city girl—or at least, temporarily, a Barren girl.

She told herself she liked it that way.

Sawyer was in the barn, grooming Sundance, when he heard a car pull up in the yard. With a last sweep of the brush over the horse's hide, he glanced out the open doors and saw Olivia's car. His pulse began to throb.

Two weeks and he'd managed not to call or see her again. He still felt ashamed that he'd marched out of her house rather than talk about Khalil. He couldn't.

He also couldn't get Olivia out of his head. The way the lamplight had shone on her blond hair, gilding it with gold. The unwilling yet concerned look she'd given him that had sent him rushing off. The gentle way she had with her son. Even Nick's comment, "You're a good doctor," had kept Sawyer from going back. He'd wondered how Nick was doing, but—

Nick raced into the barn. "Hi, Uncle Sawyer!" A bag of carrots bumped against his leg as he ran, checking each stall he passed until he stopped in front of Sawyer. Nick had violated the no-running rule and paid zero attention to Olivia's calls to slow down, but Sawyer was glad he'd come. Saved him the decision to phone Olivia—or show up again at her door.

"Where's Hero?" Nick asked with a worried look.

"Out in the corral. Taking some sun," Sawyer said. "How are you?"

Nick didn't answer. He whirled around, then shot back down the aisle and turned the corner toward the pen where several other horses were turned out, too.

Olivia stood just in the doorway, squinting into the dimly lit stable. Nick had nearly knocked her over.

"And how are you?" she asked, reminding him of his hasty retreat from her house. "I would have called before we came over, but Nick was so eager to get here, I didn't take the time."

He held her gaze, all but drinking her in. "You don't need to call. This will be Nick's ranch someday." He added, "Sorry for that– a couple of weeks ago." Then he rushed past her. "Nick shouldn't be alone out there. I don't want him in the corral."

"I couldn't agree more." Breaking the stare they'd been sharing, Olivia followed him outside. They found Nick halfway up the fence, leaning over to offer Hero a carrot. A whole one.

"That's probably too much for him at once," Sawyer said. "Here. Let me break off some pieces for you."

But Hero had already pulled the carrot from Nick's hands. It dropped to the dirt and the horse nosed it, then stepped on it with one elegant hoof. He nudged part of the mashed carrot, lipped it and finally got some into his mouth, dirt and all. Sawyer could swear he saw the horse smile.

"He likes 'em," Nick said. "Me and Ava always feed him."

"He doesn't usually eat them with dirt." Sawyer stood inches away from Nick, leaning on the fence in a mirror image of the boy. They both crossed their arms on the top rail. Nick's feet dangled off the ground but he didn't seem to care about his precarious perch. "Let's hope he doesn't colic tonight."

"He won't. He never does." Nick was obviously the expert. He eyed Sawyer. "You going to look at me again? I think my mom wants you to."

Olivia sighed. "Nick, just say what *you* want."

"I want to ride Hero."

"There's a familiar refrain." Sawyer thought of messing up the boy's hair to show him he was teasing but he didn't. His arms stayed on the rail.

Olivia stepped up to his other side, not touching him, either. Even so, Sawyer could feel her heat as if their shoulders had brushed. "Would you mind?"

Sawyer started. For a second, he'd thought

she meant for him to touch her. "So that's why you dropped by today."

"One reason," she said, nodding in Nick's direction. "He's been begging to see Hero, as you might expect."

Sawyer smiled. He turned his head toward Nick. "Why don't we let Hero work on his carrot? Bring the rest of the bag. You didn't forget Sundance, did you?"

At first, Nick was reluctant to leave his horse. He tossed carrots to the other cow ponies in the corral, but once inside the barn, he walked along the aisle with Sawyer, doling out treats to every horse, greeting each one by name.

"You're going to make a fine rancher, Nick."

He nodded. "That's what I want to do."

Sawyer heard Olivia make a small sound of distress, which he ignored. He assessed Nick as they went, looking for any signs of neurological impairment, not finding any, probing again about his headaches. Nick refused to answer. "You already asked me that."

"So I did."

"They're better," Nick finally said. "I'm all better."

"Well." In the center of the aisle, Sawyer stopped, shoved his hands into the rear pockets of his jeans and rocked back on his boot heels. Olivia kept her distance, standing beside a stall, clearly understanding this was between Nick and Sawyer. "Your mom tells me you have a doctor's appointment soon."

"Another doctor," Nick said, watching a buckskin mare vacuum up a carrot.

"True. Okay, but for now it seems to me you're in pretty good shape."

Nick almost danced up and down. The bag of carrots fell to the floor. "Does that mean I can ride? Say yes!"

Olivia stepped in. "No, really. I'd rather he didn't—"

Sawyer steered her away, raising his eyebrows. "Let me handle this." He faced Nick again and lowered his voice. "Sometimes moms get…worried," he said.

"A lot," Nick muttered, rolling his eyes. He gave Sawyer a hopeful look.

"And sometimes, we…guys have to stick together. So here's the deal. You can ride Hero today but only in the ring. I'll move the other horses to the pasture. Go get your saddle and bridle. Then we'll see what kind of horseman you are."

With a shout, Nick punched the air. His boots stomping, he ran toward the tack room.

Olivia's mouth had become a flat line "Sawyer, I don't like this. I told Nick he could come to the ranch to *see* his horse. Shouldn't that be enough?"

"Not for Nick. Come on, Olivia. I won't let anything happen to him."

"But…"

Sawyer moved the other horses. He oversaw Nick while he saddled Hero and did a pretty good job. Sawyer readjusted the cinch, tightening it as he said, "I don't know if your dad has told you this, but after you're done saddling, your gear and the horse warm up—which means the cinch can get loose. It's always good to recheck it a bit later."

"This is the first time I've saddled Hero by myself."

The kid was determined, all right. Sawyer liked his spirit, but no wonder Olivia tended to worry even when she shouldn't. "Well, then, Lesson learned. You can take him outside now."

With a lead rope slung over his shoulder, Sawyer walked close to Nick, keeping a careful eye on him while Olivia trailed after them.

In the corral, Nick swung into the saddle like a pro, making Sawyer smile. He glanced back at Olivia. One second, she looked as if she wanted to snatch Nick away and bundle him into her car, the next she seemed resigned. Or as if she trusted Sawyer? He didn't suppose she often gave up control of her son, and the realization made him…happy.

Nick gathered up his reins, then started off with a quick, light jab of his boot heels in Hero's sides, but Sawyer caught the bridle. "Hey. Whoa. Today you just sit back and enjoy the ride." He clipped the lead rope to the bridle.

"I can do it myself!" Nick protested.

"I know you can. Your mother will feel better if you don't." Sawyer gave him a man-to-man look. "Are we square?"

"Yeah." Nick looked away. "But I'll feel like a baby."

"You're on the horse, aren't you? Count your blessings."

Olivia's thank-you look was enough to melt his bones.

CHAPTER TWELVE

"FASTER!" NICK CRIED.

For almost an hour, Sawyer had guided Nick's horse around the outdoor corral in the hot summer sun, chatting to both Hero and Nick as they walked. The two, man and boy with the lovely gray gelding, made Olivia's heart ache in a good way. Here was Sawyer McCord, a cowboy again just like Logan, though they'd both turned their backs on the Circle H years ago. Though Sawyer would probably leave soon once more.

Sawyer had just urged Hero into a slow lope, much to Nick's delight. Olivia bit her tongue. Really, there was no way Nick could get hurt again. Sawyer stayed right with him, and today she liked how he treated her son even more than she had the night he came to their house. Unlike Olivia, he knew how to manage Nick's obsession with his first horse. Had he been as good with that other child in Kedar? What had gone wrong?

She was waiting by the gate when Sawyer

led Hero out, Nick still grinning. "Did you see, Mom? We almost cantered."

Sawyer sent her a look. "Not quite. Hero's got good gaits, but I doubt I could keep up with him at that pace." He wasn't even breathing hard, and Olivia looked away from his shirt, now plastered to his shoulders, chest and flat abdomen. He was saving face for Nick so he wouldn't feel as if he were on some pony ride at a summer fair. Of course he wanted to go fast. That was her son. Years ago, she had to admit, that would have been her, too, flying like the wind on Jasmine.

And that was, always, like Sawyer. His impulsiveness had cost Olivia her favorite horse. She found it hard to forget that when she was here at the Circle H, so close to Wilson Cattle and that meadow in between.

She walked with Sawyer and Nick into the barn. She watched them pick Hero's dainty hooves to remove clumps of dirt and any stones, wipe him down, then groom him before they put him in his stall.

"Thank you," she said, knowing how stiff she must sound.

Sawyer didn't seem to notice. "Come on up to the house. I think we have some Popsicles in the freezer. Sound good to you, Nick?"

Nick nodded, his dark blue eyes filled with

happiness. "I hope there's a cherry one. And I want milk in my dinosaur mug. I keep it here."

In the kitchen, which had been hers while she was married to Logan, Olivia looked around. Blossom had made a few changes, added bright new dish towels, a set of ceramic canisters with a pretty flower design and a lace-trimmed cloth on the roughhewn table. Which made Olivia smile. She could imagine what Sam thought of that. As if Blossom were here now, a pot of coffee stood ready on the counter. Had Sam made it, or Sawyer?

He handed Nick his cherry Popsicle, then put on a cartoon for him in the family room. Now he and Olivia were alone together as they'd been in her living room. Sawyer led her to the front porch and her nerves tightened.

"He's a good kid, Olivia."

"Yes, he is. I love him so much it hurts. I'm trying not to worry about him—really, I am—but Logan thinks I still go overboard. You should have seen me right before he and I split up. Believe me, I was far better controlled at Farrier General after Nick fell than I was the night of the flood here."

"Bad memories." He braced his arms on the porch railing next to Olivia. "That includes Jasmine." He added, "And me."

Olivia couldn't deny that. "Well, if you

hadn't dared me to race you to the other end of that meadow—"

"I made a mistake. Seems I keep making them," he said. "But if I never told you how bad I felt about what happened to Jasmine—and having to make that choice—I'm telling you now."

He was sorry for a lot more than that. She could see it in his eyes, the same way she had that night at her house, and she guessed Kedar was never very far from his mind. Was it better to talk about her horse—as if the mare could be more important than what had happened in Kedar? Safer, yes, she decided. For now. She owed him that much.

Olivia heard the wistfulness, not anger this time, in her tone. "She was the best horse I ever owned…"

"I've said I'm sorry. I know that's not enough, but it's all I have."

She met his eyes. "Yes, and I could hate you for that but I don't. That day, we were *foolish*—not only you—and poor Jasmine paid the price. I didn't have to accept your dare, but there was something more in the air and…even knowing the danger, the risk, I couldn't seem to tell you no. So I'm as guilty as you are."

Sawyer looked surprised. "I'm still sorry."

"As you said, there was nothing else you

could have done. I knew that then. But I *wanted* to blame you."

He straightened. "Olivia…"

"No, you were right. Putting her down was the only solution. I'm glad she didn't suffer any longer than she did." She was about to ask him what else had been driving Sawyer that day when he cleared his throat now but didn't speak. She held her tongue. Olivia could feel his warmth, so close their arms were nearly touching. From the cottonwoods by the creek, a chorus of summer locusts began to sing.

The air all around seemed charged. Reminding herself that she didn't want any closeness with him, Olivia took a step back from the rail. This was enough for today—for always, if she was smart. Sawyer had too many shadows hidden deep inside. He wouldn't stay here long, as she'd told Nick. She didn't want another serious relationship with a man, including Clint, at least not now. And with Sawyer, never. She'd tried marriage with Logan, finally started dating again with Clint and concluded all over again that love was not in the cards for her.

Olivia turned toward the screen door. "I'll get Nick," she said. "We should go. Thank you again for being so kind to him today." She forced a smile over her shoulder. "He'll probably be talking about this for the next week, asking questions…"

Sawyer had left his place at the railing. Olivia had her hand on the door. He walked toward her, his deep blue eyes serious, and he put his hands lightly on her shoulders to hold her in place. His voice was low, intimate. "Olivia. We were friends once, weren't we?"

"Good friends," she agreed, his touch warm through the fabric of her blouse, as if he were touching her skin. She focused instead on a rush of memory: Olivia and Grey, Logan and Sawyer getting themselves into trouble, riding horses and playing hide-and-seek in the barns here and at Wilson Cattle, roaming the range and pretending they were in a spaghetti Western, cowboys all day long. Until that day in the meadow when something between her and Sawyer had changed.

He asked, "Do you think we could be… friends again?"

Her heartbeat fluttered. "That sounds like a dare, more dangerous than our race across that field."

"Life's a danger," he said, then muttered a few words to himself that Olivia couldn't make out. He turned her around, and before she could think to stop him, drew her into his arms.

"Sawyer."

His gaze was intent and he didn't take the warning. Sawyer broke the stare. Then he lowered his head, angling it just so to touch his lips, soft as a whisper, to the corner of her mouth. And for a second, she wanted to lean closer, to turn her head and find him, turn the tentative movement into more with the slight, warm pressure of her mouth on his.

Then Olivia came to her senses. She pulled free, wrenched open the screen door, then hurried inside, her heart hammering in her chest, her throat tight and guilty tears welling in her eyes.

Olivia knew exactly what that something else, long ago, had been with Sawyer, and it had nothing to do with simple friendship. She tried not to hear his parting words.

"Sometimes you have to take a chance."

HE MIGHT HAVE been talking to himself.

Sawyer slung another bale of hay onto the growing pile in the loft. Hard exercise, he'd hoped, might cool his anger at himself.

Why had he said that to Olivia? Tried to kiss her? Let her know how he felt, both long ago and now? For one instant, he'd thought she might welcome that kiss, might even kiss him back. Instead, he'd be lucky if he ever saw her again, and for sure she wouldn't bring Nick to the Circle H, not before Logan and Blossom got home from their honeymoon and Sawyer wasn't needed any longer. She wouldn't want to come anywhere near him. There'd be no more heartfelt talks on the porch, no more clumsy attempts on his part...

Friends, he thought. He wanted way more than that. Always had, but even now that didn't make sense to him. Obviously, she didn't want to get involved—based on how she'd turned him down on the porch. Sawyer didn't fully understand why. And even if she did want him, how would they make it work? He was still adrift when Olivia had solid ambitions. She had her antiques shop and hoped to buy another, move to a different town, buy a bigger house for her and Nick. The simple homes in Kedar—if he went back—would shock her, the few that were still there, anyway. Ironically, one of them was his.

But because she was a kind person, maybe because at one time they had been friends—something Sawyer had hoped to change before his rash challenge in the meadow had put an end to that dream—she'd come too close to his softest spot, the tender area of guilt inside him that gave him nightmares and followed him around all day like some stubborn shadow. As if Khalil were still at his shoulder, begging him to play basketball or fly kites.

With more force than he needed, Sawyer threw yet another bale on the stack. Dust motes drifted through the air, catching the light from the loft opening and turning straw to gold.

If only it were a precious metal…he'd sell it, use the money to help people in Kedar, build them new and better houses, repair and add to the clinic, rebuild the ruined infirmary next door. *Some partner*, he thought, meaning himself. He'd left Charlie to pick up the pieces. And how could any amount of money ever repay Khalil's family for the loss of their son and brother?

With Olivia, he'd made yet another dumb mistake. A decision that couldn't lead anywhere for either of them. And then there was his absolute cowardice with Nick, not insisting the doctors at Farrier General take another look at his head injury that night, leaving Olivia to deal with her son's trauma while he escaped to try to save himself. She'd been right. Nick might be fine now, but Sawyer's silence could have had much graver consequences. Surely she hadn't forgotten that.

"What the devil's going on up there, Sawyer?" Sam's voice echoed through the barn from below. "That hay was delivered weeks ago. Willy and Tobias stacked it then."

Breathing hard, Sawyer paused to look down. Sam was standing in the aisle, craning his neck to peer up at the loft. "I'm rearranging," Sawyer said.

"That what you call it?" Sam snorted. "You want to help today, ride out to the south pasture. The boys have their hands full with the herd. All the new calves this season, we're stretched pretty thin. Could use another cowboy."

"Willy and Tobias don't seem to think I'm one of them." Sawyer leaned on the pitchfork. This was the most he and Sam had said to each other in a while. Their silent dinners were taking a toll on him, if not as big a toll as his blunder with Olivia. "Bison don't like to be herded."

Even he could see that. Except for forcing his help on Sam's men now and then and leading Nick around the ring yesterday, he'd mostly explored Sam's property alone. On his solitary rides around the ranch, he'd decided the majestic bison were also ornery, stubborn, dangerous and lived up to their reputation. Only Sam seemed bonded with the animals, and even then one bison cow had tossed him into the nearest tree last spring, breaking Sam's leg. Apparently Sam didn't hold grudges, except with Sawyer.

Sam squinted up through the shower of dust motes. "What do you know about my bison?" *You haven't been home in almost a decade.*

"I know you name them. I know Tobias and Willy think you're nuts. Sam, I don't want to debate with you. I was planning to lunge Cyclone." *After I cool off.*

Sam scowled. "Before the vet deals with him?"

Sawyer had forgotten to mention that. Tired of leaning over the edge of the loft to speak to Sam, he scrambled down the ladder. "He called the other day to postpone. He's been up to his neck lately, at summer fairs and over in Edwards County. Big horse show there this week and he's the vet on site. He had to reschedule Cyclone as a non-emergency. In the meantime, that colt's getting more agitated by the day. Turning him out doesn't seem to help his disposition. Standing in a stall all night only makes him meaner. Thought I'd try to take some of the fight out of him."

Sam's mouth set. "He's not mean."

Sawyer didn't think so either, but… "Tell him that."

"And you're the man to straighten him out? Last I heard you were off some place in the *mountains*—" Sam said the word with disdain "—not here on the Plains training horses." Sawyer could imagine him adding, *as you should have been all these years*. Sam scoffed. "Well, you want to get your head kicked in, who am I to stop you?" He turned away, then right back again. "But I already warned you. Don't think you're gonna start this, then leave with the job halfway done."

"I won't. I promise."

"Yeah, I've heard that before."

Sawyer's temper rose again. "And I'm well aware of your opinion about me. I'm sorry I let you down, left the Circle H to make my own way in the world—"

"How did that turn out?"

He flinched. "Not so good," he admitted, surprised Sam would dig that deep into his ruined soul. "But you have Logan to help run this ranch."

"You're starting to think about going back there. Aren't you?"

"I don't know yet. I don't know what I'm going to do."

Sam tilted his head to study Sawyer, as he might have done with a colt at auction. "Let me tell *you* one thing about yourself, Sawyer. When you started something years ago, you'd finish it." He stomped toward the tack room. "Whatever's eating at you, you'll need to take care of that, too. Which will leave me right where I was before." Beside Sundance's stall, he stopped. Over his shoulder, he said, "Don't let me down with that colt."

CHAPTER THIRTEEN

OLIVIA TOOK A deep breath. If what she thought about Sawyer was true, she didn't want to step on his heart. He had enough on his mind without feeling guilty for that just-missed-the-mark kiss. And he had been good to her son.

So the next morning, after she'd dealt with her email at the store, then sold a gorgeous eighteenth-century walnut armoire that would cover her overhead for the whole week—with a profit—she drove out to the Circle H again. Without Nick. He wouldn't be happy that she'd left him behind with Deirdre, but she had to do this. She didn't like loose ends.

And she didn't want a boyish audience.

The ranch yard looked deserted. A horse whinnied a greeting from the nearby corral where Nick had ridden the day before, but she didn't see anyone. None of Sam's cowhands nor Sawyer seemed to be around.

Half-grateful for more time to rehearse what she'd say, Olivia walked into the barn, stopping to greet Sundance, Ginger and a few others in their stalls. Sam and his crew must be out on the range.

The end stall belonged to Cyclone. The black colt stood at the window that overlooked the corral. When he heard Olivia, he turned his head, his dark eyes taking her in before he shambled over to the bars for a better look. Olivia almost gasped, delighted as Nick had been with Hero.

After Jasmine's death, she'd given up competing, even riding for pleasure, and she hadn't been on a horse in years. Despite the few warnings she'd heard, Cyclone had calm eyes, a liquid brown without the whites showing. A good sign, she thought.

"Hey there, boy. You lonely?" she almost whispered, not wanting to spook him. Olivia moved closer. She was an experienced rider and could tell a good horse from a bad one. Taking her time, she reached out a hand. The colt whickered, as if in greeting—

"Are you trying to get killed?" Sawyer had emerged from the tack room at the other end of the aisle.

Olivia eased back, then turned to face him. "I grew up at Wilson Cattle. I'm sure I'd know if this colt means me any harm." She added, "He doesn't."

"Then you and Sam agree. I still think he shows promise."

Still, he'd said as if he'd recently changed his mind. "Give me some credit, then. I'm not a greenhorn, Sawyer."

With slightly rumpled hair, he wore a denim shirt that made his blue eyes more blue, worn jeans and shabby brown boots. Then Olivia saw his arm. His sleeves were rolled up, and a long, angry abrasion ran from his elbow to his strong wrist. He had the arms of a working cowboy still.

"What happened?"

Sawyer rubbed the back of his neck. He studied the ground. "I had a...difference of opinion with Sam yesterday." He glanced toward the black colt. "I took Cyclone out to the corral, lunged him for a while, trying to get his kinks out. And mine. Then, when I was bringing him back in for dinner, he whirled around, nailed me against the side of his stall and scraped the hell out of my arm."

Olivia couldn't help herself. "Did you see a doctor?"

Sawyer almost smiled. "Yeah, and he's a fool. I treated myself. I knew better than to take my eyes off this colt for even a second. Just when I thought we were becoming... friends," he said with a sly look at her, "he decided to take a stripe off my hide." He touched the small scar by his right eye. "Kinda reminded me of you."

Given her opportunity, Olivia plunged in. "Sawyer, I overreacted that night at my house, and I know I've given you a hard time," she said. "I did admit I was wrong about Jasmine. About Nick, too. I can understand how you might feel about him, considering your experience in...Kedar." She hesitated. "Maybe I was wrong about you in a different way all those years ago." She cleared her throat. "I was certainly, um, falling for you then, but I never thought the reason you dared me to race was because you wanted more—"

"Never mind, Olivia. That doesn't matter now." Avoiding her gaze, he examined his arm. "It's a bit better today."

Obviously, he didn't want to talk about their past. "I think it looks dreadful. Did you clean it properly?"

He did smile. "Lucky me, Sam keeps a pretty good medicine cabinet at the house, more than most people would stock. I discovered the tack room has more than that. We're pretty well equipped."

He didn't seem to notice he'd said *we*, as if he had plans to stick around.

"Rumors in town tell me you've done a good

job subbing for Doc. And over in Farrier, they say Fred Miller is singing your praises." She frowned. "Not that he doesn't belong in jail after what he did to Grey."

Sawyer shrugged. "Maybe he and I should form a club. Two idiots who didn't watch a bull and a colt close enough."

But she could see a flicker of pride in his eyes and a hint of color in his face. She wouldn't embarrass him any further. She'd seen for herself, in the way he'd examined Nick without her son even knowing, that Sawyer had a good bedside manner.

"In spite of Kedar, I suspect you're a much better doctor than you give yourself credit for." Olivia thrust out a hand. "Friends," she said. "After almost ten years, we should leave it at that. I'm afraid I misunderstood your... intentions back then."

Clearly, Sawyer had wanted to take their blossoming romance to the next level. Olivia would have welcomed that, too, until Jasmine fell...

They shook hands, but Sawyer looked dubious and didn't respond right away. He cradled his arm, staring down at the reddish scrape. It must've hurt, but when he met her eyes again, he wore a wry smile.

"Just friends," he agreed, his blue eyes

bright, then turned to the colt's stall and stood appraising the horse as if he were indeed examining a patient. Or debating with himself. "Since you're such an expert horsewoman and I'm just a rusty cowboy, let's take this guy out to the corral. See what you think of him." His eyes were alight with the old hint of challenge. "It's like getting back on after a fall. Nick didn't think twice before he rode Hero. The longer I wait to give Cyclone another lesson, the more inclined I'll be to give up— which wouldn't please Sam."

Olivia watched him go into the stall, clip a lead rope onto Cyclone's halter, then bring him into the aisle. Keeping a close eye on him, he led the colt out into the sunlight, around the corner and into the arena. She wondered if hc'd been talking as much about a return to Kedar as he had been about Cyclone.

She kept her distance outside the fence as Sawyer put Cyclone through his paces, flicking a light whip over his flank whenever he tried to drift back from an easy lope into a walk. Sawyer kept him going on the lunge line, and Olivia had to catch her breath.

She studied the horse. Perfect conformation, she thought, with those long legs and already a good amount of muscle, that deep chest… oh, she was in love.

"He has a gorgeous gait," she called out. "A flow, really. Sawyer, he's like an Arabian with that floating trot. He'll be a dream to ride."

"He's a long way from that."

"But don't you think he will be?"

Sawyer let the lunge line out a bit, urging the horse on. "He needs a lot more work." He added, "Yes. Sam said he'd bought a good one and he has." He dared a glance at Olivia. "You like him."

"I do," she said.

He paused. "Want to help me train this guy?"

Riding wasn't all she'd done in her youth. Olivia had brought Jasmine along from birth until she'd become a beautifully mannered mare with perfect moves, working with her every day she could get to Wilson Cattle, letting Grey school Jasmine when she wasn't there. Olivia didn't have to consider it.

"I'd love to help." She was still leaning against the fence, arms crossed, grinning, heart in her throat. "He has the wrong name, though. Bad for his self-esteem. Don't you think? Would Sam mind if we changed it?"

"I'll ask him."

For a few more minutes, Olivia basked in the warm sunlight, her eyes following Sawyer and the colt around the outdoor arena. The muscles in Sawyer's arms and shoulders, the long length of his legs, worked in synch with the colt's, and she couldn't help thinking what a beautiful sight they made.

Just look at...them. Maybe she'd been too hasty in stepping back from Sawyer's kiss. No, she couldn't afford to think that way. In any case, the colt was enough to bring her back to the Circle H, even when she knew she should maintain a certain distance from Sawyer. *Just friends*, he'd agreed.

Reeling in the lunge line, he slowed the colt to a loose walk. By now, Cyclone's coat had a sheen of perspiration as Sawyer began to lead him toward the gate. He nodded at the colt, then at Olivia. "What would you call him?"

Cyclone's black hide gleamed in the sun, so black at times that he almost looked— "Blue," she said. "I'd call him Blue."

IN HER OFFICE that afternoon, Olivia was trying to reconcile her accounts when she heard the bell above the main door jingle. Part of her was still back at the Circle H, watching that gorgeous blue-black horse move around the corral. Watching Sawyer.

"Anybody home?" Grey's boot heels rang on the wooden floor of the shop.

Olivia went to greet him with a hug after

weaving her way through the crates contain-
ing a new shipment of antiques from Virginia.
One of them was an eighteenth-century game
table that had absolutely made her drool when
she first saw it. The entire shop was filled with
treasures, like Ted Anderson's, with nowhere
to put them all. "What brings you to town?"

"The usual. Feed, supplies…well, not just
the usual." He stepped back to look into her
eyes. For a moment, his hands lingered on her
shoulders. "I have news."

She clamped both hands on her hips. "You
and Shadow have finally picked a date? You
know, reserving a venue for a reception can't
be done at the last minute. Even having the
wedding at the ranch like Logan and Blossom did at the Circle H requires *some* advance
planning."

"Nag, nag."

Olivia smiled. Unable to resist, she tugged
his black Stetson over his eyes. "What are big
sisters for?"

Grey resettled his hat. If she'd done that to
him once, she'd done it dozens of times from
childhood until now. "No date yet. You'll be
the first to know."

"Then what's the news?"

"You won't like it," he said, his gaze on a
mahogany escritoire in the far corner of the

room. Grey took a long breath, then let it out. "Dad and Liza. They're coming for another visit."

Her heart sank. "So soon?"

"Apparently she misses everyone. Go figure. It's not as if we've rolled out the welcome mat. But I have to tell you, Libby, and I guess I've said this before. To me, it feels weird. I mean, being hugged as if I were six years old feels just plain strange. I know she means well..."

"It's not as if she's a bad person, Grey. But you're right. It's not an easy adjustment—and with us it's one thing. She and Dad spoil Nick. You should see the building set they gave him before they went back to Dallas. I know this sounds petty, but sometimes I wonder if she's trying to buy our affections."

"She tries too hard." Grey rubbed his forehead under his hat brim. "The thing is, I probably haven't talked to *our* mom in a year, and when I do I always come away mad. Now I'm supposed to have a second mother in Liza? What if that goes bad, too?"

"Mom is fine," Olivia said. "I admit, she was peeved with you when I talked to her last week—please give her a call—but I can't tell you how to deal with Liza. On one hand, I like her a lot. On another, I wish they'd stay in Dallas. At least a while longer. I'm not that eager to see Everett."

Grey sighed. "Unfortunately for you, he and I have an appointment with Barney at the bank this week. So he had to come. We didn't get around to that last time. Dad still plans to co-sign that new loan for me. Then he and I are going to talk with Finn Donovan. The sheriff wants to throw the book at Shadow's brother and his friends, and there's another hearing coming up, but that doesn't sit well with me. I don't want to break Shadow's heart, and if he gets sent to prison over the rustling thing, that's what will happen. I'm hoping, instead, Finn cuts him a break—and I hire Derek on to see what he's really made of."

Olivia was still trying to wrap her mind around the fact that her father hadn't broken his promise to Grey. "That's a nice idea, but is it wise? He stole your cattle. You were lucky to get them back. He and Calvin Stern—and Cal's uncle—were involved, not to mention the other kid you hired who turned out to be part of their gang. They could have driven you out of business. I'd have lost my share of the ranch, too."

He shrugged. "Maybe love and settling down have blinded me to Derek's faults. But speaking of mothers, doesn't Shadow's mom deserve a break?"

He had a point. Shadow's mother had lost her oldest son in an accidental shooting in which Grey had played a part and been blamed for ten years ago. Now, thank goodness, the whole town at last knew he was innocent, but Jared Moran was still gone. If Shadow's mom lost another son to a long prison sentence...

"You have a good heart, Grey. I hope you can convince Finn to go easy on Derek—the judge, too—if that's what you think is best."

"As long as Derek understands this would be his last chance. He messes up with me, he'll learn the meaning of the word *trouble*."

Olivia almost smiled at her brother's tough-guy stance, but he was right. And she was very happy Grey had moved on with his own life. If he got that loan, his recent financial troubles with Wilson Cattle would finally be over. He and Shadow could get married and have the family, in addition to their daughter, Ava, that Grey had always wanted. He'd have a legacy to hand on to the next generation.

Nick was part of that, too. With her share in Wilson Cattle and Logan's in the Circle H, Nick would be a wealthy man.

Olivia eyed an elaborately framed Western print on the wall. It hung slightly crooked and she fought an urge to straighten it rather than ask the question. "Are Everett and Liza staying with you again?"

"Yep. Dad may have handed the ranch to me on an official basis, but it's still his home. Guess I'll be walking on eggshells again soon." Grey looked at her as if prompting a response. Surely he didn't expect her to offer her place. For one thing, the sprawling ranch house at Wilson Cattle had plenty of space and her house didn't. For another, she didn't want to see her father more than she had to.

"I'll come to visit," she said.

SAWYER JUMPED AT the chance to have dinner the next night with Grey and Shadow. He didn't think he could stand one more meal at the kitchen table across from Sam with neither of them speaking. Several times Willy and Tobias had joined them, and the conversation had been livelier—if he ignored the fact that Sam barely said two words. Those recent moments in the barn with him, and Sam's obvious mistrust of Sawyer's intentions with Cyclone, had made the situation worse.

He arrived at Wilson Cattle, carrying two bottles of good wine and a bouquet of flowers for Shadow, who was playing hostess tonight. He'd just stepped inside the kitchen, which smelled of something delicious and homemade after too many makeshift meals at the Circle H, when he saw Olivia.

He hadn't expected her to be here, though he should have. In the room behind her sat Grey and Shadow, Everett Wilson and his wife, Liza—the guests of honor tonight—so her presence did make sense. His didn't, really. It was a family affair. Or, he supposed now, family and friends.

Olivia took the flowers from him. She was wearing a killer dress, a summery shade the color of peaches, her hair drawn back in a loose knot. "How's... Cyclone?"

"Pretty hostile right now," he said. "The vet had time today after all, so he took care of business. That colt won't have to worry about the ladies anymore."

Her eyes widened. "You gelded him?"

"Didn't have much choice. Sam doesn't need a stallion at the Circle H. Mares and geldings make better cow ponies. You know that."

"But he's such a beauty. He would have passed on some lovely genes. Poor Cyclone," Olivia murmured.

"He'll be much gentler, believe me. He's on stall rest for the next day or two. Let me know when you want to come out for a first training session."

Shadow swept into the kitchen from the dining room on a pair of awesome high heels but with a worried look. "I almost forgot the roast. I hope it hasn't burned to a crisp."

She pulled open the oven door, checked the simmering beefy goodness inside, then shut it, apparently satisfied dinner would go through as planned. She straightened to hug Sawyer. "I'm glad you could make it. If you'll open this excellent-looking wine and pour for everyone, we'll be ready to eat."

Sawyer didn't know who had made the seating arrangement, but he sat next to Olivia. At the heads of the table were Grey and his father with Liza to Everett's right. Shadow took the chair next to Grey and closest to the kitchen. Three couples, he thought, an even number of people. That was why he'd been invited.

Sawyer hadn't had a dinner date in... he couldn't remember how long. Since he'd moved to Kedar, he'd spent most of his time at the new clinic, working almost twenty-four seven with Charlie to establish the facility.

The dinner conversation seemed to ping-pong from one topic to another, everyone eager to share a funny story or factoid, and there was a lot of laughter.

Sawyer realized he hadn't heard much of that in the past few months. After the landslide, the surrounding mountains had seemed to go quiet, hushed, as if afraid to breathe in case another part sheared off and crashed into the village yet again. Even children playing in streets still filled with rubble had been mostly silent. He missed their laughter, missed seeing Khalil among his friends or tagging after Sawyer, missed *him*.

He frowned at his plate. He barely heard Shadow, Grey, Liza and Olivia, Everett—until he glanced over and saw the older man sitting frozen in his chair with one hand clutched to his throat. His face was turning blue. Everett made a motion at his opened mouth, which was gaping, but no sound came out. He was choking!

For a single instant, Sawyer felt paralyzed, too. The moments with Nick lying on the barn floor and then in the hospital, examining Fred Miller's arm, answering those phone calls at Doc's place flashed through his mind.

Then Liza cried out, "Everett!" and Sawyer bolted from his chair, rushing around the table to stand behind Olivia and Grey's father, while the others looked on helplessly.

Sawyer locked his arms across Everett's chest and applied the Heimlich maneuver, sharply lifting up against the man's diaphragm, then repeating the motion until, at last, a chunk of beef flew from his mouth.

Everett gasped, starting to breathe again.

Liza and Olivia had gone white as sheets. Grey's blue-green eyes were wide, his face flushed. Stunned, Shadow had a hand to her own throat. Then, a second later the tension broke.

Everyone grinned and a spate of talk began, including some giddy laughter. Sawyer returned to his seat, shaken a bit himself, but more than relieved. He'd done it. He'd possibly saved a life—and wasn't that a nice change?

Everett sounded hoarse. "Thanks, Sawyer. I can never repay you."

"I don't need anything except to see you sitting there okay," he said.

Everett grinned weakly. "Never hurts to have a doctor in the house."

After that, Sawyer didn't really listen to the conversation. Part of him was still back in Kedar, triaging patients after the landslide.

"Sawyer...anyone in there?" Grey's father had asked him some question.

"Sorry." He waved a hand at the table laden with vegetable dishes, a fresh fruit salad, the meat platter. "I think so much beef has put me into a food coma."

Everett appeared concerned. "I hate to bring

up a sensitive topic, but my little episode here made me think… I asked you about the landslide over there in Kedar. We saw some of that on TV when it happened, but how are things now?"

The image of Khalil, rolling a hoop down the street in the sun or popping into the clinic to say hi after school tightened his throat. Khalil flying a kite in a spring breeze, such a popular pastime for kids in the village. A rush of guilt ran through him.

"Um, I really can't say." He hadn't talked to Charlie again. Had kept away from the news and Google. "When I left for the States, it was still bad. Large patches of the only access road were blocked by rocks and debris and there aren't many earthmovers or backhoes to clear things. Much of the work gets done by hand."

Everett frowned. "And your clinic?"

"We suffered about seventy percent damage. Completely lost our hospital building. It's a tiny compound, and since the landslide, getting supplies delivered has been all but impossible. I want to send some stuff, put together a shipment, but it may just get stuck in the capital city, hundreds of miles away."

A care package, he thought. Some contribution. How could he have left Charlie there with only his wife, Piper, to help run things?

To dig out, repair, rebuild? What kind of doctor *was* he? *What kind of man?*

He and Charlie were equal partners, but Sawyer wasn't pulling his weight. No, he was sitting here, feeling guilty, in a candlelit dining room with friends—people he'd also turned his back on—having the best meal he'd eaten in a long time. Sitting beside Olivia, the only woman he'd ever loved. Still wanted to love. How could she want him, even as a friend?

As if their history wasn't enough, he'd ignored his own misgivings about Nick's condition, handed him off to other physicians, made another mistake.

Don't let me down, Sam had said about the colt. But he had. He kept letting people down.

Sawyer pushed back his chair. "Sorry," he said again. "I need some air."

Olivia laid a light hand on his arm but he turned away and left the room.

The quiet buzz of conversation—quite possibly about his mental state—didn't pick up until he'd reached the front porch. He stood there, taking in deep gulps of too-warm, even sultry, night air.

In the mountains, it was rarely this humid. Winter started early and ended late, and the growing season was shorter than it was in Kansas by months. Even in good weather, the

soil was rocky and lacked all kinds of nutri-
ents. Yet in spite of that, at certain times of
the year, the hillsides were lush and green…
until the slide had left that naked slash of gray-
brown earth.

"Sawyer." Olivia opened the screen door.
"Are you all right?"

He leaned on his arms, elbows locked, at
the rail. He studied the scrape on his arm. He
felt brittle, as if his bones might break. "Yeah,
sure." His tone didn't invite company.

He wanted to be alone, but she came outside. She stood next to him on the porch, letting the silence grow before she finally said,
"I can't imagine what you went through over
there."

"What those people went through," he said.
"What they're going through."

She rested a hand against his back. "You
really care for them."

He could only nod. His vision had blurred
and his throat clenched so tight he couldn't
speak. And still, she stayed with him. Her very
empathy threatened his control. *You're thinking about going back*, Sam had said.

"What are you going to do?" she asked.
"I mean, besides stay here until Logan gets
home." Her tone lightened. "And Cyclone
learns his manners?"

"I don't know," he said, as he had to Sam. He hadn't known anything since the landslide. Since he hadn't only let down Charlie.

Like another force of nature, he'd destroyed everything.

CHAPTER FOURTEEN

WHEN SHE REENTERED the family room a few minutes later, Olivia went straight to her father. "How are you? Okay now?"

He looked at Liza, not at her. "I've been okay since Sawyer jumped in with the Heimlich maneuver. Quick thinking. Serves me right for taking a third helping of Shadow's excellent roast."

Sawyer hadn't come back inside. While Olivia was still on the porch, he'd gone down the steps to his truck and driven off toward the Circle H. In the house, she made his excuses, which no one believed, and Sawyer hadn't asked her to do. The others had seen his distress for themselves before he'd abruptly left the dining room.

She should be more concerned about her father, who had almost choked to death at dinner. To her relief, he sat now with Liza on the sofa, her slender hand nearly swallowed up in his much larger one.

Olivia's heart clutched. Everyone in Barren knew she didn't have a good relationship with her father, and she avoided even being in the same room alone with him, but she'd never feared for his life before. In middle age, her dad looked the very picture of hale and hearty, his brown hair barely touched by gray, his blue-green eyes still sharp, like his mind. She'd expected him to live to be a hundred, but in a split second he could have been gone.

Shadow was in the kitchen with Grey, doing dishes. "Thank you, Everett," she called out. "But I should have helped you cut your meat."

He laughed. "Grey's got a good woman there," he said.

Liza kissed his cheek, then got up. "Think I'll help with those dishes."

Olivia wanted to call her back. Liza had urged her before to smooth things over with Everett. Yet she hadn't been here when Olivia was a girl, being torn apart by her parents' divorce, always privy to their disagreements and the sound of voices raised in anger. She could tell her father also knew what Liza wanted, but he was avoiding it, too—just as he'd avoided keeping his promises to Olivia, time and again.

He broke their awkward silence. "Sawyer all right? From the little I heard about that landslide, it must have been like Armageddon."

"Obviously, he's still feeling that."

"What a shame. A tragedy, for him as well as all those people." He didn't miss a beat in changing the subject. "We both missed seeing Nick tonight."

"My sitter stayed with him." She glanced toward the front door. "I need to go. I don't like her walking home alone from my house after dark."

He frowned. From the kitchen, Olivia heard the clatter of flatware, one pan being banged against another. His tone was casual. "Maybe Liza and I will come by tomorrow then."

"I'll be working all day," she said.

He tried another tack. "How's the store doing, Olivia?"

"It's doing well. I started out handling estate sales, auctions and the like, but I was doing too much travel. For Nick, I decided to stop that and repurpose, to sell antiques only, which gives me more regular hours and less running around to different places. Recently, I traded in my car for an SUV, more practical for business. I'm also trying to buy another shop, expand..."

"Well, you're obviously busy, but we can save you a sitter tomorrow. Liza and I will stay with Nick." He forced his frown into a smile. "You know she's always eager to spend time with him."

"Everett, please..."

"You think I wouldn't show up," he said, sounding disappointed.

Olivia wasn't fooled. He always took on that tone when he failed to keep a promise, as if that were her fault rather than his.

All right, then. He'd brought it up. Liza would come for sure, but him? She wasn't going to lie. "There's always that possibility, yes."

Maybe *she* should have stayed home tonight. Read books with Nick, watched *Toy Story*—all three of them—for the thousandth time, made popcorn. Instead, she'd watched in horror as her father choked, seen Sawyer save him, then all but fall apart for reasons of his own. "I'm grateful you didn't end up in the ER this evening, but—"

"Olivia, you're not a child now. When you *wer*e a kid, I was running Wilson Cattle. As a businesswoman yourself, you should have some idea of what that entails. If not, Grey could tell you. It can be a brutal job. Long hours, sick cows, money issues, hay to bring in before it rains...cowboys who quit on the spot at the worst times...rustlers," he added, then paused. "I know it was hard on you when your mother and I stopped trying to make a go of it."

Her voice quavered. "You and Mom made my life, and Grey's, miserable."

"I accept that. I'm sorry. But he's running the ranch now, and I'm…not. I have more time and he and I make a pretty good team. Why can't we, Olivia? I'd really like for us—you and me—to find common ground again. I'd like to be part of your life as well as Nick's."

"And make promises to him that you won't keep, either? Whenever some better offer for your *time* comes up first?" She said, "An opera ball in Dallas? A trip with friends to Cancun?" The words caught in her throat. "'I'm so sorry, Nick, but I won't be able to get there for your birthday party.' No," she said, shaking, "I won't allow my son to become a pawn for your attention as I was years ago with you and Mom—"

"Yes, Olivia. Your mother, too. Don't leave her out. She poisoned you against me. Liza would never do something like that—and though I'll admit I wasn't perfect back then, at least I didn't do that, either. You've gone through a divorce just as I did. You know how painful that can be, how that affected Nick. Yet you and Logan have managed to set aside your differences for his sake. Which took you a long time, I might point out."

"That's what Liza said."

"Couldn't you do the same with me? Make peace, for Nick's sake?"

"You're his grandfather, not his dad."

And tonight, she'd nearly lost him. As imperfect as their relationship might be—*is*, she thought—she only had one father. Liza had pointed that out, too. Olivia blinked back a sudden rush of tears. If only she could convince herself he was telling the truth.

For Nick's sake.

"I'm here!" Nick shouted, tumbling from the car, then running toward the barn and making Sawyer smile. "Let's ride!" The kid had scarcely waited until Olivia stopped her SUV in the ranch yard.

After Sawyer and Nick caught Hero in the far pasture, they walked the horse to the corral. This time, Nick saddled the little gray gelding by himself with Sawyer merely looking on, wondering what to say to Olivia.

He tried not to feel her eyes on him, watching his every step as she trailed after him and her son. Did she think he'd gone completely off the rails a few nights ago? That he might crumble right in front of Nick any second now?

Olivia's call to ask if they could come over had surprised him. Not because Nick wanted to ride—he always did—but because she seemed eager to get started with Cyclone. The horse was feeling much more comfortable today, so Sawyer had said yes.

Inside the ring, Nick gathered his reins, cautioned Hero to stand still, slid his left foot into the stirrup, then swung up into the saddle as if he'd been doing that every day for his entire life. Seven years, Sawyer reminded himself, and for most of them, Logan had told him, Olivia had kept him off horses, fearing for his safety. He was still a new rider, and despite his progress, needed to be carefully watched.

Nick had the same urge Sawyer had had at his age to do everything on his own, to take the next risk. He'd driven his parents nuts. Logan was more cautious. He guessed Olivia had turned away from Sawyer not just because of Jasmine, but in part because she'd hoped for a more stable relationship.

"Whoa, there," he said just before Nick trotted off. Sawyer snapped the lead rope on, as he had last time, to walk with him around the corral. Still silent, Olivia watched from the rail. She hadn't said a word to him yet.

Once, twice…on the third circuit, he reached up to unhook the lead as he might have let go of the kid's first two-wheel bicycle when he'd finally gained his balance.

Noticing that he'd been freed, Nick yelled, "Look, Mom!" To Sawyer's alarm, he booted Hero in the sides and the gelding scooted off, ears pricked as if he felt as happy as Nick to be off the lead.

"Sawyer!" Olivia had a hand over her heart. She'd finally broken her silence.

He took a step to stop Nick, but the boy was doing fine, and instead of going after him, Sawyer strolled over to the fence.

He put up a hand, palm out, to calm her. "He's okay." The lessons Logan had given him all summer had paid off. "He's really *riding*. Look at him, Olivia."

Nick's grin spread from ear to ear. Sawyer envied him. It had been a long time since he'd experienced that same rush of joy. "Would you deny him? You know how good that feels."

Or did that only remind her of them, with Jasmine, flying across the field?

Her mouth set. "How dare you jeopardize his safety?" But her tone sounded weak. Even Olivia could see that her son was okay.

"He's perfectly safe. I told you, that gelding takes care of him. Logan picked the right horse. If I didn't think Nick could handle him, I'd still be walking around this corral with them."

For a long moment, she followed Nick with

her eyes. Gradually, Sawyer saw her shoulders relax. Then, at last, she began to smile. "He's pretty good, isn't he?"

"And he'll get better. All he needs now is practice." To show his confidence in Nick, he opened the corral gate, stepped out and shut it behind him to join Olivia at the rail. If something did happen, he could vault the fence and be there in a second. He slid her a sideways glance. "You may end up with a kid in junior rodeo—a bronc rider or maybe a calf roper."

She faintly shuddered. "I hope not. And I hate to admit this, but you were right. So was Logan. I need to loosen the reins myself."

"You need to loosen up, period." To soften the words, he put an arm around her shoulders. Who was he to talk? The other night, he'd made a fool of himself. Grey hadn't wanted to accept his apology for running off after dinner but Sawyer had made it anyway.

He and Olivia watched Nick until he started to tire and the little gelding stumbled once, not enough to alarm her or Sawyer. He leaned over to lightly kiss her cheek. "Come on, a job well done. Let's get these two a treat before you and I work Cyclone."

At the house, Sam had come in for lunch. They all ate sandwiches while Sam and Olivia chatted at the table. Sawyer didn't say much and Sam didn't talk to him either, keeping his attention on Nick. Afterward, Sam fixed an ice-cream cone for him and challenged Nick to a game of checkers. Sawyer and Olivia went back to the barn to get Cyclone with Sam's caution ringing in their ears: "Don't spoil him."

Today the horse moved better. All he needed was the lightest, occasional flick of the whip at his flanks to keep him in that fluid gait Olivia liked so much.

After a while, Sawyer let her take over—and prayed. His heart stayed in his throat, but she had an easy touch with the colt, talking to him in soothing tones, praising him whenever he did something right. Letting Sawyer know he could trust her with the colt—at least under his supervision, in case things went wrong.

Why be surprised when Cyclone suddenly decided to test her?

Without warning, he broke from the slow trot. Cyclone pulled at the lunge line, dancing away from the whip, tossing his head, and Sawyer's heart leaped back into his mouth. "Hey!" he shouted, a thousand bad outcomes running through his head.

By the time he'd jumped the fence, though, Olivia had control of the line. She reeled the colt back in, waited until he stood quietly be-fore she patted the sleek column of his neck.

"Good boy," she said and Sawyer's pulse began to settle, too.

The sun shimmered along Cyclone's hide, turning it from black to blue. Olivia had been right about his color. He didn't stop her when she continued her groundwork with the colt, and to his credit, Cyclone didn't try to act up again.

When they were done, she turned to Saw-yer with a smile. "Did I pass?"

"With highest honors. You're good, Olivia. You always were."

Without a care for her own safety, as if she'd forgotten how dangerous the horse could be, she walked Cyclone to the gate. The colt blew through his nostrils and danced around, but he did as she commanded. When he was secured in his stall, Sawyer let out a sigh of relief. He hadn't realized he'd been holding his breath. In fact, he'd been holding it, figuratively speak-ing, since the other night.

They were no sooner outside the barn when, with no more warning than Cyclone had given, she said, "After dinner that night...I went home and watched a video on YouTube. About the landslide in Kedar." She stopped walking. "Sawyer, I've never seen anything like that. So horrible, so destructive. The side of that mountain came down within seconds. Frankly, it makes worrying about Nick in the corral seem silly in retrospect. Or at least, incredibly minor by comparison. I know you wouldn't have let him get hurt. You were thinking about Kedar after Everett choked on the meat. Weren't you?"

"Yes, and once your dad brought up the landslide, I couldn't stop." He put both hands on her shoulders, trying to block out the images she must have seen, the ones he would never forget. "I wish that hadn't ruined what started out to be a fun evening. If I were you, I'd try to forget that video."

"I can't. Those pictures are etched in my mind. Like they must be in yours—only I imagine what you saw, up close, was far worse than any video." She looked into his eyes. "I'm glad you weren't hurt. What happened to your partner?"

"Charlie and his wife were at the school, away from the clinic. They'd gone right before the slide to give vaccinations to the kids there. We'd had an outbreak of chicken pox, which usually goes around that time of year, and we wanted to cover as many kids as we could, those who hadn't already gotten the shot. Anyway, he and Piper got trapped at the school. In between there and the clinic was just rubble. At their end, they began digging people out. I didn't see them for another few days. I keep wondering how they can cope now, shorthanded."

"His wife really lives there?"

"And his family," Sawyer said. "In fact, Piper is pregnant again."

"And *still* there?" Olivia shivered under his hands. "I can't imagine living in those conditions—being pregnant, too—and already having small children."

"Lots of people do and she's a trouper." His mouth tightened. "Some people like adventure, helping others in adversity," he said, feeling a fresh wave of guilt.

Olivia reeled back as if he'd slapped her. "Do I sound that shallow? I like helping, Sawyer, as much as the next person. I give to charity, I teach a Sunday school class." She paused. "That sounds hypocritical, doesn't it? And it's not nearly enough. I do ache for those people, for the children who must have been hurt or died, but I wouldn't think of taking Nick there. Not that you've asked me to."

Sawyer didn't answer. He'd never thought of Olivia in Kedar, so why was he disappointed to hear her say that?

He dropped his hands from her shoulders.

"Maybe you're right, and Piper shouldn't have moved there either, helped Charlie and me at the clinic. She and their two boys could have stayed in the States, safe and sound." He spoke through clenched teeth. "But being safe is not everyone's priority." He couldn't resist adding, "Even right here in Kansas, that can be an illusion. The flood I've heard about, Nick's illness, tornadoes every spring...haylofts."

For another moment, she stared at him before something else seemed to register in her mind. Was it the same thing registering in his?

Breaking the stare, Olivia said, "You know now what you're going to do, don't you? You've made up your mind. Even if you're trying to hide it from yourself." She turned away, almost as if she were rejecting Kedar, his clinic, Charlie's family...and him. "You're going back."

CHAPTER FIFTEEN

OLIVIA SLID INTO a back booth at the diner a few days later, and Annabelle hurried over to fill her mug. "Morning. Breakfast, too?"

"No, just coffee. I'm meeting some people."

"I'll send them your way. Holler if you change your mind about food."

She rushed off to serve other customers, and a moment later Ted Anderson entered the restaurant with a man who was obviously his son. Olivia mentally crossed her fingers. She'd gone back and forth with him all week, since the night at the ranch when her father had almost died right there at the dinner table, and she hoped today would go better.

Olivia rose to greet them. After her talk with Sawyer about Kedar, she'd stayed away from the ranch, though those raw video images had replayed over and over in her mind. Because Nick hadn't ridden Hero since then, he was barely speaking to her now.

She kissed Ted's cheek, but the already-sour

look on his son's face didn't reassure her. "Please. Sit down."

Ted's son Craig sat across from her with Ted beside her on the aisle. Annabelle appeared and filled their coffee cups. Olivia folded her hands on the tabletop. "Thank you both for meeting me here today. I have a client coming in later this morning so I had a bit of a schedule crunch and you saved me the trip to your place." Then she got right to business. "Craig, I know you have concerns about the sale of your dad's shop."

"We want him to get rid of it. As soon as possible." Craig settled deeper into his seat. "Dad's unable to keep up with the accounts—he forgets to post things—and you've seen how messy his store has gotten. He can't know where half that stuff even came from, much less what it's worth."

Olivia stiffened. Ted was right here, yet Craig seemed not to take him into account. No wonder his father wasn't eager to move to Florida and become even more invisible, something Olivia understood.

"I disagree." She touched Ted's forearm in support. "I've been to his shop. You're welcome to visit mine just across the street. You won't see much difference between them." She offered a faint smile. "We antiques dealers can never resist a bargain, especially a unique piece of furniture or glassware that we know we can sell for a tidy profit. Right now, I have an incredible Georgian piece taking up an entire wall. To you, things may seem out of hand. Not to us."

Ted sent her a smile in return but Craig's expression didn't change. "You're telling me you're not better organized than he is."

"No, I'm saying we both offer our clients a wide range of choices and there's not enough room to display them. That's one reason I hope to expand."

Craig shook his head. "Then you'll have two crowded stores."

Olivia pushed her coffee mug aside. "Are we really here to discuss my presumed lack of organization in a too-small space? Your father's? Or to come to some agreement about a sale— which, if I understood correctly, you want? Whatever I choose to do with both shops will be up to me. And, Ted, you've completed a full inventory, haven't you?"

"Yes, I have."

Craig scoffed. "I wonder if he wouldn't be better off with an auction, though. Clear the whole place out and be done with it. You can find another shop to buy."

Ted winced, clearly distressed. "Craig, Olivia

is a friend of mine. She used to handle such auctions, and I bet she can tell you the prices I'd fetch might be under market value. I'm sure we can settle this without coming to blows." He sipped at his coffee, as if buying time to choose the right words. "The issue is price, not what Olivia plans to do with my inventory, my store—or hers."

Olivia had tried to bring down Ted's asking price, which she still couldn't afford. She reached into her bag. "I can give you this much right now." When Ted looked puzzled, she handed him the check. "For the Tiffany vase," she said. Olivia had borrowed from her retirement account, and included Nick's chore money.

"We're willing to be flexible," Craig said, "but not to give away the store."

Olivia bristled. Was he implying that she'd tried to manipulate Ted into accepting a low bid? She tried to tamp down her temper.

For another few minutes, they tossed figures back and forth. Ted stayed mostly silent while Olivia sparred with Craig, who seemed to feel his father was incompetent to handle his own affairs. Or was he more interested in the amount of money Olivia didn't have? And likely couldn't find? She sat back with a sigh.

"That's my best—and final—offer," she said.

Craig got to his feet. "Then I guess I'll be calling an auction house."

Ted struggled out of the booth. He knew as well as Olivia did that he wouldn't get top dollar from an auction and had said as much. He stood toe-to-toe with his son, Ted's eyes snapping. "Craig, be reasonable. You've taken over this meeting, but my shop isn't yours to make this decision about. I value your input and I know you care about me, but your mother and I didn't spend our lives building that business only to see you throw it away. Since you have no interest in running the shop yourself, and neither does your wife, I'd like to see it go to Olivia."

In spite of his support, this hadn't gone well at all. Having seen how adamant Craig was, she felt worse for Ted than she had before. No wonder he felt he was being banished to Florida to live out his days alone. Yet how could she save this deal? That no longer seemed possible, but she didn't want to completely close the door.

"Thank you, Ted." She kissed his cheek again. "Let me see what I can do."

SAWYER LED CYCLONE back to the barn. On his way he glanced down the driveway, able to see as far as the Circle H arch and the turnoff from the road, but Olivia's car didn't appear. After one last searching gaze, he went on.

Sawyer hadn't seen her since she'd said, "You're going back," and she hadn't brought Nick to ride Hero again or worked with Cyclone herself.

Maybe, although she'd brought it up, he shouldn't have talked about Kedar, which had only led to Olivia's blunt statement. *I wouldn't think of taking Nick there.* Until then, had she entertained the notion? He doubted it. Her opinion wouldn't sway his, anyway. Even if she wanted to go, he had to admit Kedar wasn't her kind of environment just now. He couldn't ask her. They were nowhere near making that sort of decision. Probably never would be.

Still, the idea teased his mind. If he went back, and she came with him, he might not feel as torn as he did now. The only things he'd be leaving behind would be the Circle H. Sam. And Logan. Unfinished business there, too. It wouldn't work.

In the muted light that dappled the aisle, he groomed Cyclone before putting him back in his stall. The colt had made good progress. Olivia had promised to help, and yet she seemed to have given up. On the horse...on him?

He hung the lunge line on a hook in the tack

room then sat on one of the trunks along the wall, pulling out his phone to compose a text. He'd tried calling Charlie yesterday but there had been no answer. The call didn't even go to voice mail, which bothered Sawyer. Communications should have been fully restored in Kedar by now. Had some other disaster befallen the area? He wished he knew exactly what to say other than to avoid his and Charlie's rift.

Hey, partner. Haven't heard from you. Any progress on the infirmary's rebuild? Sent a big box of medical supplies. Hi to Piper and the family.

Sawyer hit Send, praying his message would get through. If it didn't…

Willy and Tobias clumped into the room, then proceeded to rummage around for something. Finally, Willy hauled a saddle blanket from another trunk. "Who put my favorite pad in here?"

Sawyer suppressed a guilty twinge. He wasn't responsible, but in the weeks he'd been at the Circle H, the two cowboys had continued to shun him and Sawyer had kept out of their way. "Not me," he said. His guilt must be linked to Charlie instead. Sawyer glanced down at his phone. No response.

Tobias studied him. "That colt's lookin' good, Doc." His tone seemed grudging.

"Yeah. He is."

Being called Doc—Cyrus Baxter's nickname—sounded foreign to Sawyer. But it reminded him that he had a late-afternoon appointment at Doc's office with Fred Miller. Oh, and that toddler's mom was bringing him in while Sawyer was there. The child's raw throat was back. Sawyer would test him again for strep.

The requests for his help—or rather, Doc's—kept coming in and he kept answering them. Sawyer preferred to stay at the ranch, where the work was no less dangerous than his job overseas, but at least there were no patients here other than the occasional bison from Sam's herd—and only when the vet couldn't get there right away.

Sawyer had to admit he'd been feeling good, though, ever since he'd saved Everett Wilson from choking to death. He didn't always mess up and kill someone.

Tobias gestured at Sawyer's phone. "You busy?"

"Not very. What can I do for you?" Maybe Tobias had a wound that didn't show. On such a hot day, he wore a long-sleeved shirt with the cuffs buttoned and a red bandana around his neck to guard against sunburn.

"Me and Willy are huntin' down an ornery cow. Sam went into town, and the part-timers aren't here today. We could use another hand."

Surprised, Sawyer looked up. Were they serious? This was unexpected. He glanced at his phone. There was still no answer from Charlie.

He was getting worried again, yet there was nothing more he could do except give it time. Charlie might be at the construction site or with patients, and Sawyer had a few free hours before he was scheduled to meet Miller. "Sure, why not? I'll saddle Sundance. Be right with you."

He enjoyed ranch work. He'd done enough of it, solo, in his time here. Willy and Tobias were loyal to Sam, and so were the other cowhands that came and went as needed. But it was possible Sawyer's extended stay at the Circle H had finally softened Tobias and Willy's obvious resentment of him for leaving long ago. Maybe he was getting somewhere with Sam's men. Sam was another matter.

Sawyer rode back to the barn a few hours later, sweating from the midday heat, every muscle in his body aching from so much time and action in the saddle. There was no message waiting for him from Charlie. Yet he was grinning as he put Sundance away.

It had felt good—no, great—to chase that cow all over the place, then herd her back to the others. Then, of course, they'd discovered a section of broken fence that had to be fixed. Sawyer had remembered how to do that, his movements almost automatic until, finally, the other two men had stepped back to let him finish.

Along the way, he'd shared a few laughs with Willy and Tobias. What if things continued to improve with them? What if he stayed here instead of going back to Kedar, as Olivia assumed he would? Could he find some way to truly connect with her again, then see just where they could go?

He'd try to make a start after he saw Fred Miller.

SAWYER HAD TO ADMIT, he'd gotten used to holding office hours at Doc's clinic twice a week. Several times he'd even conferred with Max Garrett, who ran the walk-in place around the corner on Main, enjoying their interaction as they consulted about one of Doc's patients, the first being Fred Miller.

Sawyer had changed his first impression of Max; he was actually pretty good. And he gave himself high marks now for having taken charge of Miller's follow-up care rather than sending him back to the clinic.

Sawyer examined Miller's stitches, but there was no sign of infection and the man was on track to regain full use of the limb. The skin was knitting together nicely.

Miller's troubles with the local law were apparently another matter. From the minute he'd walked in, Miller had been complaining about Finn Donovan, but Sawyer said nothing. In spite of his first inclination to avoid the sheriff, he'd gotten into the habit of meeting Finn for coffee or a meal whenever he was in town. He'd been foolish to think the sheriff might have it in for him.

Miller scowled. "Wilson got his cattle back. He's satisfied with that. Why Donovan has to hassle me about this, I can't say—but I'll be durned if I end up in a cell."

"Maybe you need a lawyer, Fred."

"Just because I let my nephew borrow my truck? Leave a few cows on my land for a little while?" His reasoning only seemed to highlight his guilt. Aiding and abetting, Finn might say.

Sawyer said, "Rustling is against the law."

"Yeah, well, no tinhorn sheriff is going to

put me away. If that takes a lawyer to back him off, so be it. You know any good ones?"

"No."

"My nephew and his friend—even that other guy, Cody Jones—don't deserve time, either. Where's the harm? Those cattle are right where they started out."

Sawyer raised his head. Grey had told him he hoped to help Shadow's brother, the friend Miller had mentioned, with a job at Wilson Cattle, but that was up to him. And Finn. "I can't interpret the law for you. But these stitches can come out today. That sound okay to you?"

Apparently pleased, Miller nodded. Ten minutes later, to Sawyer's relief, Miller was out the door, cradling his arm and pushing past a woman coming in with a little boy, Sawyer's next appointment. He shook his head. Miller wasn't one of his favorite people, but that wasn't his business. It was Finn's.

"Afternoon, Mrs. Gallagher." He ushered her into an exam room. "Jesse's throat still feeling sore?" She nodded and Sawyer touched the boy's shoulder. "That's no fun, is it? Let's fix you up."

He examined him, then took a strep kit from Doc's cabinet. The result came up positive, and Jesse's shoulders were slumped, his eyes red and bleary from fever. "Let me call in a prescription. He should feel better in no time."

For a moment, after he saw them out, Sawyer gazed around the waiting room before he wandered back into Doc's small office.

And I thought I wasn't treating patients. That reminded him of Kedar, the lack of supplies and his unanswered message.

It would be easy enough not to go back. Charlie's resentment might never be possible to overcome. Instead, Sawyer could settle here. Maybe with Olivia. Make peace with Sam.

He sat in Doc's chair, leaned back and folded his arms behind his head. He studied the degrees on the wall, none of which had his name on them, but still...they could. Doc should be home by now, and would pay Sawyer for his time, yet he'd made one excuse after another. He and Ida were currently in Chicago visiting relatives they hadn't seen in years, along with one of their sons.

It would be so easy. If he stayed, he could help Doc run this practice, maybe take over one day, perhaps sooner than he knew. He could be with Olivia, with Nick. Had Doc been trying him out? Hoping he would stay? He wouldn't put it past him, but Doc had also put his own patients at risk.

Sawyer rapped his knuckles on the desktop.

As if the practice were his, he tidied the area, then locked up.

And went to see Olivia.

CHAPTER SIXTEEN

"Home invasion," Sawyer announced.

Minutes after she got home from work, Olivia had opened the door to find him standing there with a smile, holding a large pizza box. His one raised eyebrow asked her to invite him in.

The mere sight of him should have made her shut him out instead. She'd had enough bad news for one day from Ted's son, and the images of Kedar's landslide were still making her tremble inside. A reminder that she preferred safety.

Her stomach growling, she looked at the box. She'd forgotten to eat lunch. "Is there bacon on that?"

"Everything," he said. "I didn't know what Nick liked."

"As long as it's pizza, you and I will be lucky to get one bite."

"I was in town," he explained, "so I thought, why drive all the way back to the ranch, then have to cook my dinner? I figured you might be ready to eat after work."

"I'm starving." She led the way to the kitchen. Olivia pulled plates from the cupboard, knives and forks from the drawer for those who wanted to use them, though Nick preferred his hands. She poured milk for him, red wine for her and Sawyer, while he recut the pizza because the shop he'd ordered from never cut all the way through.

Nick came running down the hall from his room.

"Did I smell...pizza!"

While they ate, they talked about Nick's recent visit to his school, where he'd met his teacher for the upcoming fall semester. Classes wouldn't start for a few weeks, but he said, "She seems okay," which meant he'd given her his stamp of approval. He added, "Me and Ava are going to be across the hall from each other."

"Ava and I," Olivia corrected automatically, keeping her gaze on her plate.

Nick looked at Sawyer. "Why didn't you let me come to see Hero?"

"That's your mom's decision."

Olivia didn't appreciate being thrown under the bus. He knew why she hadn't come to the ranch. "I've had too much work to take time off. And—have you spoken to Grey?"

His mouth full, Sawyer shook his head.

"He and Shadow have actually set a date," Olivia said. "Get this—they're not having their wedding here."

"I won't get to be a ring boy like I was for Dad?" Nick asked, chewing.

"Ring bearer," Olivia murmured.

She shouldn't discuss this in front of Nick, but she certainly didn't want to talk about Kedar again or her ongoing negotiations with Ted Anderson. "No, they've decided to get married in San Diego. They're meeting Blossom and Logan there since they're already in California. They'll stand up as witnesses. A very small event."

"Wow," Sawyer murmured, having swallowed his pizza. "Guess Logan will be their best man then. Grey asked me but…" Was he glad to be off the hook?

They let the conversation die while Nick was in the room. Instead, they talked about his Lego set, which was nearly finished.

When it was time for Nick to go to bed, Sawyer went with him to see the project in the dining room on their way. When he came back, he said Nick was already half asleep.

"You know what this means." Sawyer rubbed the nape of his neck. "I'll have to stay at the Circle H longer if Logan and Blossom are extending their trip." He told her about his text to Charlie. "I didn't have firm plans to leave, in spite of what you may think, but I didn't expect this."

Olivia shrugged. "Neither did I. With Grey and Shadow in San Diego, planning to spend extra days there afterward, my dad has offered to run the ranch."

"What about Ava?"

"I'm told she's had a good time with her 'new' grandparents, but of course she wants to be part of the wedding. Liza will fly with her out there, then come back. Grey and Shadow have promised to throw a big party when they get home."

He smiled. "So Ava's along for the honeymoon."

"It won't be a honeymoon. They plan to take a trip later."

"Well. At least this is a good opportunity," Sawyer pointed out, "for you to put things right with your dad."

You only have one father Liza had said. True, but Sawyer also had one grandfather.

"And you with Sam?"

He flinched. "We'll see. Then there's Logan. I was hoping he'd come home sooner." They had bonds to repair, too. He hesitated. "I hoped you and Nick would come out to the Circle H."

"I told you. I've been swamped at the shop."

"That didn't stop you before."

She sighed. "No, you're right. It didn't, and I'm on Nick's list for staying away. But it appears my deal with Ted Anderson won't go through after all. I've been exploring other means of financing again all day—without any luck."

"You said you wouldn't give up."

"And I won't. Not yet." She told him about paying for the Tiffany vase. But that wasn't all. She'd also stayed away from the ranch to protect herself. "Sawyer, after we got home the last time, after you and I talked, I rewatched that video. How did anyone survive that landslide?"

Sawyer squirmed. "A lot of people didn't. Too many," he said. "I'd rather talk about your shop." He hesitated. "I've got some money put aside... In Kedar there's nowhere to spend it. I'd be happy to lend—"

That surprised Olivia. "I couldn't accept that." She returned to their previous topic. "So many people lost, including some people you loved." For a moment she didn't continue. She'd already said, *You're going back.* During that talk, she'd glimpsed his love for those people, his guilt at leaving them. And the aftermath of that other incident.

Olivia couldn't fault him. As a boy, Sawyer had lost his parents. Along with Sam, he and his brother had been at odds for years. Although she certainly had issues with Everett, and, by association, Liza, even with her mother at times, all her life she'd had her birth family. Sawyer didn't. She said softly, "They're your family now, aren't they?"

After a long moment, he said, "I guess they are. And what have I done? Not long after that landslide, I left. Oh, I used the pretext of Logan's wedding—which I was late to after all—but it was more than that."

"What was more, Sawyer?" At the same time she didn't want to hear anything else about such a tragedy, she knew he needed to talk it through. "What happened with the child you lost?"

He stared at his hands. "Stupid," he said, "a rookie mistake, which I told you. You really want to know the rest?" He paused to take a deep breath. "Well, then. Here it is. An hour or so before the landslide, Khalil had come to the clinic complaining that he didn't feel well. He waited his turn and I checked him over but didn't find anything obvious—and I was up to my elbows with other patients that morning. As I also told you, Charlie and Piper had already gone to the school. I was in the clinic alone. I decided Khalil was probably having a minor side effect from the vaccination he'd gotten before some of his classmates. I decided he was okay to go back to school." He shook his head. "He hadn't been gone long when that mountainside let loose."

She pressed a hand to her chest. "He was caught in the slide?"

"On his way to school, Khalil got trapped under some rubble. Not as badly as other people did because he was on the near edge of the slide, but we—some other villagers and I—didn't reach him for quite a while. Khalil was bruised and cut up, a few of them pretty deep, but I cleaned and stitched those, and miraculously he hadn't broken anything. By comparison to many of the people I was seeing, he looked pretty good. He stayed that night with me—his folks were still missing—but by morning he was running a fever. He really was sick and I'd missed why."

"What was it?"

Sawyer looked into the middle distance. "For a couple of days, I kept on missing it. I was overwhelmed with other patients and Khalil still didn't seem that bad. By the time I realized he wasn't just dealing with vaccination side effects and with a bunch of relatively minor injuries, he was much worse. He had a hot appendix, which had already burst."

"Oh, Sawyer. That's dangerous, isn't it?"

"Yeah, and I should have caught it sooner. I lost valuable time. I operated on him, but it was too late and a desperation move. I had no antibiotics left to stem the infection that had spread through his system. Maybe by then they wouldn't have helped anyway." Sawyer swallowed hard. "And that killed him." *I killed him*, she imagined him thinking, but he didn't say that.

"Afterward, I left all those people, including Charlie and Piper, who'd finally made their way back to the clinic…left everybody in the lurch."

Olivia said weakly, "Maybe you'll hear from Charlie tomorrow."

"I'm becoming afraid I won't." Sawyer looked down at his hands again. "So there you have it. I've been feeling pretty full of myself here, taking care of a few cases for Doc, but I missed a diagnosis in Kedar that any first-year med student would have spotted."

"Wrong. It wasn't that simple. Khalil's death was a tragedy, but under the circumstances— with so many other people needing your help and with Charlie and his wife trapped at the school—what else could you have done?"

"That's what I ask myself. Every damn day

and night." He shook his head. "I never seem to find an answer."

"You did the best you could." As he had with Jasmine years ago, she thought. That wasn't the same, but she moved closer to him anyway, knowing she shouldn't. Who was she to comment on Kedar, when only last week Olivia had chosen safety, security? Even the horrendous video she'd seen was a far cry from what Sawyer had dealt with.

She caught his hand in hers, warming his skin with her touch, willing whatever strength she had into him. She leaned against his shoulder, her hair sliding over his upper arm, and heard his shaken breath.

"Now do you understand exactly why I didn't want to get near Nick? He's such an engaging little guy that he won me over. I'm grateful he did, but in a way that only makes what I did over there seem worse..."

Olivia didn't know what else to say. So instead of speaking, she gently kissed the side of his neck, then his jawline, planting soft kisses along the way like little dots of healing medicine, of comfort and forgiveness. When at last he turned his head to capture her mouth with his, she became lost in the warm brush of Sawyer's lips, the teasing nips and longer,

ever more intense kisses that left them both
breathing faster.

This isn't appropriate, she tried to tell herself. It wasn't right to lean in, to give in because Sawyer was hurting, but she couldn't
seem to stop. When she drew away, Olivia
knew they'd crossed some boundary, and she
wondered if, like him with Kedar, she had lost
herself in her feelings—for Sawyer himself.

At one point, she'd thought being attracted
to Logan's twin had an element of weird, but
she could never confuse them. She would
recognize Sawyer anywhere, not by how he
looked but by his willingness to take chances.
His innate kindness. Yet she'd never dared to
kiss him like this before and that changed everything. It was enough to make her scatter
caution to the winds, to jeopardize the careful life she'd made with Nick. Almost. But she
couldn't risk that, and would Sawyer want a
ready-made family?

Olivia rested her forehead against his—and
prepared herself to destroy any chance they
might have had to love each other, to be a family of their own.

"I knew you were going back," she murmured. "But that wasn't right. You *need* to go
back to Kedar. You have to, Sawyer."

"THOUGHT I'D FIND you packing by now," Sam said the next morning, frowning. Sawyer had been feeding horses when Sam ambled into the barn, and the unhappy expression that had become his signature look around Sawyer tore at his heart again. *You need to go back.*

Yes, he did. On some level, he'd always believed that, and Sam had a sixth sense like finely tuned radar. The instant he walked down the barn aisle, Sawyer knew why he was here.

"I'm not leaving yet." Not until Logan returned from San Diego. And Sawyer still hadn't heard from Charlie. To ease his mind, he'd been doing chores since before sunup. Later he'd ride out with Willy and Tobias to round up some stray bison. Sawyer liked to think he'd won them over doing such routine jobs and working with Cyclone, which seemed to have earned him their respect.

Or was he using the ranch, and Grey's wedding, as a means to avoid Kedar?

Sam grunted. "Then I guess I was wrong. For now." What appeared to be a hopeful look flashed in his eyes, then was gone.

Sawyer measured out Sundance's feed. "I'm just doing what we always do here this time of day."

The routine had become a comfort to him. Like Olivia last night.

Sam studied the floor between his boots. "I suppose that's a nice change for you from overseas, abroad, whatever you call it. But I have a right to know when you plan to leave here. I can't run this ranch if I'm always in the dark."

"I'm not sure just when I'm going back to the clinic. Soon," he added. Hadn't he made that plain enough? Sawyer dropped a scoop of grain into Hero's feed bucket.

"Then go. Now." Sam snorted. "If you think you have to babysit me while Logan's enjoying himself in California—"

"You've talked to him. Haven't you."

"Yessir. And I know Everett's staying on to take care of things over at Wilson Cattle while Grey's off getting married." Sam dug at the dirt with the toe of his boot. "Some people love the land where they grew up, the place they inherited, built into something. They don't just up and leave other people to do all the work themselves."

"Which is exactly why I need to go back to Kedar. Why can't you understand? I abandoned what I helped to make there, I up and left the people who counted on me. Like you said the other day—I started something, Sam.

I need to finish it." Sawyer's mouth tightened. He moved on down the barn aisle. "Why can't you see that? How many times do I have to tell you there were reasons why I left the Circle H back in the day? You're right, it wasn't just to finish med school."

Sam muttered, "One reason. Think I don't know who that was? I saw from day one she wasn't right for Logan. I saw how you looked at her then. You still do," he pointed out. "And I still love her as if she was my own daughter. Why would you leave her a second time?"

Sam didn't need to say her name, but his insight surprised Sawyer. He'd hoped no one had noticed what had been going on with him and—

"That's between Olivia and me."

"You don't have to go back," Sam said.

"Yes, I do." If Sawyer hadn't acknowledged that before, he did now. "I didn't realize just how badly I need to until Olivia said it." He was still trying to figure out, after their kisses, how he was going to leave her behind, even when she'd made it plain she could never follow him to Kedar. So much for seeing where their relationship might go.

"Then you care more about some far-off country, the people there, than you do about her...about us," Sam murmured.

Sawyer swallowed. *They're your family now, aren't they?* He couldn't deny that. Sawyer had turned away from Sam, Logan…Olivia, but not to replace them. "I don't mean to hurt you—though it seems I always do—but I can't stay here."

Sam grunted, his mouth set in a stubborn line. "Whatever's 'between you' isn't one-sided, Sawyer. You really want to lose that?" He didn't say *again*, but that's probably what he was thinking.

And, Sawyer realized, Sam didn't only mean Olivia.

Sam stroked Sundance's nose through the bars of his stall. Apparently, this had been on Sam's mind for some time; no wonder he'd given Sawyer the silent treatment until now, letting his feelings build. "When your folks didn't come home after that accident, Muriel and I took you and Logan in like our own kids—if we'd had any. That didn't happen for us. I was a bachelor for most of my life until I met her. She'd already raised her family with your real grandfather. So we had our December romance and we had you boys instead."

"I'm grateful, Sam. So is Logan. You were both the best."

"And you repaid me—as if I need any payment—by leaving this ranch? I was mad enough then, and when I heard you'd changed back to your father's name, that was like another slap in the face. McCord? I won't go through that again. I admit I'm proud you stuck it out, became a doctor and did some good in the world. But I thought you'd juggle that with the Circle H. I swear, you leave this time— the *Hunter* ranch, which became that because Muriel McCord Hunter did me the honor of changing it from her first husband's name to mine—I won't let you come back."

"Then that's your decision. I've made mine." With a lump in his throat, Sawyer turned away. He started toward the feed room, then stopped.

When he turned around, he caught Sam's face morphing from a scowl into an expression of obvious sorrow, and Sawyer remembered what Sam had said before. *My other grand...son.* He was breaking Sam's heart all over again.

"Aw, Sam." Sawyer gathered him into his arms and just held on.

How could he leave? Yet how could he stay? Unless he went back to Kedar, he would never find the redemption he needed.

CHAPTER SEVENTEEN

WELL, LET'S SEE how this goes, Liza thought. Less than twenty minutes after Olivia Wilson Antiques had opened for the day, Liza walked in, probably the last person Olivia expected to see. And Liza hadn't come to buy an antique.

She kissed Olivia on both cheeks. "Is that a new sign on your front window?"

"Yes," Olivia said. "Since I'm not doing estate sales anymore, I had to change the name of my business. Thank you for noticing."

"It's beautiful. I love the gold script. And I know, I'm out early this morning," she said, then came straight to the point of her visit. "I talked with Grey last night—when I could get his attention while he packed for his trip with Shadow—and he tells me your deal to buy Ted Anderson's store has hit a snag."

"More than that. It seems to be dead. I've spoken again with his son Craig, who remains adamant about 'their' price." Olivia rearranged a stack of ivory lace place mats on a table, then straightened the Western framed print on the far wall. "I can't believe Grey was spreading gossip."

Liza flushed. "I believe he heard that from Sawyer."

Olivia rolled her eyes. "Just as bad." Her face had turned pink.

No, Liza thought, that was obviously worse and didn't have anything to do with Ted Anderson.

"I wouldn't call that gossip—merely a brother and a…friend catching up with one another. Most of *their* talk was about the wedding." Liza drew an audible breath. "Is there something I can help with?"

"No," Olivia said, eyeing the doorway. "I'm sorry to seem distracted, but a client who wanted to 'think about' a large armoire she liked promised to come by today." She paused. "Would you like a cup of coffee? Maybe you'd like to browse. Or both."

"Thanks, but before I left Wilson Cattle I drank enough coffee to float a boat." Liza followed her around the room, exclaiming over an elk antler chandelier here, a Sheraton dining room table and chairs there. "I redid our condo when Everett and I moved in and I don't plan to go through that again—but oh, now I'm tempted. This table would look lovely in our dining area." She paused. "Except then I'd have to swap out everything else. Right now, we're 'contemporary.'"

"Many people like an eclectic look." Olivia gestured at the shop, explaining that she stocked Western antiques along with Colonial pieces from Virginia and Massachusetts and currently had some art deco items from France. "Really, anything goes. I was talking to Jenna Moran the other day—Shadow's sister. She's in the process of becoming a designer and she said the same thing."

With a heavy silver candlestick in her hand, Liza turned. "Tell me more about Ted Anderson."

"Nothing to tell." Apparently, Olivia didn't want to talk. "I only need to decide whether or not to pursue this deal—as if I actually have a choice. I've racked my brain, but can't think of any solutions."

"Well, I'm here to listen," Liza said, "and not because I like gossip. Olivia, you worry me. There must be some way you can salvage things with Mr. Anderson."

Olivia gave up. "You're a good listener, and maybe I need to vent. It's not Ted, it's his son who's in the way. He seems to control his father, though Ted did stick up for himself the last time we met. But every time I call him, I get Craig instead. I have to wonder why he's so set on auctioning off Ted's inventory rather than letting someone else—me—expand my business to include his." Olivia told Liza about their meeting at the diner.

When she'd finished, Liza put an arm around her shoulders. "This is an easy fix. I'll lend you the money."

Olivia blinked. "Oh. No, I couldn't take that, Liza. I wouldn't feel right."

"Because you don't like me?"

Olivia glanced at the far wall. "I do like you, but I've already had a similar offer. I can't take your money, either." She eased away from Liza's touch. "I'm glad you and Everett are so happy…"

"But what about *you*, Olivia? Everett needs his daughter, too," Liza pointed out. "I can't say how grateful I am that Sawyer was there when Everett choked on his dinner, but that certainly reminded me that life is not only short, it's unpredictable. If it hadn't been for Sawyer, you and I both could have lost him that night."

"Yes. I know. I feel the same way you do."

Liza smiled. "Then please tell him that." *You only have one father.* "If you're worried about my money being his, you needn't be. I have my own accounts, thanks to my very generous parents, and I can easily afford to make a loan—to someone I care about." She named a modest rate of interest, but Olivia shook her head. Did she think Liza was trying to buy her love?

"I can't, Liza. I promised to prove myself, and I will."

She didn't want to be obligated. Okay, then. "Olivia. I understand about your parents. About your marriage with Logan. But sometimes we have to lean on each other, and there's no harm in that. I could have refused my family's money—we were never very close—but I decided to accept it, then use it for good. I think that would have made them happy. Please think about this. My offer will stay open."

"Thank you."

Olivia walked her to the door but Liza didn't open it. "Oh," she said, "one other thing while I'm here. Grey is concerned about Sawyer."

"You mean because he's leaving?"

"No. Because, when he does, you and Sawyer may miss out on something special together. I shouldn't pry into your personal business—"

Olivia frowned. "That's why you're really here."

"Part of the reason." Liza opened her mouth, but there was nothing else to say. She'd taken a chance with Olivia—and, on two counts, failed.

Without a word, Olivia reached past her to open the door. Liza felt her watching as she crossed the street, stopped on the other side to say hi to Jack Hancock, a chef at the nearby café, and slipped into her car. As she drove past Olivia's shop, she saw her. And tooted the horn.

I do like you, Liza thought.

Which didn't mean Olivia would take the loan.

Just as she probably wouldn't ask Sawyer to stay, even for her own good.

As soon as Olivia's SUV stopped at the barn, Nick bounded out of the car. With a wave and a "Hi, Uncle Sawyer," he blew past him into the barn, shouting, "Hero! Blossom Too!" He ran off to see his horse and half-grown kitten.

Sawyer waited for Olivia to get out before he said, "I didn't expect to see you this afternoon." Or any day, after their last conversation about Kedar.

Olivia smiled at her son's retreating back. In the barn doorway, he scooped up the cat he'd adopted months ago. "This is all he's talked about since he woke up. I had some business to take care of—a client who, thank heavens, decided to purchase a lovely armoire before I'd have had to cut the price to move it. I promised Nick a ride today." She wouldn't meet his gaze.

"I was just going to get Cyclone, but he can wait." Nick had already disappeared down the aisle and Sawyer heard Hero snuffle a greeting from his stall. "Unless you have to rush off, we can have a training session when Nick's done."

While Nick put Hero through his paces, Olivia stood with Sawyer by the rail. Nick seemed to improve every time, and Sawyer loved seeing the look of pride on his face. When he'd finished, Nick decided not to go up to the house or to look for Sam as he usually did. He wanted to watch them work Cyclone.

That was fine with Sawyer, but it also meant he couldn't really talk to Olivia. They needed to discuss last night, try to find some meeting ground in far more than shared kisses.

He'd been feeling guilty ever since his talk with Sam, but he didn't know how to resolve the situation with either of them. What might work for Sawyer would never work for Sam or Olivia. He doubted Logan would see things any differently, but he wasn't here. That confrontation was coming, too, and Sawyer had all but resigned himself to it.

For now, he tried to focus on the colt.

Unfortunately, Cyclone didn't want to cooperate. Sawyer became increasingly frustrated with him until, finally, he turned toward the fence, his back to the colt for only a second. He knew better.

Cyclone took his opportunity to scoot off around the arena, building speed until he brushed past Sawyer, knocking his shoulder hard enough to make him lose his balance.

"So much for his being quieted down after his day with the vet." Sawyer rubbed his shoulder. "I'm no good with him today. Why don't you take over?"

"Yeah, Mom!" Nick agreed from his perch on the fence, arms crossed on the top rail, his booted feet dangling off a lower board.

If Sawyer hadn't seen her with the colt before, he would never have let her step in. But right now, she seemed better equipped than he was to deal with Cyclone—until Sawyer suddenly doubted his decision. Should he risk her safety just because he couldn't concentrate? That seemed less risky, in its way, than wishing she might join him in Kedar, but Sawyer had started back into the arena when Olivia entered the ring.

As if in challenge, her eyes met his for an instant, then flickered away. With her total focus on the colt, she crossed the corral and caught him on his next pass as he glided along the far rail.

"Whoa!" she called out twice, loud enough to startle the horse into obeying her. She'd certainly gotten his attention.

Cyclone stopped and stood, blowing hard with his head hung between his front legs, but his ears stayed flat against his skull.

"Watch him, Olivia," Sawyer said, his heart in his throat.

It was one thing for him to try to train the colt, another for him to watch her and feel helpless. Or maybe he'd forgotten for a moment just how capable she was. To his relief, Cyclone's gait had leveled out into that smooth, floating trot and the colt couldn't seem to do enough for Olivia.

When she finally reeled him in and slowly coiled the lunge line, Cyclone was practically eating from her hand. As she clipped a lead to his halter, Olivia grinned.

"I needed that," she said, crossing to open the gate.

After they'd settled Nick in the family room with a glass of juice and a snack to watch a children's program on TV, she and Sawyer sat across from each other at the kitchen table.

"I saw Liza this morning," she said with a

sigh. "She offered to help me with Ted Anderson's shop." Olivia hesitated. "She wants to lend me the money."

"Which you refused. Just as you refused my offer."

She arched a brow. "How did you know?"

Sawyer looked away. "You and Grey haven't exactly welcomed her to the family. I can't imagine you accepting her help."

"I didn't, and yet…you're right. We've been unfair. I'd say my mother's influence had something to do with that, but now that Mom's also remarried and seems to have mellowed, it's all on me. I'm ashamed of myself."

"Never a good feeling," Sawyer agreed.

She tried to change the subject. "Have you heard from Charlie?"

"Not a word. I've sent his wife a message but so far, nothing." Sawyer ran a hand over the back of his neck. "I've become a news junkie. I've probably hit the world weather site and googled *Kedar* a hundred times. There doesn't seem to be anything to worry about, but I can't help worrying anyway." He squirmed in his chair. "I almost wish Grey and Shadow hadn't decided to get married in California. Otherwise, Logan would be home by now."

Olivia frowned. "You haven't heard."

"What?"

"According to his latest phone call with Nick, he and Blossom are stopping in Wichita on their way back. Logan has an interview with a new small plane manufacturer there. The money would be good and he'd only have to fly on a limited basis, which would leave him free to help run the Circle H."

"He didn't say anything to me. I thought Logan was done flying." This would add another few days to Sawyer's stay at the ranch and he wanted to pound the table.

"Logan said the extra income would provide working capital for the ranch. It may be a part-time 'offer' he can't refuse."

Sawyer rubbed his temples. "Olivia, you know I need to get back to Kedar. To find out what's going on…" He trailed off. To redeem himself, if that were even possible with Charlie. "I need to figure out what I want, too. If it's to leave Kedar for good, then I need to do it the right way. I don't want to leave Sam here without help, either. I don't want to leave you without speaking my mind."

Olivia traced the pattern on the tablecloth. She wouldn't look at him.

"I'm in love with you," he said, his voice low. "In case you never noticed, I've been in love with you since…long before that day we raced across the field. And I messed up. I'd like us to have a chance now, Olivia. Last night, I thought you might feel the same. I know it won't be easy—"

"No..." She pressed her lips tight before going on. "I have family here, friends, Nick... He's my *child*, the most important person in my life. He depends on me. He's vulnerable. I have to think of him, of making a home for us that doesn't shift and change with the prairie wind." She glanced toward the family room. "So what do we do, Sawyer? You go back to Kedar, I stay here with Nick. In all likelihood, we wouldn't see each other more than a few times a year. What kind of relationship is that?"

"Some people function that way."

Yet he knew Olivia wasn't one of them. Because he'd known her for so long, watched her deal with her parents' divorce, he understood that, most of all, she craved stability for Nick. Sawyer couldn't give her that. Still. She hadn't said she loved him, too, but he tried to take heart. At least she hadn't downplayed their feelings for each other.

"Your partner doesn't," she said at last. "His wife lives there. You and I are a long way from thinking about...marriage, and pardon me for seeming presumptuous, but I'm not sure I'd

want to try that again. I can't base my future—
or Nick's—on some kisses." She half smiled.
"As lovely as they were."

"Lovely? More than that, Olivia."

She didn't disagree. "We're at an impasse,
though. Aren't we? Even if we could work
something out between us, there's still Nick.
I could never give up my business—whether
I expand or not—and risk his security. Maybe
you're right that no one can predict another
disaster, but I can't take him away from his
friends here, his family—or leave *my* friends
and family for a place where the language bar-
rier would be only the first thing to overcome."

"I know this much—safety is an illusion,"
he insisted. "Unless we try, we'll never know
whether you and I could have a life together.
I made a bad start with Nick, but we're good
now. You and I can be, too."

Olivia held up a hand, then let it drop. "After
Logan and I broke up, I thought I'd never want
another relationship." She lifted her gaze to
his. "I've come to realize I was partly to blame
for what went wrong, and I want you to know
why. When we all started to grow up, Logan
and me and…you, and we all began to change,
I had no idea what to make of that. I'd always
loved Logan, I…cared for you, too…but in a

different way, I realized. You frightened me, the strength of my feelings for you. Then that day when you dared me to race you across the field, I must have sensed what was going on with you. I didn't want to acknowledge that, and after Jasmine fell, I think I used that as an excuse. I turned to Logan because he seemed safer to me ...steady and, well, stable. I've only come to understand that recently, and to feel guilty that I chose him for all the wrong reasons."

She paused. "I can't do that again. If I ever do remarry, I'd want someone who was there for Nick, full-time. As great as Logan is at being a dad, I won't have Nick pulled in yet another direction."

"Olivia." He rose from his chair, rounded the table and pulled her to her feet then into his arms. He drew her closer, lowered his head to hers and angled it just right to meet her lips. Keeping an eye on the door to the family room, he kissed her once, twice, a third time—and finally, felt her surrender to the embrace.

"We can make it," he whispered against her mouth. "Somehow, we will."

But Olivia had already pulled away. Her expression told him he'd lost.

"I don't want another part-time relationship," she said, then rushed into the other
room, calling for Nick.

CHAPTER EIGHTEEN

BLOSSOM POKED HER HEAD around the corner of the dining room. "All set?" she asked Olivia. She and Logan had arrived home that afternoon, and Nick had been eager to see them, so when Blossom phoned to ask them to dinner, Olivia had offered to cook. Even though Sawyer would be there and Olivia hadn't seen him in two weeks.

I don't want another part-time relationship. Ever since, she'd been dropping Nick off to ride Hero. Sawyer had brought him home but never stopped in.

In the Circle H kitchen, she stacked plates and flatware for Blossom, who looked tired from the long drive. Olivia glanced at the stove, where a pot was simmering. "Thanks for setting the table. Our spaghetti sauce should be done in a few minutes," she told Blossom.

The rich scents of tomatoes, onions, oregano and basil filled the air, making her stomach growl. From the oven wafted the enticing smell of garlic bread. The salad she'd fixed was in the refrigerator and homemade oil-and-vinegar dressing sat in a cut glass cruet on the dining room table. For once, she and Nick would be eating before seven o'clock and not their usual mac and cheese or a quick hamburger. Or pizza.

She hadn't seen Sawyer since she'd arrived tonight.

It seemed strange—and oddly satisfying—to make a meal again in this kitchen, where she'd cooked for Logan and Sam until the flood, but the result pleased her. Another part of her peacemaking efforts with her ex-husband.

When Blossom came back for more serving pieces, Olivia said, "You've done enough. Sit down. I'll call the others."

She turned the burner off under a huge pot of pasta, then hunted through a lower cabinet for her favorite strainer. It wasn't hers, really; Sam's wife, Muriel, had bought it and Olivia had left it here when she moved out.

"We can't wait to hear all about your honeymoon," she added, "and, of course, Grey and Shadow's wedding in San Diego."

"The beach at Coronado was divine," Blossom said, one hand on her stomach. "But I can't help wishing we'd been able to come home a bit sooner. This baby is kicking me to pieces. I think he wants to be born. I bet Logan that I won't make it to my due date."

"I know the feeling. With Nick, I was so uncomfortable by eight months that all I could think of was being thin again, having my body to myself."

They shared a smile, Blossom's a bit wry. "I'm making at least two dozen trips to the bathroom every day. Did that happen to you?"

With a quick pang of might-have-been, Olivia slid the pasta into a large bowl. Nick would be an only child. "Sure did."

Once the baby was here, maybe she'd invite Shadow, Annabelle and some others to her house for the baby shower, a celebration after the fact. Everyone, she knew, had gifts ready for Blossom and Logan's little one, including the layette Sherry would provide from Baby Things. Maybe she'd also invite Liza, unless she and Everett had already gone back to Dallas by then.

They could all take turns holding Blossom's baby boy. And Olivia would try not to cry. By the time Nick was turning four, she'd stopped hoping for another child with Logan, and after the flood just before Nick's birthday that year, she'd left the Circle H.

Now the memories assailed her. This had been Nick's first home, and tonight he was drinking milk from his favorite dinosaur mug, which he used whenever he came to what he now called "my other home." His toddler silverware was still in the kitchen drawer. She'd come across it when she took out the table settings. His crib, stored in the attic, would soon be repainted for Blossom's baby and Nick wanted to help with that. He seemed excited to be having a half brother, but then enthusiasm was his middle name.

She wondered how he'd react if she asked him about visiting Kedar.

Olivia carried the pasta bowl to the dining room. She didn't have to call the others. Following the aromas of dinner, they had already showed up to eat.

Without looking at her, Sawyer fetched the salad. Blossom brought in the garlic bread wrapped in a cloth napkin. After Nick said a quick grace, everyone dug in.

Like the night at Wilson Cattle when her father had choked, people talked over other people in their eagerness to share experiences or ask another question. Logan and Sawyer weren't exactly beaming, but they didn't argue, either. Although Sam didn't seem his usual talkative self, he made a comment now and then, his gaze avoiding Sawyer. Olivia did, too, trying to ignore the undercurrents between them.

Sawyer wasn't here to stay. And neither was she at the Circle H. Although she and Blossom had become friends, this wasn't her family any longer—except for Nick.

The thought made her feel unaccountably sad.

And she kept thinking, *Sawyer loves me.*

AFTER DINNER, SAWYER helped Olivia with the dishes. Then, while she and Blossom talked about babies, and Sam and Nick watched a rodeo on TV, he and Logan walked out to the barn to make a nighttime check of the horses, which wasn't their only reason to slip away. Sawyer expected they were about to have *that* conversation, just as he had with Sam. And Olivia. Neither had ended well. He assumed his departure for Kedar would be the starting point, but Logan surprised him.

"You and Libby," he said. "What's going on there?"

Sawyer didn't know how to answer.

Logan trailed a light hand along the bars of the stalls they passed, talking to each horse in the now-darkened barn. A single overhead light penetrated the gloom. "C'mon, you think I'm blind? I always knew you cared about her.

Seems to me you still do." He stopped to pet Sundance's nose. "Hey, pal. Did you miss me?"

The horse's ears had pricked up and he offered a whickered greeting.

Sawyer shifted his weight. As Sam had said, his feelings for Olivia were no secret, but when he'd shared them with her, she'd rejected him. "Nothing's 'going on.' I hadn't seen her in weeks until tonight. She brings Nick to ride Hero, but she never comes in. I was bowled over when she actually made dinner here tonight."

Logan snorted, as if he was getting only half the story. "Libby's a good woman. We were never right for each other, but that doesn't mean she doesn't deserve to be happy with someone else."

To the sounds of hay being munched, water being slurped from buckets, an occasional hoof stomping the ground, Sawyer wandered down the aisle.

"Meaning me?"

"If you're what makes her happy." Logan paused. "That's how it seems."

"Where'd you get that idea?" Sawyer stopped at Hero's stall. Had his brother seen Sawyer looking at her during dinner, or Olivia sneaking wary glances at him?

The little gray came right up to him, nuzzling his hand for a treat. Sawyer reached into his pocket for the stub of a carrot. Then moved on. "If we had anything, that was before I had to put Jasmine down—before Olivia chose you instead." What was the use of talking about her? Why didn't he and Logan just have it out at last over Sawyer's long-ago defection from the Circle H? Sam sure hadn't hesitated to tell him how he felt.

Seemed like Sawyer had alienated everyone during his stay.

"I'm leaving," he said. "Guess that's what you'd expect." Sawyer told him more about the landslide in Kedar, and that he still hadn't heard from Charlie. "I was only waiting till you got home."

He could be gone tomorrow morning.

"Yeah, well. Things have gotten complicated. You know we stopped in Wichita. Stayed at my apartment there. I should let it go, but my interview went pretty well. I'm still waiting to hear their take on that, but if I'm offered the job, I'll grab it. Sam also needs your help, Sawyer, especially when I can't be here. More than that, he wants you home."

"Didn't seem like it last time we talked." Sawyer told him about the day in the barn with Sam. How for a moment, he'd thought they might find common ground until Sam had all but disowned him. "When I leave this time, I don't know for sure, but... I probably won't come back. Maybe that's for the best all around." Even if that choice meant losing Sam, too. The man who had raised him, loved him, begged him to stay.

"If I were you, I'd think twice about that." Logan walked closer to the end stall. "Any luck with this colt?"

Sawyer didn't stop to think. He went right up to the stall and stuck his hand in. Cyclone lipped his palm for another piece of carrot. "See? He doesn't bite. I've been spending time with him. Groundwork, remedial classes, you might say. Oh, and while you were gone, we had him neutered." He hesitated. "Olivia's been helping with his training. When I go, she can take over. With you."

Logan half smiled. "I can't see us—her and me—working together. I wouldn't want to risk our peace treaty. Apparently, you didn't have any trouble."

"With the colt, no." Sawyer leaned against the stall door. He crossed his arms. "Olivia wants a nice, secure life. That's all she's ever wanted. I can't blame her for that, but where I'm going—where I have to go—I have no idea what I'll find."

"So—just like that—you're done." Turning away, Logan put one hand up to the bars of Cyclone's stall. And, teeth bared, the colt tried to take a piece out of him. Logan examined his finger. "Hey. Thought you said he doesn't bite."

"He doesn't bite me." Sawyer almost wanted to smile. They'd always been competitive. "You have to win his trust, big brother."

"Thanks for the advice, Tom." Logan started back toward the open doors. In a shaft of moonlight, he turned to face Sawyer, probably not realizing he'd used his old nickname for him. "You know, our world got shaken up pretty bad when we were kids. But after Mom and Dad died, we did all right with Sam, didn't we? You were the one who planned to stay then, to take over the Circle H. I left to fly—part of the reason I finally lost Libby. She never signed on for that, but you had it made right here, Sawyer." He shook his injured finger as if to ease the pain. "Why in hell did you run off? Just to lick your wounds after Libby married me? Why didn't you stay before—fight for her? But, no. Now you're racing off again as if someone is chasing you. If that's Libby, you're never going to find what you really need somewhere else." He said, "I know I didn't. And I didn't go as far as Kedar."

"NICK, WE NEED to go home." Olivia had told him at least twice to get his things together, and still he hadn't moved. He and Sam were watching a marathon of some cartoon series on TV. Nick's eyes were drooping, but he refused to give in to sleep or to Olivia's reminders that it was getting late. Finally, she went outside to load the car herself.

She was backing out of the SUV's rear seat, having stowed Nick's iPad and backpack there along with the light sweater she'd insisted he bring in case the night air carried a chill, when Sawyer appeared out of the darkness.

"Olivia."

She turned, nearly bumping into his chest. The starlight had turned his hair the color of obsidian, deepened the blue of his eyes, chiseled his cheekbones and made her heart speed. She looked at his mouth, set in a straight line, unsmiling and hard, but all Olivia could think of was the heated softness of his lips on hers and Sawyer saying, *I'm in love with you.*

She sought safety in small talk. "Tonight turned out well. It was good to see Blossom and Logan. Where did you guys go after dinner?"

"Down to the barn. He tried to convince me I'm doing the wrong thing. I wish I could stay, Olivia. You know that, don't you?"

"No, this is what you have to do. And I have to think of Nick. Neither of us would benefit from waiting after you leave, hoping to see you again."

She had no doubt that, once Sawyer reached Kedar, he'd get caught up in the lives of the people he loved there, the surrogate family he'd adopted in place of Sam and Logan, the daily crises at his clinic. For an instant, she wanted to resent those other people. Yet they needed Sawyer and he obviously needed them.

Olivia gazed up at him, standing so near, and in spite of her thoughts felt almost sheltered by his broad shoulders, his strength, as if that were something she and Nick could trust in, rely on, and that would be enough. In the time he'd been at the Circle H this summer, he'd built new muscle from hard work. Wasn't he still, in part, a cowboy? She'd thought so before, but she guessed not, after all.

"I'm glad you've been able to…restore your faith in yourself as a doctor—"

He cut her off. "Doc and Ida are coming home tomorrow."

He didn't say the rest, but he didn't have to. He'd sought her out in the yard for a private goodbye. Her voice trembled. "I hope you find what you're looking for, Sawyer."

"What?" he said. "To be forgiven for what

I did? That's not what Logan thinks I should do." Without warning, he framed her face in his hands, and even knowing how futile this was, Olivia welcomed his warm touch. "I'm not sure, either—except that I have to do this first before I make any other decisions. Before I can—" He broke off.

Decide about me? Olivia had already made her decision.

Sawyer was a highly skilled, talented physician. Medicine was his calling, not helping to run the Circle H. He hadn't forgotten those skills—watching him with the black colt had quelled any doubts she might have had about that—but how could she ask him to give up his practice, his passion?

"The clinic is your…home now. I can almost see you driving down the road tomorrow morning, heading for Kansas City and the airport, reviewing case files from Kedar in your mind. That's who you are, Sawyer. And I'm… Nick's mother."

"A very good mother," he said, still holding her face in his hands.

Yet—she'd never had the thought before—was that enough for her? Olivia blinked back tears.

From the nearby creek, just through the stand of cottonwood trees that had edged the wooden dance floor at Logan's reception, she could hear crickets singing, the deep gulp of a bullfrog's call, the faint rush of water flowing between its banks. The same creek that had overflowed, then flooded, trapping her with Nick at the ranch three years ago.

Still, she'd had good times here. With Logan, their childhood friends…Sawyer. More good times recently with him and Nick, with the colt. What if, having made her choice, she never saw him again?

"Olivia. You can be Nick's mother and a woman at the same time."

She bristled. "I am a woman." She didn't need him to tell her that. "One with a business to run, a house that's too small for us, a dozen issues at once, every day, but…what's best for Nick is best for me, too."

"So you won't even try. With us."

"I am trying," she said. *I'm trying to let you go.*

With a slight shake of his head, Sawyer drew her against his chest. If only she could trust him to come back, to be more than a temporary presence in her life…

She didn't get the chance to say so. He lowered his head and his mouth took hers in a long, slow, lazy kiss as if they had all the time in the world. Then the moment gradually changed, and grew, into something lush and splendid and loving, filled with need, and by the time they finally broke apart, she was aware of nothing but the way he felt against her. His hands on her shoulders now, gently kneading, caressing, the sound of his shaken breaths and hers in the stillness of the night.

The crickets were silent now. The bullfrog had stopped croaking, but the creek still burbled along in its channel like another reminder, whispering of her past mistakes. When Sawyer kissed her once more, he spoke, the words hoarse, into her mouth. "Trust me, Olivia. Make a commitment. We can work out the details later. Trust in us—in yourself."

Oh, he tempted her. Until now, she'd focused solely on Olivia Wilson Antiques, the deal for Ted Anderson's shop and, above all, Nick. She wouldn't be a three-time loser, after her parents and Logan, with Sawyer.

But still...what about *her* happiness? Maybe she needed more than to be the best single mother on the planet. Maybe she needed something for herself.

She had the words on the tip of her tongue, had moved deeper into Sawyer's arms to say them, to ask him to reconsider leaving before they could come to some agreement, when she heard a familiar chirp from his pocket.

With a soft curse for the interruption, Sawyer pulled out his phone.

By the light of its screen, she watched him read the message. In the dark all around them, she couldn't see his face turn pale, but she could tell by his expression that it had. His hand shaking, he turned the phone for Olivia to see the shocking text.

Possible cholera next village. Charlie.

CHAPTER NINETEEN

SAWYER HAD WATCHED Olivia reread Charlie's text. Then she'd gone back to the house. She needed to take Nick home, she'd told him, her eyes downcast. It was late, and he didn't disagree. He'd also run out of time.

Sawyer didn't think more discussion would do either of them any good at this point. Instead, remembering his talk with Logan, his brother calling him Tom for the first time in years, he went down to the barn again to see Cyclone. He stepped inside the stall.

"Hey, boy. Doing great. By the time you're ready for a saddle, you'll be a star," he said, keeping a close eye on the black colt. If he twitched a muscle on those powerful hindquarters, Sawyer would dance out of the way. He didn't need to get kicked tonight. Olivia had already done that. "Sure wish I could take you with me…"

The only horses that thrived in Kedar were the tough mountain ponies, bred through the ages from Mongol stock, with blocky bodies and short legs. Cyclone would stand out there like the proverbial sore thumb. The rocky ground would soon cripple him, ruin his elegant legs, and then Sawyer would be forced to put him down as he had Olivia's horse.

No, this had to be yet another goodbye. Until now, he hadn't realized how hard that would be, and not only because he'd grown fond of the colt. In his weeks on the Circle H, he'd managed to slide back into his place here, to become a gradual part of the ranch and sense its heartbeat again deep inside him. Where did he truly belong?

He heard footfalls and, hoping it was Olivia, turned toward the stall door. Sam shuffled up to the bars and peeked in. "Talking to yourself?"

"Horse whispering," he said, stroking Cyclone's sleek, dark neck. "I hate to leave him, Sam." *Hate to leave you, too*. He patted the colt once more, the sound echoing through the barn. "I know you think I'm running off, and I wish I could be here to finish him properly for you. I know I promised. But I can't."

Sam's mouth set. "I won't try to change your mind." He half smiled. "I was kind of hoping Olivia would do that for me."

"Well, she won't." *She didn't even try*, and he already missed her. Still, he respected her decision. Once she'd seen Charlie's text, she must have known any argument for Sawyer to stay would be futile. Because how could he let his partner down—again? What a grim irony that he was letting other people down here in order to return to Kedar. "I probably won't even see her before I leave."

Sawyer tilted his head, listening for the sound of her car, the crunch of gravel beneath her tires, but heard only the faint chirp of crickets and the throaty song of a lone frog by the creek. The chorus had started up again.

"She's having a hard time getting Nick to budge," Sam said.

A lump had lodged in Sawyer's Adam's apple. He already missed Nick, too. For a man who'd never thought much about having a family, who had destroyed someone else's, he'd enjoyed being with Olivia's son, seeing Nick recover from his fall, watching him ride and improve his skills, hearing his little boy giggles over some silly joke or a children's TV show. He glanced at Sam. "Thought you and he were watching cartoons."

"I've already seen *Curious George*—with Nick, with you and Logan years ago…" He paused. "I figured you might be gone before I wake up tomorrow."

Sawyer straightened Cyclone's forelock, then slipped out of his stall. His hand still felt warm from the colt's flesh, the smooth ripple of muscle on his neck. In the aisle, he faced off with Sam, who seemed at a loss for words. There was no need to tell Sawyer again not to come back.

He sighed. "You said what you had to. I never said you were wrong."

Sam cleared his throat. "I heard there's more trouble over there." Olivia must have told him about the cholera outbreak. "You sure you need to get into that? Seems to me when you came back this summer you'd had enough."

"The clinic is likely still in bad shape. I've been gone too long and now, because I left in the first place, Charlie's burned out."

Why in hell did you run off? Logan had asked about Olivia. *Now you're racing off again.* Sawyer had no choice, really, but his brother was right.

He held Sam's gaze. "All my life, I've given in to the urge to run away—from the pain of my parents' deaths, losing Olivia to Logan… the landslide…" And what he'd done to Khalil. Maybe he'd never be able to atone for that, but the trip would be a first step. He had to try. "I even ran from Nick after his fall." Olivia had rightly called him selfish then. "I'm done running."

Sam studied him, then shook his head. Sawyer thought that was the end of that, but Sam wasn't through after all. "Guess I was pretty hard on you last time, huh?" He scanned Sawyer's face and his sharp blue eyes softened. "God gave me two fine grandsons," he said. "I don't want to lose either of you. My boys." Another pause. "But sounds like those people over there need you more than we do right now. I hope when all that's done, you'll see a way to come home, Sawyer."

"But you said—"

"I'm an old man. Ashamed of myself. Shouldn't have taken you leaving again for me to see I've treated you wrong." He shifted from his good leg to the other, which had worn a cast not long ago. And Sawyer remembered him saying he wasn't a quitter. "Before I'm done, I hope to see you on the Circle H again."

Sawyer surprised himself then. "I'll try." He pulled Sam into an awkward hug, the lump in his throat as big as a boulder. "Take care of yourself."

Sam hooked an arm around Sawyer's neck. "You, too…son. Especially you. That's how I see you, you know. " He rested his forehead against Sawyer's, and Sawyer thought of one way, at least in part, to atone right here, to Sam, too.

He straightened. "I love you, Pops." The

term was one both he and Logan used to call Sam because he'd really been like a father to them just as Sam thought of him more as a son. It seemed to fit now. "But how wedded are you to this colt?"

OLIVIA WAITED BY her car for Sam to leave the barn. Then, watching him trudge up the slight rise to the ranch house, she took a deep breath. After reading Charlie's message, she'd felt too stunned by the situation in Kedar—the reality of Sawyer leaving—to say a word. She couldn't let him go without saying more.

She entered the mostly silent barn. A single light glowed overhead, casting shadows everywhere, and in his stall Hero whickered a soft greeting. Sawyer met her halfway, his dark blue eyes like ebony in the dimness and looking surprisingly moist.

"Did you and Sam make peace?" she asked.

Sawyer didn't quite answer. "I keep thinking. What if that was the last time I see Pops? He said he's not getting any younger. His accident—his broken leg—set him back for a while. He's not limping now, but if something else happens or he gets sick—"

"He's a tough old guy," she said. "I'll keep an eye on him for you."

Sawyer leaned against the nearest stall door.

He crossed his arms over his chest and studied her. "You're pretty tough yourself, Olivia Wilson."

"I've had to be—for Nick."

He sighed. "I wish things could be different. For us."

"So do I." But he probably had his flight booked already. She could see in his eyes that Sawyer was already halfway out the door.

"Before I go..." He straightened, squared his shoulders. "There's something else I need you to know. About Kedar. I've already told you about Khalil, my mistake, but..."

"Stop blaming yourself."

He shoved a hand through his dark hair. "You haven't heard the rest, Olivia. I figure you have a right to know and tonight I need to get this off my chest." He held her gaze. "That little boy—Nick's age—wasn't just a kid from the village, although I love all of them. I was more than close to his family, close to him." He glanced away, then back again. "At times he seemed like my own...child."

Olivia had a bad feeling.

"I was his godfather," Sawyer said. "His parents entrusted him to me, and Khalil trailed me around like a shadow. We flew kites together, played ball...and played tricks on each other." Sawyer faintly smiled at the memory.

"He loved knock-knock jokes, especially his own, which never made sense but always made us laugh like crazy. He wore a ball cap I'd given him—the Kansas City Royals—until it literally fell apart. He was still wearing it, torn and crusted with dirt, when he was brought into the clinic after being dug from the rubble."

She could barely speak. The pain he must feel went much deeper than she'd imagined. "You did your best. I know you did."

"Not good enough." He studied his crossed arms. "They believed in me—*he* believed in me. The last thing he said was 'You can fix me.' His parents weren't there. I was holding him in my arms when he took his last breath." She started to speak but he held up a hand. "Olivia, Khalil—my godson—he was Charlie's boy."

"Oh. Dear God." After that, she didn't know what else to say, could say, except, "Come here," but Sawyer didn't move. When he sagged back against the stall door, she went to him and drew him close. He began to shake.

Sawyer dropped his head against her shoulder and openly wept, which she had never seen him do even when his parents died, even when he'd euthanized Jasmine. Now she understood *why* he had to go back. "Surely they don't blame you—Charlie and his wife."

His voice sounded thick, muffled by her shirt, as his warm tears soaked through it. "They should. Because of me, he isn't there anymore."

"You're being too hard on yourself," she said, stroking his hair as she might do with Nick. After another moment, she tilted his head up, took his face in her hands and looked into his eyes. "*I* don't blame you, Sawyer."

"No? What if it had been Nick?"

She gently wiped a tear from Sawyer's cheek. "I still wouldn't."

"Not even if, after his fall, he'd...died because of me?"

"No." Olivia rubbed his back, up, then down again. Clearly, he didn't believe her, and why should he? At first, she had blamed him for not speaking up about Nick. And all those years she'd spent holding a grudge about Jasmine.

His dark lashes were spiked with tears and glistened in the low light, and Olivia faced a sudden truth she had tried to deny. She loved this man, loved him all the more because of the burden he still carried. How could she let him go? She could only pray that in Kedar he might find the salvation he so badly needed.

That wasn't up to her to give. "It's going to be a hard journey," she told him.

Sawyer nodded, his gaze still on hers. He seemed to be asking for something she probably couldn't give…until Olivia looked deeper into his troubled eyes, then angled her mouth to fit his and kissed him.

Soft and warm, it started as a kiss of healing, of the forgiveness he couldn't seem to find for himself. She'd thought they'd said goodbye before. But this might be their last moment, together, standing here outside a stall with Sawyer's back against the rough wood boards, his body heating hers, his kiss changing, taking her deeper, then deeper still until she felt they were closer in a different way that wasn't just physical.

When at last he raised his head, he was almost smiling, his eyes still sad.

"You really know how to scnd a guy off," he said, then reached into his back pocket to pull out a folded sheet of paper. His gaze fell just past her. "Here's my itinerary. I've given one to Logan, too, so you'll all know where I am this time. Or at least which flights I'll be on." He pressed a finger to her lips. "Olivia, don't say it."

Goodbye.

Trying not to cry, she stepped back. "Let me know. Text or call…"

"I will." Sawyer straightened from the stall door. Inside, Sundance shuffled around, perhaps hoping for a midnight snack. Finally, the horse gave up and Olivia heard the gelding slurp water from his bucket.

Without a word, Sawyer took her hand and drew her with him down the length of the barn aisle to the end stall where Cyclone lived. She felt as if they were a married couple, touching base before a business trip. "I hope you'll keep working with him. Or he'll slip back into his bad habits."

"I'll do my best." She added, "Just like you."

He turned her toward the stall, and stood at her back, almost touching but not quite. If they had, she wouldn't have been able to let him go. "I want you to make that deal with Ted Anderson. Build your business—for you and Nick." He hesitated, then his voice was almost a whisper. "And I want you to have one more thing. I've talked to Sam. I asked—and he agreed. He'll board him for you right here. I'll write a check before I leave." He paused, obviously sensing her confusion. "Let me make up for Jasmine, okay—as much as it's possible—for that mistake at least."

"It wasn't a mistake. I told you, you were right then."

"I'm right now," he said, then pointed upward past her shoulder.

Olivia lifted her gaze to read the hand-lettered sign written on cardboard tacked above the stall. And felt her heart crack wide open.

The sign said: Blue.

IT SEEMED THAT Olivia now owned a beautiful black colt. She'd been unable to refuse the generous gift. Sawyer had even ordered a new brass nameplate for the stall, but of course that hadn't come yet and she already loved the change of name.

In the ranch yard, they'd said their final goodbyes before Olivia had driven home with Nick, away from the Circle H, fighting her own tears the whole way. She could still feel the warmth of Sawyer's last kiss. Fortunately, Nick hadn't seen; and by the time they reached their house on Liberty Street, he'd been asleep in the back seat.

Olivia sat in her darkened living room, replaying the night and wishing there was some other outcome for her with Sawyer. At least, in his absence, she would make time to train Blue— as if that might bring her closer to Sawyer—

and she'd try to text or phone or email, hoping her messages might reach him. But his gift held more importance than an apology for Jasmine.

It was an expression of love.

And in a different way, Blue would help to heal Olivia. Her memories of the spring flood that had nearly killed Nick and ended her marriage to Logan no longer held the same power to hurt or to frighten. Compared to Kedar, the isolated ranch didn't seem all that remote now. Next door, her brother, Grey, would set up house with Shadow, a family at last with their daughter, Ava. Nick's best friend would be nearby. At the Circle H, he and Olivia had Logan, Blossom and Sam, if not Sawyer now. Nick could ride Hero and Olivia would work with Blue...

The thought made her smile. Life went on, and as a girl she'd ridden horses every day. Had she become, with Nick, like her own mother after her divorce? Overly protective, keeping her son from his father and the ranch Nick loved? She'd thought she was making progress, starting last spring, but had she really?

Not, of course, that she could change her whole life or stop Sawyer from leaving. He shouldn't give up his clinic work, and she wouldn't think of taking Nick, or herself, to such a faraway country. Following Sawyer to Kedar might give her that something she'd thought about just for herself, but what about her son's schooling? Leaving the ranch, their hometown, family and friends behind? What if things with Sawyer didn't work out? Or he couldn't cope and fell apart? Could she trust him with her son? Rely on him herself? She might risk everything only to lose it all again.

But this wasn't about her. Or even Nick.

It was about a broken man whose tears had shattered her heart, who would face what he'd done in Kedar. Alone.

And she remembered him saying: *Sometimes you have to take a chance.*

CHAPTER TWENTY

IN THE RANCH YARD, just as a rosy dawn broke in the big sky to the east, Sawyer propped both hands on his hips. "Olivia," he said again, "you are not going with me."

"Too late." With a definite sense of purpose, she popped the trunk on her SUV, then pulled out a roll-on suitcase and set it on the ground.

He'd already loaded his gear into Logan's truck. Then he'd glanced up to see Olivia barreling up the drive, a plume of dust billowing behind her. Nick had tumbled out of the car, saying one of his quick hellos to Sawyer before he ran into the house calling for his dad. If they'd come five minutes later, if Logan hadn't forgotten his keys and walked back to the house to get them, Sawyer would have been gone.

Still stunned by Olivia's sudden appearance, he couldn't seem to find a good argument for her to stay behind. "What about Nick?"

"Logan and Blossom will watch him while I'm gone. Nick is thrilled."

He understood that. He was more surprised that Olivia would leave her child. "You don't have tickets."

"I do now." She patted her carry-on bag. "Booked online. At four a.m.," she admitted, looking bleary-eyed. Sawyer remembered giving her his itinerary. "Same flight as yours. We're not sitting together, but—"

"You're not going. It isn't safe." His mouth set. Yesterday he'd wanted this, but things had changed. "You saw Charlie's text."

She gestured toward Logan's truck. "It's not safe for you, either."

He rubbed the back of his neck. "That's different. I'll be there to treat patients, but I won't have you exposed to disease, never mind the rigors of just getting to the village. I have no idea what conditions are like there now. I'll be playing it by ear. Considering the possibility of cholera, there may not even be fresh water available. You haven't had any of the necessary shots."

"Yes, I have. I googled that, too. My mother wanted to see Thailand last summer and I went with her, so I've had most of what I need. You're a doctor. You can give me whatever else may seem necessary, but I think I have that covered."

"Are you kidding me?" Sawyer lost his

temper. Or was this his fear for her talking? "You're not getting it. You'd need those shots weeks *before* a trip. Without them, the government may not let you in the country."

"Then you'll find a way to talk them into it."

He glanced at the long driveway. And rubbed his neck again. *Who are you?*

"As far as a visa goes," she said, "I'll be able to get that on the plane. The US has an agreement with Kedar—"

"To facilitate all the aid workers who go back and forth."

Well, she'd done her homework. But Sawyer tried again. "You're probably thinking 'what could go wrong?' But standing here, still safe and healthy on the Circle H, is literally a world away from where I'm going. You'd be risking your life, Olivia. I won't let you do that. There may still not be navigable roads between the capital and the village. This isn't a school field trip we're talking about."

"Don't patronize me!" Her temper had snapped, too. Her eyes blazed though she kept her voice low. "This is not your decision. It's mine. I was awake all night making up my mind—and I won't change it. I'm going with you."

The one word seemed to burst out of him. *"Why?"*

Their gazes locked. From the house, Logan's laughter floated on the early morning air along with Nick's giggles. Sawyer smelled bacon frying, fresh coffee. Normal, everyday things. And his mind filled with the memory of last night, of their kisses, soul deep and heartfelt and life changing for him—and, it seemed, for Olivia—with the memory of his confession about Khalil, his tears while she held Sawyer in her arms. This morning, because of all that, they were again diffcrent people.

"I can't—I won't—let you go by yourself," she said.

His shoulders sagged. In the next instant, he was picking up her roll-on case to stow in Logan's truck. His brother came out of the house and called, "Ready?"

Sawyer lifted his free hand then started for the truck. He wanted to deny her but he couldn't. More cowardice on his part?

Sawyer dreaded what he'd find in Kedar. What if Olivia hated it there?

But he'd failed to change her mind. And he was glad not to be going alone.

"ARE WE THERE YET?"

Olivia was teasing, trying to draw Sawyer from the mostly somber mood he'd been in since they took off from Kansas City. The twenty-six-plus hours to reach Kedar had seemed both exciting to her and interminable.

Beside her, Sawyer reached for her hand. "Almost there." Their first flight to Chicago had left on time, and the one after that, but their connecting flight in Abu Dhabi had taken off late. Because of that, they'd just been treated to an impressive sunset—the following day. Now they were in the highest of the Himalayas. Fortunately, the plane wasn't full and they had managed to change their seats to be together. In spite of her excitement, Olivia had slept off and on with her head on Sawyer's shoulder.

"Look," she said, leaning back so he could see out the window. "These mountains are so beautiful! I've never seen any this high."

Sawyer obviously shared her enthusiasm. "I've loved the area from the first time I laid eyes on it. Awesome. And treacherous," he pointed out.

"There's so much snow on the peaks. It's only August!"

"Always. They're snow-covered year round but fall does come early here."

Olivia spoke with her face pressed to the glass, trying to see below. "How do we get to the village when we land?"

In Abu Dhabi, Sawyer had done some calling around. "If I'd told you that part, I might have talked you out of coming with me."

"No, you wouldn't. I want to understand your life away from the Circle H." If they were going to have any chance at all of finding some compromise.

"They tell me the road to Sitara is still blocked in places— as I expected." He paused. "So I've chartered a helicopter."

She felt her face turn pale. "I've never been up in one."

Sawyer lifted her hand to kiss her knuckles. "Then you're about to have another adventure."

Olivia might have preferred slightly less adventure than that, but when they skimmed over the snow-capped peaks in the helicopter, then low through the deep passes where greenery dotted the mountainsides and hardy sheep could be seen frolicking on the hills, Olivia nearly forgot her fears.

It was almost midnight local time when they finally reached the clinic. And by then, she was dead on her feet. Sawyer left her in his hut to rest. He gave Olivia his bed—little more than a cot, but covered by a silky-soft sheepskin for a blanket—and insisted he could use his sleeping bag on the floor. Then he went in search of Charlie. Olivia didn't ask to go with him.

Almost before her head hit what passed for a pillow, she had fallen fast asleep. Tomorrow would be soon enough for her to explore the village.

"CHARLIE." THE NEXT MORNING, Sawyer followed his partner through the clinic's small anteroom past several waiting patients and on into one of their two exam rooms. He'd knocked at Charlie's door last night but received no answer, and Sawyer had quickly stepped back from the small hut, not wanting to wake everyone inside. Now, his mind fuzzy, he was fighting serious jet lag. And Charlie wasn't talking to him. "Before you leave, you need to tell me what's going on here so I can take over. I didn't see our appointment book— and where are the charts for those people sitting outside?"

Charlie stopped at the exam table, then spun around to face Sawyer. The sight was shocking. His face looked haggard, gray with fatigue, his brown eyes pale and haunted. Even his almost-black hair appeared washed-out and thinner. Grief had aged him. So had the load of work in Sawyer's absence. Charlie was about to let him have it.

"Why?" he asked. "So you can play doctor for a couple of days—then take off again? Disappear just when things get rough? I've been covering for you all summer, McCord. I can keep on doing that, thank you very much, without *your* help."

"You sent me the text. I've answered it."

"Something I never expected," Charlie said, his mouth set in a hard line.

"I assumed you wanted me here."

"I did—until I saw you. That just made me mad." Charlie dragged a hand over the stubble on his face. "You know, at first I understood. I figured you'd go home, look around that ranch, realize how much better you could serve people here in Sitara, and come back after your brother's wedding. Every day, then every week—for *months* I thought that." He took a breath. "Until I finally knew you weren't coming back."

"I probably deserve that, Charlie. I'm sorry. I couldn't—"

"What? Leave that woman you brought with you? Who knew," he said bitterly, "that Sawyer McCord, the guy who turned his back on his family years ago, who never showed any interest whatsoever in a woman over here, whose only emotional contact was with *my*

family, my kids—would finally fall for someone after all?"

Sawyer blinked. "How do you know that?"

"The village is buzzing." Sawyer should
have expected that. "And, really," Charlie went
on, "it's obvious. This goes way back, doesn't
it, my friend?"

Charlie stalked over to a cabinet, pulled out
some supplies, then crammed them into his
medical bag. Sawyer might have smiled. That
bag, like Doc's, had been with Charlie ever
since they'd graduated from med school, and it
bore all the signs of his experience since then
too—scrapes, gouges, faded black leather—
but Sawyer couldn't smile.

Charlie snorted. "Apparently you've brought
a 'golden goddess' with you. That's what people are calling her. The kids are hoping for a
first sighting." He paused. "It's Olivia, isn't
it?"

"You have a good memory." In the painful
days after Sawyer had left the Circle H, he and
Charlie had had more than a few late-night
discussions. Olivia's marriage to Logan had
been a fresh wound then, and Sawyer hadn't
been able to hide his sorrow.

"She's always been the one." Charlie added,
"But to bring her here—"

"She didn't give me any choice."

Charlie shoved a stack of charts at him. "Here's what you need to know." His back to Sawyer, he closed his bag, hefted it in one hand, then brushed past Sawyer to the doorway. With a nod at the charts, he rattled off the names of several patients, most of whom Sawyer didn't recognize, which told him how long he'd been away.

"Don't believe Nara when she tells you she took all the antibiotics I prescribed two weeks ago. When pressed, she'll try to blame that still-festering leg wound on the malevolence of some long-dead relative who gave her the evil eye." He hesitated before stepping out into the hall.

"Charlie," Sawyer said. "Where are you going?"

"Piper and I will be in the next village all day. I'm leaving now. In a while, she'll meet me there."

"Cholera?"

Charlie shook his head. "I don't believe it is now. Still waiting for the cultures to come back from the lab in the capital. Seems more like some particularly nasty virus to me, one that will hopefully run its course." Charlie's gaze slid past his. "So far, it hasn't killed anyone."

And, flinching, Sawyer took his chance. He'd half expected his partner's cold shoulder, but about something entirely different. "When will you be back? When can we talk about..." *Khalil*.

All Charlie said was "Good luck. Don't work too hard."

Trying to forget his sarcasm, Sawyer spent the morning treating patients.

The gash on Nara's leg was quickly dealt with. Sawyer changed her antibiotic. Thankful that the supplies he'd sent had gotten here along with a fresh delivery of drugs to the clinic, he gave her a shot, a bolus to start, then ordered her to come back tomorrow for another injection. Obviously, the other antibiotic Charlie had prescribed had had little effect on the bacteria, and the leg looked only slightly better than Fred Miller's arm had weeks ago. He hoped to see improvement when Nara came to the clinic again.

By nine o'clock, he was whistling to himself between patients. It felt good—more than good—to be back.

Sawyer patted a small boy's shoulder and gave him an encouraging smile. "That stuffy nose will be gone soon, Amir." He spoke in the local dialect, the words coming back to him as if he'd never been away. "Just remember. This is how to cough into the crook of your arm." He demonstrated, then turned to the boy's mother, who'd been staring at him from liquid dark eyes as if he were an alien from another galaxy. "I'd keep him home from school for a few days. Will that work for you, Fatima?"

She mumbled something about her work with the other women who had formed a weaving group to make rugs. Sawyer wasn't certain she'd understood. "I will try," she said with a shy, upward flick of her lashes.

"See you next time, then."

Her look turned dubious, but Sawyer tried to ignore it. He couldn't blame the local people, or Charlie, for their mistrust. He would have to prove himself, gain their confidence, all over again. If he stayed, he would have to put Olivia on a plane home, knowing that goodbye might be a final one. He thought of her sleeping against his shoulder during their flight, her blond hair on his chest, wondered what she'd been doing this morning other than catching up on her rest.

His jet-lagged stomach was rumbling—for lunch, dinner, breakfast?—when Charlie's wife walked into the clinic.

Formerly, she'd been their receptionist and sometime nurse, but since the landslide, like Charlie, she'd been pulling double duty. Sawyer drew her into an empty exam room. He had a final patient with a bellyache waiting in the other. Sawyer kissed Piper's cheek, pleased when she didn't draw away, drop her gaze or lash out at him like Charlie had. He glanced at her swollen abdomen.

"Coming along," he said as a mental image of Khalil crossed his mind. *Boy or girl*, he wanted to ask but didn't. He was no more certain of her feelings toward him than he was of Charlie's, but at least she hadn't turned her back on him. In fact, Piper smiled and her green eyes lit up. Even her dark red hair shone, like the healthy flush in her face.

"This pregnancy has flown by—maybe because we've been so busy here. I would have come sooner, but C.J.'s home with the cold that seems to be going around and I had to wait for a sitter." She paused. "You saw Charlie?"

"How long has he been like this?" So much for the happy homecoming he hadn't expected.

"Since you left."

Not much else had changed. The village of Sitara looked little better than when he'd gone back to America. Rubble still lay in piles by the side of the road and in the village streets, and the well in the square was covered with a sign that read in Kedarese, Warning: Danger. Do not Drink. Every other person he met, it seemed, still bore scars or healing wounds from the landslide.

Sawyer couldn't keep from glancing out the window at the naked mountain, devoid of trees and houses and the goats that had played on the hillsides before being swept away as if the rocky face had turned into a raging river. People here were suffering, and he'd been living like the King of Kansas. Teaching a horse to behave, falling in love with Olivia all over again, playing uncle—even surrogate dad, in Logan's absence—to Nick. A world away. A world apart.

"I know he didn't show it, but Charlie's happy you're here," Piper said.

"When does he sleep?" His partner had always been able to keep going, his work hours even more extreme than Sawyer's, but this seemed manic—and obviously meant to shut him out.

She shrugged. "Whenever he can, but that's not only because of his patient load."

Sawyer heard the unspoken words. *Because you weren't here.*

Or worse: *Because when he tries to sleep, he only thinks of Khalil.*

She absently stroked her stomach, then winced, reminding him of Blossom at the ranch. "I'm being kicked. Again. I doubt this baby will wait much longer to make C.J. a big brother." He was barely three years old. Sawyer hadn't seen him playing in the street earlier with a bunch of other kids on his way to the clinic, but according to Piper he was apparently confined to the house. He might not even recognize Sawyer.

He frowned. "Maybe you should get back to the States."

Her mouth set. "I won't leave him. Charlie needs me here." She paused, then said, "He needed you."

Sawyer tried to suppress another wave of guilt. "Well, I'm here now." They were much the same words he'd said to Sam at the ranch. He wasn't leaving—if he did—until the clinic was fully restored and he straightened things out with Charlie.

Piper studied him for another moment. "Olivia?" she said with one eyebrow raised. "Charlie assumed that's who she is. I can't believe you brought her to Kedar."

He half smiled. "I think she brought me." Yet he should have warned Olivia, better prepared her for what she would find here— no, he should have insisted she stay behind.

Maybe he'd simply been buying himself a bit more time with her.

If anything happened to her, Sawyer would never forgive himself.

CHAPTER TWENTY-ONE

OLIVIA WANDERED ALONG Sitara's main street, the tiny village nestled in a bowl rimmed by jagged mountains. Unlike in Barren, the dirt path didn't seem to have a name, or at least there wasn't a sign, but maybe one wasn't needed and the simplicity appealed to her. No Olivia Wilson Antiques in gold script here, no shop filled with pricey furniture. With only one street and several short byways dotted with homes, getting lost here would be difficult—unless she left the outskirts of town and ventured into what would be for Olivia a wilderness.

She raised her face to the morning sun, then stopped to watch a group of children kick a half-inflated ball around the little square that was centered by the now-closed village well. She wondered where the people who lived here got their water.

When the ball rolled her way, she returned it to the laughing girls and boys. Their excited chatter and bright faces, their shy gazes, made her happy. Her walk in the warm sunshine had also helped. Olivia couldn't sleep. Even with the time difference between Kansas and Kedar, there was something else about this new environment that didn't allow her to keep her eyes shut. Excitement, maybe.

At dawn, she'd heard Sawyer leave the hut and was ready to begin the day herself. Olivia had started out for the clinic to see if she could help, but she wasn't making much progress.

She joined the kids' laughter. "What do you call your game?" she asked the children, but no one understood her. That was, until a girl about Ava's age caught the ball and stopped in front of her. *"Gafoun,"* she said, then in English, "it means keep-away."

"Ah. We play that in my country, too. My son does."

They chatted for a moment in halting phrases about Nick and the little girl's family and their school before Olivia moved on, having learned everyone's name. The children were beautiful with dark eyes, silky dark hair and smooth, dusky skin. Olivia felt a pang of homesickness for Nick, but by the time she'd covered the length of the street, stopping to greet and be greeted by a number of women along the way, her spirits had revived. She wouldn't be here long and she wanted to make the most of her stay. Learn as much as she could.

She had finally neared the clinic when she noticed a small group of women gathered around what appeared to be a makeshift loom. In the increasingly warm day, they were talking, laughing, obviously close to each other as they worked. Olivia stopped again to admire the brilliant colors in the piece they were making, blues and reds and yellows.

"What lovely work," she said.

One woman, who'd been at the edge of the group, stood and said in English, "They've recently formed a cooperative." Tall, red-haired and slender except for the rise of her stomach, she held out a hand. "You must be Olivia. I'm Piper, Charlie's wife."

"I'm—but you already know my name."

"We've heard a lot about you. From Sawyer." She shied away, though, from that discussion to gesture at the loom. "I was on my way from the clinic to the next village but I just had to stop, see how my friends were doing. The dyes are all natural, plant based. The yarn, handspun, is goat—cashmere—and several of the women do the designs for the rugs. They're all modeled after traditional patterns handed down for generations."

"Where do they sell their rugs?"

"It's a fledgling operation. A few have sold within Kedar and a shop in the capital city carries them now. I'm trying to find a bigger market, to expand."

Olivia could understand that, yet in the past few days, she'd nearly forgotten about Ted Anderson and his shop or the potential move from Barren before Nick's school year began.

"Maybe I can help," she said. "These designs would complement the Western-style accessories people like in my area. And I have a friend there who's studying to become a decorator." Jenna Moran, Shadow's sister, could make great use of the rugs. "She could probably help spread the word, too." She paused. "Does the group have a website?"

"Not yet. Online would be great, though." Piper grinned. "We're open to all suggestions." She tapped a finger against her lips. "Hmm. Why don't you and Sawyer come for dinner tonight? We can talk more then."

Olivia wasn't sure that would please Sawyer. How had his reunion with his partner turned out? She hadn't seen him all morning, but this opportunity to help women in Sitara—and, perhaps, Jenna's new business—made her feel a part of things.

It was as if, in this tiny village, her whole world had opened up.

Though she missed Nick, she was having the time of her life.

Already, she knew it would be hard to leave.

IN THE MIDDLE of the night, someone pounded at the door.

With a groan, Sawyer rolled over, awake in an instant as he'd learned to be during his internship and residency. Across the room, Olivia was sleeping, and he didn't want to wake her.

Sawyer got up and went to the door. "Who is it?"

"Piper." Her voice shook.

He and Olivia had eaten dinner at her and Charlie's place. Halfway through their meal, Piper had put little C.J. to bed, still snuffling from his cold and cranky. Sawyer cracked open the door. "The baby?" Piper had thought he was running a slight fever and Sawyer had agreed.

"*This* baby," she said, a hand over her stomach.

He stiffened. Charlie hadn't come home for dinner. Feeling like something of a third wheel, Sawyer had listened to Piper and Olivia talk about a new website for the weavers' group, their enthusiasm for the project growing. "Charlie's not back?"

"No, he stayed in the next village overnight.

I came home to be with C.J.—and for dinner with you." Piper grimaced. "I guess it's just you and me, Doc." She held her breath. "My pains are pretty regular. Tonight's the night."

A shiver ran down his spine. "Piper—"

"I left C.J. with one of my neighbors." She'd already turned away from the door, expecting him to follow.

Instead, he stood there, feeling as frozen as he had the night Nick fell from the hayloft. In Barren, he'd treated Fred Miller, cured the toddler's strep throat. But those people were near strangers, and with Olivia's son he'd hesitated to help. And there was, of course, Khalil… What if he failed now?

Yet he had no choice. Coming back to Kedar had been his first step in finding redemption. He couldn't run again. Especially not from Piper. From Charlie's family. He *had* to act.

Olivia stepped up behind him and put a hand on his back. She seemed far more alert than he felt. Earlier, to his surprise, he'd thought she actually looked comfortable in these surroundings.

"I'm coming." She was already dressed. "Don't try to tell me no. I've had a child. I know what to expect."

At the clinic, Sawyer hurriedly scrubbed, then snapped on his gloves. He glanced at Olivia, who was hovering near the door. "You were right," he said over his shoulder. "You should scrub, too." He gave her directions. "I may need your help."

On the makeshift delivery table, Piper looked wan and frightened. She seemed to have anticipated that her baby might come early.

"Have you had contractions before?" Sawyer asked.

Her voice sounded weak. "Off and on," she admitted.

"Any bleeding?"

Piper hesitated. "Some," she said.

Sawyer's gaze sharpened. "When?"

"A few weeks ago. Just…spotting. Remember, I had that with C.J. It stopped on its own."

He frowned. The light bleeding didn't necessarily mean anything was wrong, but he didn't like the sound of this. "That was the only time—this pregnancy?"

"Um, no." Her face pinched as another contraction began. "Last week. Nothing serious, and again it just…stopped."

He wanted to groan. "You didn't tell Charlie," he guessed.

"Sawyer, you know why I couldn't. So many people need help." She didn't have to say the rest. *You weren't here.*

Sawyer moved closer to the table. "Sorry, Piper, but I need to examine you. See what kind of progress we're making." Which was awkward, to say the least. His partner's wife. He silently cursed Charlie for being gone, then realized he probably deserved this. He'd abandoned Charlie first.

His heart sinking, he stepped back a minute later. These hadn't been harmless Braxton Hicks contractions, a routine rehearsal for childbirth. Piper was roughly halfway to delivery—and the baby's safe route into the world was blocked.

With a worried glance at him, Olivia stroked Piper's damp hair from her face.

"What is it?"

Piper asked, "What's wrong, Sawyer?"

He held her gaze, not wanting to deliver the bad news. "Placenta previa," he finally said. In most women, the placenta attached to the top or side of the womb, but in some people, it attached instead to the lower part, blocking the birth canal.

"That's dangerous," Piper murmured, her eyes wide.

He rubbed her shoulder. "Don't panic. In your case, from what I can tell, the placenta only partially covers the cervix. You really didn't know?"

"I've had two babies. I thought…or maybe hoped everything was fine." She tried a smile. "Many women here don't bother to come to the clinic."

And some of them don't survive. But he wasn't about to say that.

"Charlie didn't do an ultrasound?"

"Our equipment was destroyed in the slide," she reminded him.

"But that was only a few months ago, Piper. No regular exams to check on you—the baby?" He couldn't imagine Charlie being that negligent.

A guilty expression crossed her pale face. Then so did the obvious pain of yet another contraction. She panted through it. "Only in the beginning. Then we were swamped here from dawn till dark. I kept telling him I could wait. Other people were more important. There was time," she said. "A natural process, I thought."

"And Charlie bought that? Piper, you should have been on bed rest."

"I couldn't stop working. He was already so stressed out…"

Sawyer tried to suppress his own guilt. He hadn't been here. They'd been grieving. *Because of me…* "And where did you get your medical degree, Mrs. Banfield?"

She laid a hand over her forehead. "In a cereal box, I guess."

"Piper."

"With my marriage license," she said.

Yet this wasn't the time to tease or scold. She was frightened.

"Do I need a C-section?"

Sawyer didn't respond. Ideally, yes, she did, but there could still be room—barely—for the baby, which felt small, to deliver in the usual way, and frankly, he had little choice. He glanced toward the wreckage of the hospital building next door.

To operate on Piper under nonsterile conditions without the right surgical instruments—or anesthesia—at hand would be more than dangerous. He hadn't even dared to sew up Fred Miller's arm that day at the Bar B&J. The stakes were higher tonight; two lives were on the line.

"No," he finally said. "These things happen. I think we're good." *I sure hope so.*

He hadn't said the last word before Piper moaned through still another contraction. They were coming closer now. And as luck would have it—and the saying went—in the next few hours everything that could go wrong did go wrong.

When Piper reached the last stage of labor

and was beginning to push, Sawyer turned away for a second. While his back was to the table, Olivia cried out.

"Sawyer, she's bleeding!"

He rushed to Piper's side, apologized for having to hurt her, then applied pressure to her abdomen. And swore. He'd been careful during his brief exam before, as gentle as he could be, but he might have caused some damage. Or the stress of the baby entering the birth canal could have caused the sudden bleeding. Or both. This had been a calculated risk.

He didn't have time to consider the reasons. His heart pounding, he barked orders at Olivia and tended to Piper. He didn't have the capability here to deal with any crisis, including one this serious. The ruined ultrasound machine wasn't the only missing piece of equipment. He had only his hands.

First, do no harm. He prayed he could staunch the flow of blood. If not, both she and the baby could die.

Piper tried not to cry, but she couldn't keep from pleading.

"Don't worry about me, Sawyer. Please. Save my baby," she said.

For an agonizing time, it seemed touch and go, even after the bleeding slowed, then stopped, and Sawyer's shaky confidence abandoned him.

What if this baby died under his watch? As Khalil had? He would break Piper's heart, set Charlie against him forever. What if Piper didn't make it, either? But he kept hearing Sam in his mind, saying, *I never thought you were a quitter.* Sawyer refused to lose either of them.

When the tiny form was born at last, he called out the sex and time of birth with a shout of joy. To his relief, the baby took a first, sharp breath and began to cry. So did Piper. His eyes wet, too, he passed her baby to Olivia to be weighed, then wrapped in a blanket. And prayed that Piper wouldn't hemorrhage again, postdelivery.

To help her uterus contract, Sawyer gave her a dose of oxytocin. As the next minutes passed and she remained stable, he gave thanks to a higher power for sparing her and the baby. Then with a hug and more tears all around, he thanked a worn and shaken Olivia. She had followed his every command, at the same time keeping Piper as calm as she could.

"Thank God," he murmured again.

"Yes," Piper said with a weak smile. "And thank *you*, Sawyer."

He sat—or rather, sank down—next to her

on a stool by the table. His legs wouldn't hold him any longer. "You know, there was a time when I thought of myself as, well—yes, kind of a god who could do no wrong."

"You and Charlie both," Piper said.

"I prided myself on rarely losing a patient—and then, only the most hopeless of cases with no real chance of recovery." He shook his head. "I'll never think of myself like that again. I wish I could have prevented that bleeding somehow…" Yet it could have been worse. Much worse.

"I've helped Charlie with a few delivery complications. There was nothing else to be done." Piper blinked back tears. "Just as there was nothing you could have done for Khalil," she said, reaching out a hand. "As a doctor, Charlie especially must understand that. It's your turn to believe it, too."

His throat closed. He shook his head again.

But that brief moment of forgiveness—at least from Piper—was over as soon as she said the words. In the next breath, she actually laughed a little. "Now go and bring me my baby. I haven't met him yet."

IN HIS HOUSE, Charlie bent over the cradle some local women had made for the new baby. He peered in at his son, then glanced up at Sawyer. "Quite an experience, isn't it? Never gets old," he said.

"No. It doesn't," Sawyer agreed. The miracle of life. He had seen it often, beginning as a boy when he'd watched his first calf being born or a foal slipping so sleekly into the world. Yet nothing beat this little human, a bare handful of a being with red hair like his mother's and a pair of newborn, ocean-blue eyes that would surely darken in the coming months. And a whole lifetime of experiences ahead of him. He'd weighed in under five pounds. In the States, he'd likely be in an incubator. "His Apgar scores were off the charts—and he's breathing well on his own."

"Must be the mountain air here in Kedar." But Charlie's voice sounded choked and his faint smile missed the mark. "Piper's sleeping now," he said. "You're sure she didn't need a transfusion?"

"I'm sure." A woman's blood supply increased by roughly fifty percent during pregnancy. She could tolerate the loss. "Her count's a bit low, but—"

"She'll make that up in the next few days."

"Then we're in agreement, Dr. Banfield."

"We are." Clearing his throat, Charlie tucked a blanket around his son, then walked with Sawyer to the door of his hut. "I can't thank you—and Olivia—enough."

"No need," Sawyer said, but Charlie didn't say goodbye or shut the door behind him. They stepped into the yard, and he led Sawyer to the patch of dirt where Piper insisted upon trying to grow flowers. A few fledgling marigolds had thrust through the earth, giving birth themselves, in a way. He motioned for Sawyer to sit on a log that had been fashioned into a rough bench.

"Time for that talk, McCord," he said. "I'll go first. This morning—yesterday, I mean— I acted like a jerk. I sent you that text, all but asking you to come back, then treated you very badly."

"You have every right."

"No. I don't. You know how I grew up—in the rarest of circumstances, in Boston on Beacon Hill. I never wanted for anything. Except," he added, "a friend who saw me for myself, not for where I came from, who my family was or how much money they had. You were the first person who ever just called me Charlie, did you know that?"

"No, I didn't." Sawyer slanted him a look. "You just seemed like a Charlie to me."

"Which I am. Now. Charles Worthington Banfield the Fourth is no more. Instead, I'm a guy just doing his job here in Kedar. Stitching up cuts, knocking down fevers, delivering babies." He hesitated. "I'm the luckiest man on earth tonight." He studied the sky. "They don't always survive here, as we both know. The mothers, either. But my new son has, and I have you to thank for that."

"But Charlie…about…Khalil."

He blinked. "Ah, yes. What a great kid he was, huh?" Another blink. "He worshipped you, Sawyer. One time he was so mad at me for telling him he couldn't do something—I've forgotten what—that he actually packed a bag, then announced he was going to live with you, that you'd be his father from then on."

Sawyer put his head in his hands. "I'd give everything—my own life—to have saved him."

"You couldn't," Charlie said. "I know that now. I've known it for a long while."

"I loved him, too. And you," Sawyer said. "I should have stayed here."

"I understand why you didn't. I'm sorry for earlier when I should have said how glad I am to have you back, see you, talk again the way we used to do…instead, I took off for the next village. Which makes me as guilty as you think you are." He paused. "Oh, by the way, the lab results are in. It wasn't cholera, thank heaven. And the cases we saw today seem on the mend without many others coming in. I think the outbreak will be under control in the next week or so." He said, "I'll be back here full-time then."

Sawyer heard the unspoken question, but he was still grappling with the notion that no one seemed to blame him for Khalil's death—except Sawyer himself. "I don't know what I'm going to do, Charlie. I need some more time."

"Because of Olivia, too," Charlie said, sounding like some wise sage.

"She was a great help with Piper. For a while there, I even hoped she might be willing to…stay."

"And if she isn't?"

Unable to speak, Sawyer shrugged, then tried to change the subject. "That's for later. I promise. I'll let you know about the clinic. In the meantime, what are you and Piper planning to call the baby?"

Charlie fought a smile that kicked up the corners of his mouth, then gave in to his grin. "We haven't decided. We're leaning, though— how does this sound?—toward Benjamin Sawyer."

And he punched Sawyer in the shoulder.

CHAPTER TWENTY-TWO

Two weeks later

OLIVIA OPENED HER shop for the day. While basking in the morning sun that streamed through the front windows, she tidied several displays of small *objets d'art*, dusted the George III side table, then went into her office to brew a cup of coffee. But these little elements of her daily routine didn't satisfy her.

For one thing, business had been slow since her return from Kedar. At the moment, people seemed to like midcentury modern rather than the more traditional pieces Olivia tended to carry, and which she most certainly preferred. For another thing, she missed Kedar. The trip with Sawyer had changed her worldview. He'd accompanied her as far as Kedar's capital so Olivia didn't have to travel there alone, but Sawyer had stayed behind to spend more time at the clinic, and for now things between them seemed to be on hold.

Although she was glad to be home with Nick, she couldn't forget the faces of the children there, the sound of their laughter and the easy camaraderie she'd developed with the village women.

She was sipping her coffee and studying the latest version of the weaving collective's new website, which was under construction with Olivia as an advisor, when the bell jangled over the main door. A customer? She hoped so.

Instead, Ted Anderson walked in. For weeks, Olivia had been far removed from any thought—or hope—of expanding her business. By now, she had pretty much abandoned any notion of being able to buy his store.

Olivia rushed to greet him. "Ted, how nice to see you again."

He returned her hug. "I came by before, but there was a Closed sign on your door. Were you ill?"

"I've been away." She noticed his son wasn't with him. "How have you been? Planning that move to Florida?"

"No," he said, his mouth firm. "I wanted you to know. I've told Craig I'll stay right here. For as long as I'm able," he added, putting an end to Olivia's dream of running two stores. "Why would I move south when my family is nearby? And I'd like to spend time with my grandchildren."

"I think that will make you happier," she agreed.

He sent her a rueful smile. "So. How can we do business?"

Confused, Olivia shook her head. Did he still want to sell his store? "I've tried, Ted, but there's simply no way I can come up with the money."

Ted prowled her shop, picking up a crystal paperweight before stopping to admire a handsome mounted elk head on the wall. "While you were gone, my son and I had a serious discussion. I hated the thought of leaving my business, going away...and I finally told him so. He's not happy, but I think he does understand my decision." Ted tested the linen fabric on a tablecloth trimmed in Brussels lace. "Perhaps you and I can come to some agreement, too."

Her mouth watered. "Ted, I can't afford—"

"The higher figure we talked about. Yes, I understand. And I couldn't bear to give up my shop. So. What would you think about becoming partners?"

"Partners?"

"I need some help," he admitted. "Craig is right about that. But if you'd come in with me—half of what I was asking, for an equal share—I can manage. You'd still be able to expand your reach from Barren, and I'd still have…a job."

"Part-time." Olivia started to smile. "Yes, I think that would work."

Her spirits soared. Not that she had the money—yet. Olivia didn't want to approach Barney again and she'd already told Sawyer no about a loan but….

There might be a solution after all. That would mean first eating some crow, and she was reaching for the phone on the front counter to call Wilson Cattle when the door opened again and Liza herself breezed in, wearing a new fall outfit and a sassy fedora.

"Good morning!" Then she stopped, seeing Ted. "Oh. Sorry, I don't mean to intrude. May I wait in your office, Olivia, while you tend to business?"

"Actually, the business involves you." Olivia introduced her to Ted. "We'd very much like to form a partnership—the amount of my share would be much less than before…" She drew a deep breath. "Are you still willing to give me a loan?"

"Did you really need to ask?" Liza's eyes lit up. She grinned then lowered her gaze to dig in her purse. "I have my checkbook right here."

Olivia and Ted exchanged glances before he moved away to give her and Liza some privacy.

Liza's standing offer was more important than a simple exchange of funds, though. Olivia should have seen that before. It had been Liza's way of trying to bond with Olivia, who had rejected her offer not merely of cash but of friendship. No, far more than that, it had been Liza's effort to become part of the family. Olivia and Grey had made that harder for her than it should have been, but after Olivia's trip to Kedar, the world looked bigger, broader, more inclusive. She had been unfair to Liza, just as she'd once blamed Logan for the spring flood that had nearly taken Nick from her. And she'd blamed Sawyer about Jasmine. It was time to make amends.

Olivia looked at the checkbook. "Keep the money until our agreement is drafted." She kissed her stepmother's cheek. "Thank you, Liza." Then she paused. Why had Liza stopped by in the first place? "Were you looking for something special today? I just got a shipment of beautiful Paul Revere–quality silver. There's a lovely serving set that might be right for your Dallas condo."

Liza's smile broadened. "That's one reason why I came in, to tell you we're not going back. I've convinced Everett we should sell the condo and stay at Wilson Cattle. There's plenty of room for us. I couldn't bear to leave that sweet little girl—my granddaughter—and frankly, your father's enthusiasm for Dallas may have been mainly to please me. Yesterday, I watched him ride out to look at fences or something, and I knew. This is where he really belongs." She added, "I hope I do, too."

Olivia couldn't catch her breath. This was a surprise. She would need to deal with her father. Strange, but the notion didn't repel or even scare her, as it once had. Years ago, she'd sided with her mother, but that pressure to choose where her loyalty lay was no longer there. Her mother lived in a different state with her new husband. And Olivia had been unfair to Everett as well as Liza. If she truly wanted to be part of the family herself, to belong and not remain invisible, she had to bend a little. Maybe more than a little.

Liza was grinning again. "The other reason I'm here—I was on my way to the hospital when I passed your shop and had to stop in. Great news. Logan and Blossom's baby was born a few hours ago!"

Olivia remembered the night in Kedar when

she'd helped Sawyer with Piper and Charlie's newborn son. "That's wonderful. Is everyone okay?"

Liza's smile slipped. For a moment, she seemed wistful. "Blossom looks like a Madonna, Logan said on the phone."

Olivia caught her hand. "But Liza, you seem…troubled."

"Oh, silly me. I'm slightly envious of Blossom, I suppose. I love Ava and Nick, I love babies, but I've always wanted…a child of my own."

Olivia expected to feel less than enthusiastic, particularly with what would be thirty years between a new sibling and her and Grey, but the idea actually made her smile. "What does my father think?"

"I haven't asked him."

Olivia hugged her. This was her chance to do something for Liza. "Then you should," she said, offering her support. "I don't know what he'll say, but if that's what you want, tell him."

For a moment, Liza didn't speak. Then, she straightened and said goodbye to Ted, who came to shake her hand. "Congratulations, you two. I do love such a positive start to the day. I'm off now to see Nick's baby sister."

A girl? Blossom had insisted for months that she was having a boy. With a new lightness of heart, Olivia watched Liza go, speeding away down Main Street toward Farrier General Hospital. A fine morning, for sure. A new baby, a sibling for Nick. And for Olivia, a partnership with Ted. She and Nick could move after all. Olivia had everything she'd wanted.

Except Sawyer.

SAWYER STOOD AT the nursery window, staring through the glass at his brother's new baby and fighting jet lag again. He'd flown in from Kedar last night to see Olivia—to settle things between them—and just in time for another birth. In the way of such events, everyone in the house at the Circle H had been wakened before dawn as soon as Blossom had gone into labor. Logan had all but begged Sawyer to go with them to the hospital, and he was feeling groggier now than he had when Charlie's son arrived. Beside him, Logan had his hands shoved in his pockets.

"Talk about miracles." Logan laid a hand on the glass. "Isn't she perfect?"

"No question about it," Sawyer said, grinning, too. "Did I say congratulations?"

"Only about a hundred times." Logan looked at him, then into the nursery again. "You think the baby's really okay? I mean, she's beautiful, has all her fingers and toes, those gorgeous blue eyes, but…"

"She's fine. Stop worrying." Benjamin Sawyer Banfield was also doing well. Sawyer had just gotten a text update from Charlie. "This must be Baby Month."

Logan shifted his gaze to Sawyer again. "You already miss it there, don't you?"

"Yeah, but I missed the Circle H when I was gone. Olivia doesn't know, but her being with me there helped a lot. Turns out, I'm the only one who really blames me for Khalil's death."

"And you brought a new life into the world over there."

Sawyer rubbed his neck. "Nothing could ever make up for Khalil, but I feel better now about Piper and Charlie. Glad I could do *something* for them, at least."

"A big something," Logan insisted. "And your timing here was perfect."

Sawyer's face heated. "I didn't plan that. I flew back to see Olivia, but I'm glad I didn't miss your baby's birth—the way I missed your wedding."

Logan shook his head. "Don't be so hard on yourself. You were here last night. That's what matters. Now the question is—what are you going to do? About Olivia, too."

Sawyer contemplated the tile floor. "Olivia

liked Kedar but that doesn't mean she'd consider living there." She'd said before the trip she wouldn't. "Then there's the fact that you wouldn't like her taking Nick so far away."

"Sawyer. No, I wouldn't like that, but if that would make you happy, Olivia, too, we'll work it out." He paused. "You and I are doing all right, aren't we?"

Sawyer touched Logan's shoulder. "Yeah, we are. That's another thing—the Circle H. I know Sam wants me there…"

"So do I." Logan gave him a one-armed hug. "So do I, Tom."

When Sawyer saw Doc Baxter step out of the nearby elevator, he welcomed the interruption. Things had been getting…too touchy-feely. Doc had delivered Logan's baby and was likely here to check on her and Blossom. Another round of hearty congratulations followed, but before Doc headed for the maternity rooms after Logan, Sawyer stopped him.

"Hey, Doc. Got a minute?"

"For you, Sawyer? Always."

The older man looked well rested. He had a new glow and a lighter step.

"I know what you were up to," Sawyer said. "Leaving town with Ida, dropping your office keys in my hand, expecting me to cover your practice while you were gone…testing me."

Doc's gaze fell. "Would I do that?"

"You would. And you must have known how I'd react."

Doc nodded. "I've had a few calls since I got home. Mr. Miller is grateful to you. He was doing a second cutting of hay when I talked to him. No problems with his arm. My other patients say you did a fine job, Sawyer. I thank you for that."

"But you weren't sure then."

"I could only hope," he said. "You needed a small trial by fire. I'm told you also performed well at your clinic abroad. With Olivia." Doc smiled. "Word gets around. If I were you, I'd take care of business now right here."

"HOME SWEET HOME," Sawyer said, standing in Olivia's doorway that night. He hoped he wouldn't lose his nerve.

After he'd left the hospital, he'd run into Liza—and learned an eye-opening fact that made him forget everything else. Olivia's deal with Ted Anderson, Liza had told him, would go through after all. Had Olivia already made her decision about him—about them—too?

Clearly surprised to see him, she threw her arms around his neck. "When did you get back? I didn't know you were coming." She drew him into the house.

"Can we talk, Olivia?"

"Of course," she said.

He'd been mulling over his options ever since he'd taken off in Kedar, fearing those few weeks would be their one and only trip, their last time together. Having learned about her new shop, he felt depressed all over again. He glanced around but didn't see, or hear, Nick.

"We're alone," Olivia explained. Excited about his new little sister, Nick was staying overnight at the Circle H. Blossom and the baby were coming home tomorrow morning and he wanted to be there. "I already miss Kedar," she said.

"So do I. Always." Her comment surprised him. Was she testing him, like Doc? Now that his partner had forgiven him, he could go back tomorrow, stay there, work with Charlie, watch baby Benjamin grow, teach little C.J. to fly kites…instead of guiding Nick here to ride better, working shoulder to shoulder with Logan and Sam on the ranch, seeing Blue turn into the horse he knew he could be. But was that what he wanted? To leave again? To lose Olivia?

In her living room, she sat in her favorite armchair, Sawyer on the sofa. He wished they were back in his hut with Olivia sleeping a few feet away from him, walking along the street in the village together, chatting with the locals. He cleared his throat. "I hear you've finally made a deal with Ted Anderson."

Olivia blinked. "A good one, I think. As it turns out, he's not ready to fully retire—that was more his son's idea—and I was in no position to pay full price for his business anyway. Thanks to Liza, we can now draw up our agreement and I'll have the funds I need." She smiled. "And, apparently, a stepmother I admire, but not because of the loan."

That sure sounded to Sawyer like she meant to stay. A silence followed.

"But about Kedar," she said, clearing her throat. "I didn't think about this when I was there, yet I've been wondering. Sawyer, why was Charlie's oldest son called *Khalil*? Before I knew that, I always thought he was one of the village children, not Charlie and Piper's child."

"When he was born, they named him Charles Worthington Banfield the Fifth. Then they moved to Kedar, and he wanted to be part of the group of kids there. But not with that name, which set him apart. You saw them all playing in the street. So in order to fit in, he decided to rename himself Khalil. Insisted upon it, much to his parents' amusement." He paused, remembering he'd done the same, changed his name to separate from Sam. "I never thought to mention that. I didn't mean to deceive you, Olivia."

"You didn't." She said, "That's kind of a sweet thing he did."

"He was a sweet kid." Sawyer shifted on the sofa. "I'll never forgive myself for Khalil, but that won't bring him back. And you know what else I did? Charlie was right. I made yet another mistake. Instead of staying to face him, Piper and what had happened to Khalil—instead of facing myself—I just cut and ran."

"Sawyer, you did what you felt you had to at the time."

"But *did* I have to? Khalil's death was terrible, and I've felt more than ashamed of myself for that, but I never realized—until now—that I've felt equally ashamed for having run away."

She smiled sadly. "Maybe that's not much different from me shutting out Everett. Maybe it's time we both stopped making mistakes."

She was right. As Logan had pointed out, running had been a lifelong habit for him. *Why didn't you stay? Fight for her?* Instead, he had gone to Kedar. Yet when Piper had needed him, he'd stuck around. He hadn't lost her or the baby. He wouldn't lose Olivia. Not this time.

Able to forgive himself at last, in part because of her, Sawyer felt his whole body relax. He had to make her see his side. To find some compromise.

"Listen. Here's what I want to do. I'm going to talk to Charlie. We could continue our partnership in the clinic, and we'll always be friends, but being here all summer in Barren, playing cowboy again…feeling, after so many years, that I do belong on the Circle H…that's important, too." He said, "I know you're intent on this deal, moving out of Barren to be closer to Ted's shop…" When she didn't answer, he went on. "I mean, I understand that living in Kedar, even part time, wouldn't work very well for you and Nick, but—"

She cut him off. "You don't know that at all."

OLIVIA SAT UP straighter in her chair. This was the talk they'd needed to have when she left Kedar. Was he trying to say goodbye again? But, *home sweet home*, he'd said. Just as he'd announced on his first visit that he was making a *house call*, and later, a *home invasion*. The notion of belonging seemed more important to him than she'd imagined, far more than his teasing words had suggested. She watched his face, his eyes, but he looked serious now.

"Why not?" she said at last. "Nick would be part of that group of boys and girls playing in the street."

Sawyer touched the scar by his right eye. "You'd really consider that?"

"I've been considering it—ever since our trip to Kedar. It wasn't the part-time marriage I had with Logan that was the real issue. It was being with the wrong man for me. All I had to do today was see Logan with Blossom and their baby to know how true that is." She paused. Earlier, she'd thought she had almost everything she wanted—just as she'd thought she did when she married Logan—but that wasn't true. It was Sawyer who'd been missing from her equation. In all their years apart, he had always been here in her heart.

And now, she could tell, his heart was in his eyes. She could see him holding his breath. "You think I'm the right one?"

Olivia reached for his hand. "Yes. You are."

"I'm not talking about us living apart."

"Neither am I." Olivia's mind whirled. Months ago, she'd assumed love wasn't her strong suit; that she had tried a serious relationship but failed; that she would raise Nick by herself with some guidance from his father. Once, Olivia had been overprotective, quick to find fault with Logan's parenting. Yet she'd managed to alter their relationship, and earlier today she'd bent with Liza. It was more than time to take another chance. With Sawyer.

"Ted will continue to work at his shop some of the time, and I can talk to Jenna Moran—Shadow's sister. She's divorced, working to become a decorator in order to support herself. She might like to help out there as well as my store in Barren. Gain some firsthand experience."

He smiled. "Then I'm going for broke. Nick's at the ranch right now. So is Blue. Makes more sense if you and I stay there, doesn't it?"

This might have been the deal breaker but it wasn't. Olivia answered his smile. "Well, it is only a fifteen-minute drive into town."

His voice gained strength. "I know the house will get crowded with Logan and Blossom, the new baby and Sam there, but we could build another place on the property. There's plenty of land, and there's a spot I love on the other side of the creek with a view of the trees and, well, all the bison."

"What about your clinic?" Neither of them should make a mistake this time. "You wouldn't really give that up?"

"No," he said, taking a breath. "I hope Charlie will be okay with me spending three, four months a year there—not all at once—and the rest here. I'm going to ask Doc about buying his practice, too. That will keep my hand in on the medical front here."

"You really think Doc is ready to retire? I'd bet he's more like Ted Anderson."

"At least for the next few years, we can share the practice like you and Ted will do with your two shops. Later on, we'll take over. In the meantime, that frees us up to keep doing what we love." He added, "As for Kedar, Max Garrett isn't only a doctor at the walk-in clinic here. He's a big outdoorsman. He just might like to help Charlie, have an adventure himself. I'll need to sound him out—as you will Jenna."

She hardly dared to hope. "You're sure about this?"

"I want us, Olivia." He drew another breath. "I want to marry you."

With those words, no doubt remained. She was out of her chair, across the space between them and into Sawyer's arms. They exchanged a long kiss before Olivia eased back to look into his beautiful deep blue eyes. "I do have one condition," she said.

"What's that?"

"When you spend time in Kedar, Nick and I go with you."

There. She'd taken the ultimate chance.

Sawyer shook his head, as if to marvel at all of this. "You're serious. And amazing. I love you, Olivia."

He'd told her so before, and this time she didn't hesitate.

"I love you, too, Sawyer. Yes, of course I'll marry you."

When he drew her even closer, Olivia melted into his embrace. Bending his head so his mouth could meet hers, he kissed her for a sweet moment, each of them making silent promises for their future together, a future that had been a long time coming.

Or maybe, Olivia thought as she sank into yet another kiss, it had been waiting for them all along. For her.

CHAPTER TWENTY-THREE

THE FAMILY ROOM at the Circle H could hardly hold another person. That morning, Blossom had come home with the baby, who was being passed around and was now in Olivia's arms. She wasn't sure she belonged here, but she'd come to pick up Nick, then gotten drawn into the impromptu party. She gazed down at the infant's sweet little face and felt her heart melt all over again.

The past day and a half had been amazing. First, her agreement with Ted, then Olivia's "reunion," if she could call it that, with Liza. The new baby. And, of course, the crowning touch: her engagement to Sawyer, who had promised her a ring as soon as the celebration died down.

Olivia wasn't that eager for the party to end. She'd never felt more at peace within herself or happier—she never would have expected this in the very house she'd shared with Logan. She studied her ex-husband's tiny new daughter, the perfect bow of her mouth, the baby blue of her eyes, the coppery glints in her hair, which reminded Olivia of Blossom.

"How precious is this?" she murmured to no one in particular, touching the little multi-colored knitted cap on the baby's head. It had a cowboy/cowgirl design woven into it. Until Kedar, and today, it had been a long time— seven years—since she'd held a newborn. She felt a pang of longing.

The noise level in the grand old ranch house seemed to shake the rafters. Olivia didn't hear her father's footsteps, but suddenly he was there, peering over her shoulder to examine Blossom's baby. And her heart skipped a beat.

"Never know what to make of a newborn," he said.

Olivia turned to face him—and, in a knee-jerk reaction, fell back on her usual stance. "You never knew what to make of me."

Everett glanced around, as if searching for Liza to rescue him, and Olivia regretted her unkind words. Hadn't she promised herself to make an effort with her father?

He reached out to trace a light finger over the baby's cheek. His tone softened. "I remember almost the very minute you were born. You looked a lot like this little girl—except your hair was blond, not red. Your mother whisked you right out of my arms the first time I tried to pick you up. I'm not blaming her, understand, for how you and I went wrong later on. But it occurs to me, maybe that's where it began. It's hard to connect with your own child when you can't even…hold her."

He'd obviously sought her out today, perhaps at Liza's urging. "Are you sure you really tried?" Olivia asked. "All I remember is watching you ride off into the sunrise every morning, coming back after dark. Often when I was already in bed."

"You know why, Olivia." He hesitated. "The ranch took much of my time. And I had a wife who hated the place. Your mother always wanted a house in town, to be closer to her friends, to shop and grow a garden without the occasional cow trampling the plants…or a spring flood wiping everything out. I think I often stayed away to avoid another argument. I wasn't that surprised when she left me."

The way Olivia had left Logan? She felt tempted to be offended but the feeling refused to take hold. There were similarities in the two situations.

"How is your mother?" he asked, surprising her. "We haven't spoken in a while. Not that we need to, but I doubt we'll ever forgive each other and I regret that." He managed a smile. "After all, she gave me a wonderful son and daughter, my bond with her for life. Whether she likes it or not."

"She seems happy enough." Olivia chanced a smile at him. "Of course, there's always something to complain about. Often these days, that's me. I don't call, I don't come to visit, I mailed her birthday present late—as usual. She's right about that, but honestly, I can't bring myself to fly to Denver just to hear more of the same."

"She's worse with Grey. You both love her, but…"

"I do," she admitted. There seemed to be something missing after that. "I can handle Mom. I doubt there are many mothers and daughters who don't clash now and then."

"But you and I… Olivia, I'm grateful you and Liza have found some way to connect. She's a fine person. I think you'll discover just how good she is." He glanced down at the baby, then back at Olivia. "What can I do to change your mind about your old dad?"

She blinked. "You're not old. It's not easy for me, though, to forget what it was like when I was a girl, growing up in Barren with Mom instead of at Wilson Cattle where Grey was still part of things, your buddy, the guy who would take over from you. You have every right to feel proud of him." She smiled through sudden tears at the baby in her arms. "I always felt...invisible."

Everett reeled back. "Invisible? Olivia, you're my daughter. Maybe we haven't been as close as we should be—maybe that's still my fault—but I... I love you. I see you. Never doubt that. Just because I don't know how to express it doesn't mean I don't care."

"That's no excuse, Everett." Liza glided between them, having obviously heard part of their conversation. "Maybe you should try harder."

Olivia sent her a grateful look. "I should, too."

Her stepmother took the baby from Olivia. "My turn. I'm having the best time," she said, reminding Olivia of their talk at her shop. "Would it be okay if we take Nick home with us for the day?"

"He and Ava are joined at the hip," her father agreed. "We'll take Hero with us, too. Borrow Sam's trailer. I've already promised the kids a ride later."

He was testing Olivia. Would she trust him with her son? His grandson.

"Of course you may."

"Then I'll leave you two to straighten yourselves out," Liza said and disappeared into the crowd. Olivia heard more cooing over the baby

Liza carried. Then Olivia turned to Everett. For too long she'd thought only of making a stable life for Nick. Yet all along, she had been missing that same stability for herself. She needed that, but so did her father.

"How do we start?" she asked.

"Like this." He pulled her close, tightened his hold on her and let her bask in the warmth of his embrace. "Olivia." He kissed the top of her head.

And Olivia murmured, "Dad."

STILL CARRYING THE BABY, Liza made her way through the crowd. In a quiet corner, she gazed down at her and blinked. Several times. Once for this new little life, twice for Everett and Olivia. Clearly, they were trying to mend their relationship. She blinked again for herself and her dream. She didn't realize he had joined her until Everett reached out to wipe a tear from her cheek.

"Happy occasion," he said. "Why are you crying?"

She swallowed. "I love babies. Don't you dare tease me for it."

"Would I risk my life? No, I wouldn't." His hand joined hers on the baby's head. His voice was hushed. "Today I'm far too happy—probably more than I deserve to be."

"You and Olivia," she murmured.

"You and me, too," he said. "There's something troubling you, though."

Liza couldn't meet his eyes. "A foolish daydream, that's all." But she remembered Olivia's advice. She studied the baby's face, her rosebud mouth, felt the slight, warm weight of her in her arms. Her heart ached but Liza forced a smile. "How silly I'm being. Grey and Olivia are grown. How could I expect you to indulge my fancy? Start all over again?"

His gaze captured hers. "You…you want to have a baby? Us?"

It was now or never. She'd come this far.

Liza planted a soft kiss on the baby's head, then handed her to Everett. "Yes," she said. "I do."

He laughed. Actually laughed, and for a second her heart froze. She thought he would turn away, reject the notion, but he didn't. Liza heard the faint buzz of conversation in the room, or was that in her ears? She thought she might faint. Everett jiggled the baby he held.

"I'm trying her on for size. She's beautiful, isn't she?" he said.

"An angel," Liza murmured, wondering, hoping now…

"I'll get it right next time—from the start." Then Everett leaned over the baby to lightly kiss Liza and said, his lips on hers, "I like your idea."

She drew back in shock. "You do?"

"Let's go home as soon as we can," he said, forgetting for the moment that Nick and Ava would be with them.

"You're sure," she said, hardly able to believe he wanted a child with her.

"I'm sure."

They had time. Plenty of time, Liza thought, for the love they shared.

LEAVING THE PARTY BEHIND, Sawyer wandered through the house, out the back door and down to the barn, where he said hello to Blue. The black colt seemed to grow muscle every day and was becoming one handsome horse. Sawyer was grooming him just for the fun of it when Sam joined him in the aisle.

"Lot of noise up there," he said, gesturing over his shoulder toward the house. "Never seen people make such a fuss over a six-pound baby."

"That baby will probably make a fuss of her own tonight. All night."

Sam picked up a currycomb, then started on Blue's other side. "I'm a great-grandfather again," he said. Then, "Hear you and Olivia have an announcement to make."

"How'd you hear that?"

Sam didn't quite answer. "Can't think of anybody in this house or at Wilson Cattle who'll be surprised. Except you, I suppose."

"I'm the one who asked her to marry me."

"Should have done that years ago."

Sawyer smiled. "Yes, I should have."

"Hope you're done running from all your problems. Like you said you were."

"Pops, I don't need a lecture, okay? Yes, I am through—and…" He paused to find the right words. "If it's all right with you—" he knew it would be "—I'm staying at the Circle H." He told Sam about his idea to build a new house on the property for him and Olivia. "So you'll have Nick here again, too, running back and forth."

Sam drew the currycomb along Blue's side one last time.

"Nick with both his parents in one place. I'm a happy man," he said. "Glad to have Olivia here, as well."

Sawyer grinned over the horse's back. "So am I."

Before he left the barn, Sam rounded the colt's rear end. He hooked an arm around Sawyer's neck. "Welcome back…son." Sam grinned but his eyes looked damp. "I'm not only happy. I'm lucky. I'll have both my boys here. Both my boys," he repeated, then seemed to pull himself together. "Quite the legacy we're building. If Grey and Everett think they're ahead with Wilson Cattle, they'd better think again."

As Sam left the barn, Olivia walked in, blinking to adjust her vision. "What was Sam crying about?" she asked, as if Sawyer were responsible.

He guessed he was, but not for the reason she might think.

"We weren't arguing. We came to an agreement. Just like you and Ted. Sam knows I'm here and that I'm not leaving again." He arched an eyebrow. "That message is for you, too."

Olivia didn't bat an eye. She moved around to kiss the colt's head. "Thank you for Blue," she said. "I'm calling him an early engagement present. Better than a flashy diamond ring."

"You have no idea how flashy it's going to be. You should thank Sam. I talked him out of this horse."

She stepped back to assess Blue, ran a hand along his neck, then down his side to his foreleg. "You know, I think he might make a good barrel racer."

"You'd go back into competition?"

"You never know. We'll see."

Sawyer laid a hand on her shoulder. He

leaned over to kiss her. "Making a lot of bold moves here, Ms. Soon-to-be-changing-your-name-again-Wilson."

She grinned. "Then I'll be Olivia Wilson Hunter Wilson McCord."

"Wow. Sounds like some royal family."

"Why not? You're Sawyer McCord Hunter McCord. You need one more."

"Not gonna happen." Or maybe it should. Sam would like him to be a Hunter again. He'd have to think about that. In the meantime, he kissed her once more, lingering, hardly able to realize she was his. And, after all these years, he was finally hers. When he raised his head at last, the taste of her still on his lips, Olivia was smiling through her tears.

"What?" he said.

"I talked to my father. I think Dad and I will be okay."

For that, Sawyer had to kiss her one more time. Then he unsnapped Blue from the crossties and together they walked the colt back to his stall.

"Good," he said. "Good for you."

Good for us, he thought.

LATER IN THE AFTERNOON, Olivia and the others were in the family room when Blossom came down the stairs with the baby after taking a rest. Logan had been right; she looked like a classic Madonna, and Olivia almost envied her. No, she *did* envy her, even if that wasn't an admirable trait. Once, she'd planned to have more babies with Logan, but that hadn't been in the cards and Olivia had tried for three years to make her peace with the notion of Nick remaining an only child. Seeing Blossom as a new mother brought back her own fantasies, as it had for Liza.

In the center of the room, Grey and Shadow were holding court. The newlyweds had come home and her brother looked as if he no longer had a care in the world. Shadow simply glowed. They were wrapped in each other's arms, their eyes only for each other.

Olivia tapped him on the shoulder. "Hey. How was San Diego?"

Grey winced. "Great. Sorry you all missed the wedding. Our fault."

Olivia kissed both of them. "No hard feelings. Best wishes."

Shadow said, "We're happy for you and Sawyer, too." They had made their official announcement earlier. She leaned closer to Olivia. "Just don't let the past keep you from having a future. We almost did—"

"But we stopped that from happening," Grey put in.

Satisfied that her brother was with the love of his life, Olivia glanced across the room. Even Finn Donovan had just stopped by and was talking to Annabelle from the diner. Which gave Olivia an idea. "Shadow, I'm thinking we need a girls night out. You, me, Blossom, Annabelle, Sherry from Baby Things...and Liza. Maybe we'll form a group."

"Don't forget Jenna. Living in a small town—or on a ranch—can get lonely."

Olivia agreed with Shadow. After all, she'd spent years on the Circle H feeling isolated, years, too, at her dad's ranch feeling invisible. A better social life would be more than welcome. She already had a new sister-in-law in Shadow and was friends with Blossom. Plus, now she and Sawyer were engaged.

She sent a smile toward her dad, who was talking cattle—or was it bison?—with Logan in the corner, then waved at Liza, who joined in now and then. Her stepmother had already taken to ranch life. Nearby, Nick and Ava were playing a board game in the middle of the family room rug. Olivia and Sawyer had already told him there would be no move after all, except to the Circle H, and Nick was thrilled. Life was good. It could hardly get any better except—

Olivia didn't finish the thought. Logan had

left her father's side and was coming toward her. "Well, here's the new daddy," she said with only a small twinge of disappointment. She *was* happy for him, happy for Blossom…

She could tell he felt the same for her. "I hear more best wishes are in order. You and Sawyer really getting married?"

"That's the plan."

"All good things, Olivia. Sawyer and I have had our differences—but we're past that."

Sawyer joined them. "We are." He glanced at Sam, standing in the archway to the dining room with a beer in his hand. He toasted Sawyer with it. "All of us," Sawyer added, an arm around Olivia. "I have to say, whether it's black Angus or bison, we've got a great team. Kansas—"

"Cowboys," Logan said and winked at Olivia. "Cowgirls, too. I've heard about your plans for Cycl—for Blue."

They were still laughing when Blossom brought the baby to them. It was Sawyer's turn to hold her and it was he who asked the question that Olivia had been wondering about all afternoon. He gazed down into that sweet little face. "What's her name?"

Logan said, "We finally decided. It's Daisy."

Sawyer smiled. "Blossom and Daisy, huh? You've got a flower theme going."

"Don't forget Blossom Too," she said. "Nick's kitten." That little cat was "helping" Nick and Ava play their game, occasionally scooting a token across the board as if playing with a mouse.

"Blossom spent her pregnancy convinced she was having a son named Aaron. I sure hope the next one's not a boy, then," Logan murmured. "You know, all these flower names…"

Blossom almost shuddered. "I'm not ready to think about that. Daisy was a pretty easy birth, I'm told, but still…"

Logan drew her close. "Maybe it'll be twins next time."

Grey wandered over again with Shadow. "What are we missing here?"

"Family planning," Sawyer said.

Shadow smiled. "Just what we were talking about last night. Ava's nine, and we've missed out on so much time together…" She sent Grey a private look, the kind happily married people shared. Olivia hoped she and Sawyer would be just like them.

Sawyer spoke near Olivia's ear, his voice low for her alone. "Nick's already seven."

And her heart soared. "You're talking about—"

"A little girl. Or another boy," he said.

Grey grinned. So did Logan. Shadow and Blossom rolled their eyes.

"How will we keep everyone straight?" Olivia asked with a laugh. "Logan, Daisy is your daughter and Sawyer's niece. Nick is our son but also Sawyer's nephew. When we get married, you will not only be my ex-husband but my brother-in-law, just as Sawyer once was to me. If he and I have a baby—"

"Whoa," Sawyer said. "Let's get married first."

He rocked Daisy in his arms. She cooed a little and Olivia watched him fall in love. Her big, strong cowboy. Or should she say, the town's new doctor as well as Charlie's partner in the clinic?

She knew Logan had taken the flying job in Wichita, but his occasional days away from the Circle H shouldn't trouble Blossom at all, and he was already talking about buying a small plane to keep at the ranch, putting in a runway in a nearby field.

Maybe Olivia was the only one who had ever felt isolation here, reminding her of her often-absent father. He winked at her now across the room. And Olivia smiled just for him.

She had no doubts. He and Grey would bring Wilson Cattle to profitability again, then probably send it flying even higher, like one of Logan's jets streaking across the sky. Who had her father been fooling? Like Doc, he wasn't one for retirement, either.

Liza didn't seem to mind at all. In fact, she was talking about getting a job herself: helping Shadow at Mother Comfort. And having a baby of her own.

That left Olivia and Sawyer. It wouldn't always be easy juggling her two shops, his work with Doc in town and trips to Kedar, but they would manage. Olivia was already involved with the women's cooperative. Nick would love it there. She and Sawyer loved each other, and that was all that mattered.

Logan and Blossom. Grey and Shadow. Olivia and Sawyer.

"I jumped the gun before," he said for her ears only. "We haven't really talked about a family." He glanced down at the baby, then up at Olivia. "You okay with that?"

Olivia didn't have to think. "I'm all for it, but—" She also knew something else. "We're already a family, Sawyer."

"Yeah. We are."

And they kissed.

"Not only that," he said. "We're home."

* * * * *

For more stories in Leigh Riker's
KANSAS COWBOYS *miniseries,*
check out
LAST CHANCE COWBOY and
THE RELUCTANT RANCHER

Get 2 Free Books,

Plus 2 Free Gifts—

just for trying the *Reader Service!*

Get 2 Free Books,
Plus 2 Free Gifts—
just for trying the Reader Service!

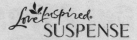

Get 2 Free Books,
Plus 2 Free Gifts—
just for trying the
Reader Service!